Officer Of The Watch

By DW McAliley

D. W. McAliley

Copyright 2015

This book is dedicated to my father,

Joseph P. McAliley, Sr.

He stood the watch.

Oct 14, 1953-Feb16, 2008

A Brief Note To The Reader

What follows is a work of fiction. All events and characters in this work are fictitious, and should be considered as such. However, the events are based on a very real threat that confronts modern society. The United States Congress formed the Commission to Assess the Threat to the United States From Electromagnetic Pulse (EMP) Attack to investigate the reality of this threat and to attempt to address it. The report that resulted from that Commission is available at a link found at the end of this book.

To date, the most critical recommendations of the Commission remain undone.

God Bless.

DWM

"Now, I am become Death, the destroyer of worlds."

~J. Robert Oppenheimer

Table of Contents

Ch. 1

Watch Room, USCENTCOM, Norfolk, VA

Joe Tillman sat at his desk, his Bible open and a cup of fresh coffee steaming next it. He watched two talking heads take turns interrupting each other for a few moments, a smile twisting the right corner of his mouth up just a touch. Neither of the two "experts" had the slightest clue about real domestic defense policy, which was probably why they were the ones on television this morning.

The people who really knew what they were talking about were also the ones who could never talk about what they knew.

Joe flipped the screen back to the multi-paneled watch mode that kept live streams from twelve of the largest news agencies, both domestic and international, active at all times. Part of his job as Senior Watch Officer (SWO) was to make certain that none of the troop movements he was responsible for ever made it onto those screens before their intended time. Carefully managed "leaks" had become an integral part of the information delivery system these days, and they made tight secrecy all the more important.

A quick glance at the time on his personal terminal, and Joe smiled. Only one more hour until the morning briefing where he would fill in his relieving officer and the assembled four star generals and admirals of the condition and alert statuses, then he could head home for twelve hours of peace and quiet. Joe sat back, picked up his Bible again, and started thumbing through to the page for this weekend's Sunday school lesson.

Suddenly, the wall-sized screen at one end of the watch room went dead black, and two high-intensity strobe flashers at the back of the room began pulsing. Joe slapped a bookmark in his Bible and shoved it into a desk drawer as he brought his terminal up. The two junior watch officers also rushed to their keyboards and began hammering in commands. All three men moved with practiced efficiency and urgency; if they scored a bad result on a readiness test, it could mean disciplinary action and even a drop in pay, and no one wanted that.

Joe was just finishing his log-in credentials to access the Secure Emergency Action Comm. system when the alert prompt began buzzing and a message flashed across the main screen. When they read the words scrolling down, all three men froze for a brief moment and stared—first at the screen and then at each other.

It read:

*****EMERGENCY ACTION ALERT*****

FLASH: NORAD Air Defense Protocol: Priority: ALPHA ZULU TANGO 113

Simultaneous launch detected------- Four medium range ICBM-------- Point of origin unknown------Target designation unknown---------

*** *********

Joe sat down and pulled the sheet off the printer as it rolled out. He checked his authentication card, and then the paper slipped from his numb fingers. Suddenly, the room seemed to spin and he gripped the edge of his desk hard to try and stop it. He looked around, and finally snapped back to the present moment. Only a few seconds had ticked away, but it seemed an eternity.

"Tom, Chris," Joe said, and his two associates jumped as if pricked, "we have to get on this. Tom, get NORAD on the horn *now* and make sure this isn't some damned drill. Chris, get the Chairman of the Joint Chiefs on your line and see if he has any details that we don't. The President is going to be looking for answers, and that means we are the ones who have to find them."

The two men nodded once and began punching commands into their keyboards and talking into their hands-free headsets. Joe, meanwhile, tapped into the NORAD radar defense shield and brought up the threat tracking display that eliminated all known radar sources, both commercial and military. There, on the screen, he watched as the four lines tracing the hostile contacts climbed towards the sky. One was arching up from the corner of Washington state, one from southern California, one from the New York area, and the last from near Miami.

Joe frowned and blinked. He sat down at his terminal and accessed the telemetry on the radar sources and did some quick calculations. The computers had read the result as a computational error and listed the point of origin as unknown because it couldn't accept the answer that the math had given it.

The four tracks had each originated within three miles of the US coast line.

The track that was arching up from what looked to be the Seattle area of Washington bent a bit towards Idaho as it climbed. Then, at exactly 200km altitude, there was a flash on the radar screen, and the radar track disappeared. One by one, the other three tracks followed the same pattern of arching towards the US heartland, then exploding at 200km.

As the final missile flashed, there was a brief flicker of darkness, and the lights dropped off completely. Two heartbeats later, the fluorescent panels overhead flickered back to life, but all of the computers in the room showed dead black screens.

Joe felt a cold knot begin twisting in his gut as he looked at the pale faces of the two junior watch officers and said in barely more than a whisper, "Gentlemen, I think we are under attack."

The red phone at the front of the room started to ring.

Ch. 2

Ground Zero

Joe stood and said, "Tom, get the systems back up and running. Chris, you go and start warming up the briefing room. We're on the clock, guys. Let's get it done."

At the front of the watch room, Joe paused and took a deep, slow breath. He could feel his pulse pounding in his neck and temples, and his palms itched. Calmed as much as he could manage, Joe picked up the receiver.

"Cent-Com, Joint Special Ops Command, Captain Joe Tillman speaking," Joe said.

"This is Sec. Def. Davisson," A familiar voice said, "You the SWO, Captain Tillman?"

"Yes, sir," Joe replied.

"Good. What's the status over there?" Secretary Davisson asked.

"We lost grid power," Joe said. "Backup generators are up and running, but we're doing a hard reboot on all systems. Codes will be changed once all the systems have been brought back up and connections reestablished. The briefing room is being prepped for video conference."

"Sounds good, Captain," Secretary Davisson said, his voice strangely calm. "Once your systems are up and running, get as much info as you can from the field. You'll give a briefing in thirty minutes. Stay calm and stay focused, Captain. There's a lot riding on your team, and I have every confidence you'll carry the load."

There was a click, and the line went silent.

Joe went back to his desk and took a seat as his computer terminal came slowly back to life. The random code generator immediately began whirring, beeping, and growling as it crunched unbelievably large algorithms to generate several random sixty four character long access keys that would control access to one of the most secure networks on the planet. Once the access keys had been generated and entered properly, the systems began making connections and printing out automated status reports.

"Systems are up and running, JT," Tom reported. "I'm getting status reports and….well….. I don't know, JT. There's got to be some kind of error in the system. Something got fried in the power surge or something."

"Show me," Joe said and followed Tom to his computer terminal.

Tom pointed to his alert status screen. "Look, I've got status updates from Hawaii, Alaska, and D.C., but that's all as of yet. None of the other twelve defense sectors have reported anything, but there should be some kind of status listed on the screen. All twelve continental defense zones are just blank. This system is designed not to give a blank return, JT. No matter what, there should be a status listed."

"Okay, keep at it, Tom," Joe said, the twisting knot in his gut turning tighter. "If you can't get anything on the system, get on the phone and start calling people."

Chris came in from the secure briefing room, and nodded. "Video feeds are up and running, JT."

"Good work," Joe said. "Now, see if you can access and bring up the east coast defense satellite feeds. We need to get a bird's eye view of this thing if we can."

Chris swallowed hard and bent over his computer, tapping in commands. Joe turned back to his screen and started scanning the secure wire channels and civilian media broadcasts. Already, the media in Europe and Asia was reporting some large scale catastrophe in the U.S., though no hard facts were available yet. Unfortunately, nothing as trivial as facts had ever stood in the way of good wall to wall media coverage and the talking heads were already working hard to get in their two cents. Joe tried to check the domestic news channels, but none had a feed up and running. That sent a shiver through him as he cycled through channel after channel of static and dead-feed marker screens.

"Oh, God," Chris whispered, and the color drained from his face. He tapped some commands into his keyboard and a satellite image popped up on the main screen. "This is from a geo-synch satellite over New England…"

Chris trailed off as the image zoomed in on New York City. The outline of the massive metropolitan area was clear, and the two rivers that framed the city looked like dark ribbons set down among the glowing gems of the high-powered sodium vapor street lamps. As the image played, small lights moved on the bay and the rivers.

Joe started to ask why they were watching this, when there was a brief flash from the Upper New York Bay near Liberty Island. The three men watched as a dim speck of light climbed through the pre-dawn sky above the city, turned and arched away from the satellite's field of view.

Suddenly, the image on the screen flashed a bright, blinding white, and digitized static scrambled the view as the satellite's image processors were overloaded. A few seconds later, the image cleared, and a massive fireball rose what had once been lower Manhattan. A mushroom cloud spread slowly as the fireball climbed into the sky. Joe felt hot tears running down his cheeks as he sat, transfixed by the scene of unbelievable devastation.

The only sound in the room was Tom noisily losing his breakfast.

Ch. 3

Star Light, Star Bright

Eric lay back on his sleeping bag, watching the sky overhead. A few meteors still flashed through the waning darkness, but it wasn't nearly as spectacular as it had been a few hours earlier. Just past midnight, the Perseids had peaked with nearly a hundred meteors an hour streaking through the starlit sky overhead. There had been so many bright meteors flashing overhead that it had been hard to decide where to look. As the night wore on, the flood of falling stars had slowly thinned out. Now, with the edges of the horizon off to the East beginning to glow that unique shade of grayish-purple that the night sky gets just before dawn, the meteors overhead were getting dimmer and more difficult to pick out.

Christina shifted position and mumbled something in her sleep, and Eric smiled. She had her head on his chest, one arm draped loosely over his stomach. Her sleeping bag covered both of them and had helped keep off some of the dew. Eric leaned down and kissed her on the forehead. Christina smiled and blinked up at him a few times, half-heartedly trying to wake up.

"If you wake up now," Eric whispered in her ear, "we can watch the sunrise before we have to hike back down to the camp."

Christina smiled and nodded, then stretched her arms and legs as far as they would go. Eric smiled to himself, reminded of how her fat-bellied tabby cat back home would do the same maneuver every morning. Christina shifted her position and scooted into a sitting position with her back pressed against Eric's chest. He wrapped his arms around her and they watched the last few meteorites flashing through the sky.

Eric's phone began buzzing, and he pulled it out to shut off the alarm. Just then, there was a bright flash of light from the south side of Crowder's mountain that momentarily cast the entire plain below them in what looked nearly as bright as daylight. A heart beat later there was another flash off to the north east. The light was bright enough that Eric and Christina both brought hands up to shield their eyes momentarily.

Eric cursed as the cell phone in his hand suddenly became nearly hot enough to blister his fingers. The phone made a sizzling sound similar to frying bacon as he dropped it to the grass, and a thin plume of grayish blue smoke rose from it. Eric cursed again and stuck his fingertips in his mouth, hoping they wouldn't blister.

"Was that lightening?" Christina asked with a voice sharp and on edge. Her eyes were wide open now, and she was a bit breathless as she looked around, waiting for the thunder they both knew should have hit by now.

"I don't think so, Tina," Eric replied, shaking his head. He picked up his phone, which was still warm and examined the shattered touch screen. He tried to power it up, but nothing happened. Puzzled, he said, "Whatever it was, it completely fried my phone."

"I never heard of light—look!" Tina suddenly exclaimed, pointing down the mountain.

Eric turned and watched as one by one whole sections of the power grid went completely dark below them. As each new sector blacked out, there were flashes and sparks from transformers blowing. The two watched as the power outages rolled from horizon to horizon. Even the towering Charlotte skyline in the distance went completely black. Along the tracks of transmission lines that ran through the forested countryside, there were pockets of flickering light and smoke to mark where high-voltage switching stations had once stood. The huge transformers used to handle those massive current and voltage loads began exploding in flashes of fire and sparks.

Eric caught a glimpse of bright yellow light to the northwest and pointed it out to Christina. "Look," he said, "I think that's the Coalogix power plant. Something doesn't look right, though. I've never—"Eric cut off midsentence as a huge, bright fireball rose from the power plant.

Several seconds later, the deep and resonating thump of the explosion's pressure wave hit them. Even this far away, the shockwave was strong enough to rattle Eric's chest and it made Christina's eyes water. As Eric watched, the plant underwent two more small explosions, and then a final blast that dwarfed the others lit up the entire western horizon briefly. The pressure wave from the last detonation was strong enough to make their ears ring and pop.

"Eric, what's happening?" Christina asked, tears streaming down her face as she clung to him, trembling.

Before Eric could answer, there was another bright flash off to the East, and a fireball rose from the woods a few miles away. The now familiar boom of a distant explosion rolled over them at just about the same instant that another explosion lit up the sky a few miles to the north. More explosions were happening all around them at seemingly random intervals and in random directions.

"Are they bombs?" Christina asked, bordering on hysteria.

Eric shook his head and pulled Christina close, burying her face in his shoulder. He watched numbly as the pre-dawn light silhouetted a huge shape as it plummeted towards the ground. A few seconds later, a new fireball rose into the sky.

"No," he whispered softly, "they're airplanes."

Ch. 4

The Morning Brief

Captain Joe Tillman stood at one end of the seven foot long conference table. At the other end of the room was a one hundred and twenty inch panel screen divided into six sections. In each section was the image of a high ranking official or a top military officer. Behind Joe, the entire wall served as large projector screen which currently showed the recorded satellite feed of New York Harbor as the missile streaked up from the harbor and the nuclear weapon that detonated at ground level.

Once the video played twice, Joe clicked the projector and the image shifted to a slide with bullet points outlining the known information. Unfortunately, there were more questions than facts.

"We know that four weapons were detonated at exactly 200km altitude," Joe continued. "We know the high-altitude EMP bursts have caused significant damage to electronics and to the power grid. Our systems were protected because we use all optical transmission lines with hardened electronics on the repeater stations. We're not sure at this time what the long term impact will be, and we can reasonably expect failures on the diesel backup generators from faults introduced in the wire windings. As it stands, we have limited power available at critical points, but communications have been slow and intermittent with domestic and international bases."

"What kind of exposure are we looking at overseas?" Admiral Fitzsimmons, the Chief of Naval Operations asked as the blood drained from his face.

"As I said, Admiral, our communications overseas have been intermittent at best," Joe replied. "No current reports of attacks as of yet. All staff members have been placed on the highest alert readiness status. Per our established disaster protocol, there should be active combat air patrols over all foreign bases at this point."

"Who hit us, and how did they get in without our knowledge?" Defense Secretary Davisson asked.

"I'm sorry, Mr. Secretary, but we just don't know yet," Joe admitted. "There are several front runners, but we'll need spectral analysis of the radioactive material to determine where the bombs were manufactured, and the only place we know that is available is GZ1."

"You mean New York," Secretary Davisson interrupted, his voice hard and cold.

"Yes, Mr. Secretary," Joe continued without breaking stride, "and as of yet, we don't have the means to coordinate that kind of search and recovery effort."

General Alexander, Army Chief of Staff, cleared his throat and asked, "Is this thing over yet, or are we expecting another hit?"

Joe shook his head. "General, I don't know how to answer that. We haven't been able to re-establish communications with half of our bases here in the U.S. NORAD's comm. link is flashing in and out, and we have intermittent radar coverage at best. Most of the info we're getting is from our secure satellite links. From those images, it looks like New York, Los Angeles, and Miami were all three hit with ground level nukes. There are clear indications of widespread fires over most of the area our geo-synch satellites cover. Beyond that, we just don't know. We're gathering data currently and as soon as we have more information we'll deliver it. That process is slow given the current state of the power grid and the lack of any reliable communications."

Secretary Davisson sighed heavily. "So basically, what you're telling us is that we don't know how bad it really is, we don't know who hit us, and we don't even know if it's really over yet? What do you suggest we tell the President, Captain?"

"Pray," Joe said when nothing else would come to him.

"Thank you, Captain Tillman," Secretary Davisson said in a strained voice. "Keep at things on your end, and we'll continue working at it from ours. I want another brief in 2 hours, and keep us updated as new information becomes available. Our first priority has to be establishing communications outside the secure optic network. Get on it, Captain. Dismissed."

One by one, the panels on the screen went dark.

Ch. 5

Morning After

Eric rolled Christina's sleeping bag up and tied it as tightly as he could then set it off to the side. As gently as he could, he moved Christina off his sleeping bag and onto a nearby boulder. Christina moved woodenly, staring off into space without really acknowledging his presence. Tears streamed silently down her cheeks. Eric rolled up the remaining sleeping bag and then tied both of them to the frame of his hiking pack. After doing a quick sweep of the area to make sure they hadn't left anything behind, Eric shouldered his pack and grabbed their hiking sticks.

Eric knelt in front of Christina and handed her stick to her, patting her knee, and said, "Tina, the sun is coming up and we need to go. We've got to get down off the mountain and get back to camp, okay?"

A brief look of confusion passed across Christina's face, and then her eyes seemed to focus on Eric for the first time as she blinked.

"But what about the people?" Christina asked in a whisper.

"What people, Tina?" Eric asked, confused.

"The people," Christina repeated with heat in her voice. "The people on the planes! The planes crashed, but they had people on them. What about the people?"

Eric took a deep, slow breath through his nose and had to swallow past a hard lump his throat to answer. "I don't know, Tina. But we can't worry about that right now. We have to focus on getting down off this mountain, okay? I'll help you the whole way, but we have to go. One step at a time, and we'll get it done. Once we're back in camp, then we can worry about other stuff."

Christina nodded slowly, and Eric helped her to her feet. Carefully, the two made their way down the winding trail and off Crowder's Mountain. The 'mountain' was barely worth the name at hardly more than 1600 feet elevation. Still, compared to the surrounding flood plains, it was a towering giant. The trail wasn't difficult, but it was deep in shadows for the most part, and there were stones and roots exposed enough to trip over if you weren't cautious. Christina stumbled several times, but Eric managed to catch her before she hit the ground.

It was a little more than a mile down Pinnacle Trail from the peak to where the side trail that led to their campground split off from the main path. After nearly an hour of hiking, the sun was well up, and Eric and Christina were both soaked with sweat. As they approached the sign marking the camp trail, a uniformed park ranger stepped out of the brush with his gun drawn.

"DOWN!" The ranger yelled, pointing with his free hand at the ground, "DOWN! On your knees, hands where I can see them!"

Eric froze and Christina screamed collapsed in a sobbing heap. The ranger blinked, not quite sure what to do. Thankfully, a second ranger came running up the trail from the direction of the park office. She looked a bit older and had several stripes of rank on her uniform.

"Jesus, Mike," the woman said. "Put your damned gun away! Can't you see these people are terrified?"

Mike hesitated for a moment, then holstered his pistol as the woman walked the rest of the way to them.

"Look, Claire," Mike said, "they were on the trails after hours, and we don't know who they are."

"Did you ask?" Claire demanded with her fists on her hips. Mike didn't say anything, and Claire shook her head. "I didn't think so. You folks camping up here?"

Eric nodded and pointed towards the campgrounds. "Our stuff is back in the camp area. We just went up last night to watch the meteors."

Claire nodded and knelt in front of the still sobbing Christine. She took Christine's hands in her own and squeezed them reassuringly. "It's okay, honey," the matronly ranger said in a soothing voice. "Mike's just scared and nervous. I guess we all are. You are safe, okay? No need to cry now, honey. What's your name?"

Christina tried to answer, but she was crying too hard to get words out, so Eric said, "I'm Eric, and that's Christina, my fiancée."

Claire put her arms around Christina and held her as the younger woman shook and cried. Mike mumbled something under his breath, then turned and walked back down the trail towards the park office. Eric wasn't quite sure what to do, so he stood and waited in the uncomfortable silence. After a few long minutes, Christina finally cried herself out and wiped her wet cheeks with the back of her hand. Sobs still shook her shoulders, but she had settled down enough for Claire to help her to her feet.

"Eric, you take Christina here back to camp," Claire said, patting Christina on the back reassuringly. "Get her some good cool water from the pump, and you two get some rest."

Claire started to turn away, but Eric reached out, caught her sleeve, and stopped her. "Do you know what's going on?" he asked. "We saw... Well, we saw a lot of things. Have you heard anything at all? Any news?"

Claire patted Eric's hand as she gently unclenched his fingers. "We're trying to find out as much as we can. As soon as we hear something, we'll let you know. For right now, though, we're asking everyone to stay close to their campsite so we know where everyone is for safety reasons. Y'all just concentrate on getting something to eat, staying hydrated, and getting some rest. We'll take care of everything else, okay?"

Eric nodded and half carried Christina as they walked down the short trail to the campgrounds. Each camp site was sectioned off from the others with a thick hedge-row. The individual sites had their own electrical outlets under a small lean-to style picnic shelter. A circle of large, rounded river stones marked the campfire area, and each site had a hand-operated pump that gave fresh, cold water from the naturally filtered subterranean springs in the area.

Inside their medium-sized six person dome tent, Eric spread out a foam pad and then opened Christina's sleeping bag and lay over top of it. He helped Christian onto the pallet and then stepped back outside. A wave of exhaustion rolled him, but Eric shook it off and went to refill all of their water bottles from the hand pump. He set the full water bottles and coolers under the picnic shelter out of the sun.

With the water supply replenished, Eric carefully and quietly stuck his head in the tent and retrieved his phone charger, Christina's cell phone, and the small weather alert radio he always carried when camping. He first tried to power on his phone again but couldn't get any life out of it even after plugging it into his charger and plugging the charger into the outlet under the picnic shelter. Christina's phone also had a shattered touch screen and wouldn't respond to any of the buttons he could press. Discouraged, Eric tried to power up the small alert radio with similar results.

Drained, Eric folded his arms on the picnic table and leaned forward to rest his head on them. He closed his eyes briefly and tried not to relive the last moments of the night before as he and Christina had watched airplane after airplane crash to the ground. He wondered how many people had been on board those flights. He'd stopped counting after fifteen explosions, but there had been many more. At least a couple of thousand passengers, probably more, had perished in front of them in the space of a few minutes.

Eric shuddered hard, and the tears he'd been holding back by sheer force of will finally broke through, and he wept.

Ch. 6

The Kindness Of....

Eric woke with a start and winced as the muscles in his neck cried out in protest. He blinked and rubbed the sleep from his eyes as he looked around, trying to get his bearings. His eyes fell on the line of water jugs underneath the table, and the reality of the night before crashed down on him. Eric sighed heavily and pulled himself to his feet. He made a quick round of the camp and collected everything together under the picnic shelter. He began packing the coolers and getting things ready to haul back down the trail to the parking lot. Once Christina woke up, he wanted to be ready to hit the road.

When everything was packed for travel, Eric took all of the disposables and the trash he'd collected and tossed it in the two large round metal trash cans by the trail. He looked at the shortened shadows around the trees and the shelter and guessed it was probably close to noon. The sun overhead was beating down, and his shirt was soaked with sweat.

There was no sound or movement from the tent, so Eric stuck his head in the door to check on Christina. As soon as his head hit the inside of the tent he caught the sharp, acrid stench of vomit. Christina lay on her side, and there was a stain on the floor of the tent where she'd gotten sick. She was breathing in rapid, shallow gasps. Eric put his hand to her forehead to check for a fever, but her skin was slick with sweat and cold to the touch. Her cheeks were pale, and her lips had a light bluish tint to them. He nudged her, gently at first and then with more force, but Christina didn't budge.

Suddenly, Eric's pulse was pounding in his ears, and he felt tears well up in his eyes. He clenched his fists and bolted from the tent.

"HELP!" he yelled as loudly as he could. He ran to the picnic shelter and grabbed two of the pans they'd used to cook dinner the night before and he began banging them together, yelling at the top of his lungs, "HELP!"

After a few minutes, a barrel-chested man with a vast paunch hanging over his faded denim jeans and straining the buttons on his bright red shirt came shuffling down the path from one of the other campsites. His head was completely bald on top, but a fringe of long silver hair around the sides was pulled back in a ponytail and a broad gray and white beard fanned out over his massive chest. Leather suspenders helped his wide leather belt hold his pants up, and he wore cowboy boots that matched his belt.

The man was out of breath, and his face was almost as red as his shirt when he made it to Eric.

"What's the problem, son?" the man asked in a winded Texas drawl.

"I don't know," Eric said as he dropped the pans. "My fiancé is in the tent, and she's sick or something. I can't get her to wake up!"

The man placed a large, heavy hand on Eric's shoulder. "It's okay, son. Let me take a look, alright? You show me where she is."

Eric nodded and led the man over to the tent. There wasn't room for both of them plus Christina, so Eric held the tent flap as the man worked his way half inside the tent to check on her. After a few moments, the man grunted and grumbled as he struggled back out of the tent and into a kneeling crouch just outside the door.

"Looks like she's in shock, son," the man said. "We need to get her feet up and get her warm. Listen, back up the trail is Site 3C. My wife is there, and her name is Imogene. You tell her Bill needs her help and bring her back, okay? Then you run back down the trail and get one of the rangers."

Eric shook his head and grated through clenched teeth, "I'm staying with her."

Bill reached up and put his hand on Eric's shoulder again. "I understand, son, but I need help here. Now, you look at me. Which one of us can go, get help, and get back quicker? I know you're worried and you're scared, but right now I need you to trust me."

After a brief hesitation, Eric nodded. He turned and sprinted up the trail, looking for site 3C. After a few hundred yards, he found the sign and ran up to the very petite woman stringing up linens on a clothes line between two trees. She had curly hair that was brushed and teased into a perfect cap of steel-gray ringlets. As Eric came to a skidding halt, she turned and smiled at him, wiping her hands on an apron that hung down the front of her pale green cotton dress.

"So you were the one makin' all that racket?" Imogene asked in a sweet voice.

Eric nodded out of breath, as he panted, "Bill needs help. My fiancé. Site 3A down the trail. On left. I have to get rangers."

Imogene nodded. "I'll get what I can and take it to him. You run on now, dear."

Eric nodded again and bolted back down the path. The trees passed by in a blur as he ran. Twice he tripped and slid on the loose gravel, but he jumped back to his feet and continued down the path. Finally, out of breath and bleeding from a few cuts on his hands, Eric leapt up the three wooden steps to the front porch of the ranger's office. He started pounding on the door, hard, and didn't let up until the knob turned and a disgruntled Mike opened it.

"Jesus, don't beat the thing down," Mike growled. "Oh, you. What do you want?"

Eric was breathing hard but managed to say, "Christina's sick, in shock maybe. There's a guy helping, but we need you. She won't wake up."

Instantly, Mike's facial expression changed. He nodded once and opened the door wide enough for Eric to enter. Mike went to one wall and grabbed a red and black medical bag that he slung over his shoulder.

"Site 3A, right?" he asked, already moving towards the door. "Okay, let's go."

Mike led the way out the door and shut it behind Eric. He locked the deadbolt and followed Eric up the trail. The ranger moved surprisingly quickly up the trail and soon passed Eric and kept running. When Eric reached the campsite, he was panting and soaking wet with sweat. His side had started to cramp, and he bent over trying to catch his breath.

Mike jogged up to the tent and got a brief rundown from Bill and Imogene. He stepped into the tent and got a look at Christina, who was still lying on her side, panting and sweating. Eric watched through the back window as Mike took Christina's pulse and listened to her heartbeat and respiration with a stethoscope he pulled from the kit. Mike carefully lifted her eyelids and checked her pupils with a flashlight.

Finally, Mike backed out of the tent and turned to Eric. "She's dehydrated and in shock. We need to get fluids in her to get her electrolytes balanced and her blood pressure stabilized. That means an IV, okay?"

Eric nodded, "Whatever you have to do."

Mike nodded and ducked back into the tent. Imogene came over and patted Eric on the back, gently leading him away from the tent with Bill.

"Bill," Imogene said, "you take this young man over to that shelter and get some water in him before he dries up like a raisin, okay?"

Bill nodded and draped a massive arm around Eric's shoulders, ushering him away from the tent. "Yes, mother," he called warmly back over his shoulder as they walked. "Don't worry, son," Bill said to Eric as they walked. "Imogene there spent just shy of forty years as a nurse and EMT in Galveston, Texas. She knows her stuff, and they'll take good care of your fiancé."

Eric nodded and stuck out his right hand. "I never introduced myself," he said, somewhat shakily. "My name is Eric Tillman. Thank you for coming."

Bill's hand swallowed Eric's, and he shook it with enthusiasm. "I'm Bill Daley, Texas Ranger....retired, of course," Bill said with a wide grin and a slap on his massive belly. "If they tried to squeeze me back in my old uniform, I swear one of us'd split down the middle."

Bill roared with laughter at that, and Eric couldn't help but join in. The two took a seat on opposite sides of the picnic table and talked while Mike and Imogene treated Christine. Eric rubbed his eyes as he felt exhaustion creeping back into his muscles and bones. Then, suddenly, Bill stopped mid sentence, and stood. He breathed in deep through his nose, and a serious frown creased his face and broad forehead.

Bill looked down at Eric and said, "Do you smell smoke?"

Ch. 7

The Fog of War

"Guys, quiet, check this out" Joe called out as he transferred the main viewing screen to a full image of the *Russia Today* broadcast.

An English speaking reporter had just finished a recap of the "troubling news" out of America, and the shot transitioned to a view of an ornate press room in the Kremlin. Three massive, elegant crystal and gold chandeliers hung from a high ceiling. A crowd of reporters sat in a semicircle in front of a simple platform that held a single podium with a bank of microphones. Vladimir Putin entered from a side door to applause and flashes from cameras. He stepped up to the podium cleared his throat and began speaking.

"Today, there has been a tragedy of unprecedented caliber. The United States of America, our ally and friend, has come under direct nuclear attack. Four weapons were detonated in the upper atmosphere above the United States, resulting in Electromagnetic Pulses, and crippling their infrastructure and disabling much of their modern and industrialized society. At the same instant, nuclear attacks were carried out against New York, Los Angeles, and Miami. The destruction in these cities is nearly complete."

The Russian President paused and took a careful, slow sip of water as cameras flashed.

"We have reason to believe that this attack was ordered, orchestrated, and executed by North Korea in an open act of aggression. We have partnered with China and will be issuing a direct and immediate response of force. Our fighters and bombers are in the air as we speak, and our justice will be as sure as it is swift."

Joe looked over at Tom and pointed to the screen. "You tap into every feed we have from our Eurasian satellite fleet and get eyes on this. Something doesn't smell right here. How could they know this quickly who it was?"

Tom nodded and bent over his computer to work. Putin looked directly into the cameras and continued, "We will offer any and all assistance we can to our friends in the United States as they cope with this massive disaster and tragedy. Russia will do what we must to rebuild and remake America, the land of the free, and home of the brave."

Suddenly, Tom stood and took the remote From Joe. He keyed in some commands, and the screen split to show four different satellite images. The top left image showed a satellite radar image of the Korean Peninsula, the top right image was a true color image of the Bearing Sea and Alaskan coastline, the bottom left showed the western border of Russia, and the bottom right showed an image of a Russian naval base in northern Siberia.

"Look at the radar map," Tom said, pointing to the top left panel. "We've got tracks on about forty targets that have no transponder identification. That's got to be what ol'Puddin Pop was just talking about, but look at the flight paths. We've got twenty five coming in over the Sea of Japan, and fifteen approaching from the Yellow Sea. If you wanted to hit N. Korea, there are much more direct routes to get there, so why fly over open water?"

Chris frowned and squinted at the telemetry on the targets, then pointed. "Look at the altitude! They're coming in at less than a hundred feet off the water. Why would they come in on that vector to hit North Korea? All of the North's defensive capabilities are concentrated in the south. They could fly in over China and have an open pathway for the most part."

"They've got to be headed for the South. For our bases," Tom said, pointing to the map. "Look, they can come in from the southern coast and skip all of the anti-air installments along the DMZ."

Just then, a red alert light started flashing on the radar image. Tom raced back to his computer and brought up the message and cursed loudly.

"We've got multiple launches from Russia, China, Korea." Tom said, "Christ! They're all over the place."

"What are the targets?" Joe asked, tapping commands furiously into his computer terminal, trying to pull up the radar telemetry. Before he could enter the commands fully, though, his question was answered for him.

The satellite radar image of the Korean peninsula suddenly flashed to static. A few seconds later, the same happened to the image over the Russian border with Europe.

"The Sat-net," Chris said. "They're going after the Sat-net."

Joe stood and watched as the last two satellite images went dark. He fell back into his chair as his knees gave out.

"Russia and China just blinded us," Tom said quietly. "Only one reason for that. War is coming."

Joe just shook his head and whispered, "No, Tom. It's already here."

Ch. 8

On The Road Again

Mike and Imogene stepped out of the tent, sweaty and tired. Bill saw them and nodded to Eric. Eric walked over to the tent and looked through the back tent flap. Christina was still asleep, but her breathing was slower and deeper, and her color already looked better.

"Is she okay?" Eric asked when Mike walked up to him.

"She's stable," Mike said with a small shrug. "Her blood pressure is going up and her pulse and breathing are going down, which is all good. She still hasn't woken up though, and I can't figure out why.

Did she hit her head or anything?"

Eric shook his head. "No, nothing. She was fine when she lay down. Well, as fine as she could be."

Bill coughed loudly enough to get their attention and looked a bit sheepish when both men turned his way.

"I hate to interrupt," the bear of a man said, "but I think we may have a larger problem at hand here. There's the smell of smoke all over the wind, and if the breeze is carrying the smoke to us, eventually it'll carry the fire to us too."

Imogene nodded and patted Bill on the back.

"Is there any way out of here?" Eric asked, and Mike shook his head.

"We had two Jeeps at the ranger station," Mike said, "but after last night, the engines won't even turn over."

Bill cleared his throat again, somewhat self consciously. "I got a '61 Dodge pickup down in the parking area. I guarantee she'll crank. Hell, I spent twenty years trying to kill the damn thing on the farm back home. I finally realized anything takes care of you for that long deserves to be taken care of." Bill tossed a set of keys to Eric. "She's sky blue with white trim. And I promise she'll crank. If we gotta run, she's the best bet."

"Is there anyone else camping up here?" Eric asked.

Mike shook his head. "Claire went out to check some of the trails, but she was coming back to the office. I can't leave her here if there's a fire coming."

Eric nodded. "Okay, here's what we do. Bill, you and Imogene, do you have any food at your camp?" Bill nodded, so Eric said, "Good. Go get that and any water you have and bring it back here. Imogene, bring all the sheets off your line back too; we'll need them. Mike, you go back to the station and get Claire and any guns and ammo you can find and bring it all back here. If you have maps or med kits, bring that too. Anything you think we can use. This will be our rally point. I'm going to go test out Bill's pickup. Okay?"

Everyone nodded, so Eric took the keys and trotted down the gravel path towards the public parking lot. The trail was only a quarter of a mile long, and it passed quickly. Eric walked out onto the flat pavement of the parking lot and spotted the old Dodge across from him in the shade.

When Eric was almost to the truck, though, a man stepped out of the edge of the woods. He staggered a bit as he walked up and put one hand on the hood of the Dodge. In the other hand he held a black pistol.

"Don't care what you have," the stranger said, "but you best drop it, and now."

"Look," Eric said, his eyes dropping down the gun, "I don't want any trouble. My fiancé is sick, and I need to get her to a doctor."

"Don't see anyone but you," the man said, pointing with his handgun. "Now, whatever you got, drop it."

"I don't have time for this," Eric grated through clenched teeth, and he took a step towards the truck.

The man raised the gun and leveled it at him. "I don't want to shoot you, but I will," he said. "I've been walking all morning. You smell the smoke, right? You hear any fire trucks? You hear anything at all?" the man asked, and when Eric didn't reply, he shook his head. "I didn't think so. That's cause there's nothing out there. Nothing but fire and death. Now whatever you got, you drop it and you back up. I don't want to shoot you, but I--"

Suddenly, there were three shots from behind him, and Eric jumped. The man stumbled forward, dropped to his knees, and fell face forward on the pavement. Eric turned in time to see Claire step pale-faced out of the brush behind him, her gun in her hands. She walked up to the stranger and kicked his pistol away, then knelt to check his vitals and shook her head.

"I walked out to the road," Claire said in a whisper. "This man shot two people and took everything in their pockets. He was a couple hundred yards down the road and out of range, so I circled around and tracked him back here."

Eric bent and picked up the man's gun. He checked the chamber, and it was loaded.

"Thank you," Eric said, and Claire jumped as if she'd been pinched. "You saved my life. Listen, there's a fire coming--"

"I know," Claire said. "I smell it on the wind. But I don't know what we can do, Eric. None of the cars on the highway would start, and he was right. There's no one coming to help."

"I know," Eric said softly, "but if I'm right, we might have a chance."

Eric walked over to the pickup and unlocked the door. He climbed in the cab, stuck the key in the ignition, and paused. Eric closed his eyes, said a short prayer to the God he desperately hoped was listening, and turned the key.

The engine cranked easily and roared to life on the first try. Eric leaned forward and rested his head on the steering wheel, his eyes closed and he whispered, "Thank you."

Ch. 9

Pissin In The Wind

"Mr. Secretary," Joe said through clenched teeth, "I don't think you understand. We don't have any information because we don't have any way to get it. The Sat-net is down, and it ain't coming back up, sir. We don't have good numbers on exactly how many of our birds they shot down, but judging by how difficult it is to get a signal from anywhere, you can bet if they didn't get all of them, they came damned close. We're blind, deaf, and dumb, sir. And there's not a damned thing we can do about it."

Secretary Davisson's face got redder with every word. "You listen to me *Captain* Tillman. We're going to track down whoever did this, and we're going to make them pay. That's your job right now, son. Find who did this."

"It doesn't matter," Tom said softly, and everyone on the screen and in the briefing room turned to look at him, surprised and confused.

"Doesn't matter?" Secretary Davisson growled. "Just what the fu--"

Suddenly, Tom stood, walked to the far end of the table, and grabbed the small black box that served as the connection hub for the video conference. He ripped the cords from the wall, and the screens went instantly black. Tom threw the CPU against the wall, and the casing cracked with a loud snap.

"Tom," Joe said carefully, "you okay?"

Tom just started shaking his head, and for a long time, he didn't say anything. Then, his head snapped up, and he started to laugh. It was a chilling sound.

"They don't get it," Tom said at last, wiping tears from the corners of his eyes. "They just don't get it, Joe. It doesn't matter *who* did this. They did it! And it worked, too; that's the b-&*$ of it all. It actually worked. Whoever it was, they hit us fast and they hit us hard enough to knock us out; not down, *out.*"

"We'll come back from this, Tom," Chris said soothingly, and Tom shot him a glare that would have withered an oak tree.

"Really?" Tom grated. "How will we come back, Chris? I've got a bachelor's in electrical engineering and a masters in semiconductor physics. Before I joined the Rangers, I was headed to be a *scientist.* Do you know what an EMP does to a circuit board? Cause I do. The voltages spike in time intervals so short that the circuit breakers and fuses don't have a chance to flip. Silicon heats instantly to vaporization points and all of the nice fancy little trace wires in processing chips melt straight through their housings. Stuff isn't just messed up, Chris, it's FUBAR'd beyond all repair."

"Tom, you gotta calm down," Joe said, taking a step towards him.

"Screw you, Joe," Tom shot back. "I've got a wife and four kids out there right now. Don't tell me to calm down. I can't talk to them, don't know where they are or if they're okay. We can't talk to any of our bases anywhere, so we don't know what's happening. We don't know what the next hit's going to be, or where. So don't tell me to calm down!"

"I hear ya, buddy," Joe said, easing his way towards Tom. "Chris here has a wife and a sixteen month old daughter. I've got a wife and two kids myself. We know what you're going through, okay?"

"Your kids are grown and out of college," Tom said dismissively, and Joe laughed.

"Jesus, Tom, you think you worry less about them once they're gone?" Joe asked. "Give it time, and you'll see. If anything, you worry more. We're going to get through this, Tom. Together."

"They don't get it, Joe," Tom said again, turning to look at the blank screen. "Those brass nutted idiots in D.C. don't get it. They're sitting behind their marble and granite walls, feeling safe and secure. They don't get it yet.... but they will. They're trying to hold onto how it was... what they had... who they were. But that's just pissin in the wind now. And if you're from the country, like you and me, well... heh... you know what that gets you."

Joe was close enough to make his move. In two steps, he was behind Tom. Joe's left arm went under Tom's and then up at a sharp angle while at the same time Joe brought his right hand around, locking his arm under Tom's chin. Tom struggled and tried to get out, but the lock was tight.

Joe put just enough pressure on the back of Tom's neck and under the point of his chin to pinch off the blood supply to his brain. He waited, carefully counting the seconds until Tom's arms went limp and he was unconscious.

Joe carefully and gently laid Tom down at the end of the table. Then, he took off his belt and Tom's. He wrapped one around Tom's wrists and one around his ankles. Tom was a highly trained Operator, and it wouldn't be a good idea if he woke up with a grudge and free range of motion. When he stood, Chris was staring at him.

Joe smiled. "You know when I told you I was in the Navy?" Chris nodded, and Joe shrugged a little. "Maybe I didn't tell you the whole story. I was stationed on an aircraft carrier for a few months, but right after that deployment, I applied for BUDS. I spent the rest of my career as a frogman."

Chris shook his head in disbelief and looked at Tom. "Man he really lost it, huh?" Chris asked, his face a little pale.

"Yeah, he did," Joe said, "but he was right too. Listen, Chris, when Tom wakes up, there are going to be some tough things to talk about and decide. You'd best get ready for it."

Joe turned and headed for the briefing room door.

"Where are you going?" Chris asked.

"To get my Bible," Joe said, never breaking stride, "and pray."

Ch. 10

Over the River and Through the Woods

Claire headed for the ranger's office to help Mike collect supplies while Eric carried the truck keys and good news back to his campsite. Bill and Imogene were there already, stacking food and water under the picnic shelter. Bill had a six shooter on his hip.

"How is she?" Eric asked, glancing through the back window of the tent. Christina hadn't moved much, but her breathing was easier and the IV bag was nearly empty.

"She's resting easier now," Bill said, walking over to Eric. "Still hasn't woken up yet, but she was making noises and mumbling. Mother says that's a good sign and that once her body's rested enough she'll be up and around."

Eric breathed a sigh of relief and headed back towards the picnic shelter with Bill. He stopped at the pump long enough to splash cool water on his face and neck and to get a quick sip to cool off his throat.

"I keep it with me when I'm out of town," Bill said when he saw Eric looking at the pistol at his side. "Been years since I hung it on my belt, but you never know. How'd the truck do?"

"Started right up," Eric said, flipping the keys to Bill." Just like you said she would."

Bill laughed a good, hard laugh that shook his shoulders as well as his massive paunch, and he slapped Eric on the back so hard it nearly knocked him over.

"I told you that was a hard truck to kill," Bill said. "It'll be a tight ride, but we should all fit."

"There's something else," Eric said softly, watching as Imogene folded sheets and blankets into carefully crafted bundles tied with bungee cords. He took Bill by the elbow and led the ex-ranger a few yards away to make sure they were out of ear shot and said in a low voice, "Claire had to shoot someone."

Bill just nodded. "I heard the shots," he said and put his hand lightly on the grip of his Smith and Wesson. "That's why I went and got the Mag here. Wasn't sure who was doin the shootin, and I didn't want to be the last one to the party, if you get my meaning."

Eric nodded. "This guy, looked like a drifter, came into the parking area and drew down on me. He wanted everything I had, and he looked like he meant it. Claire was in the bushes, though, and she shot him. She saw him out on the road and he killed a couple and took everything they had. If she hadn't been there..."

Eric pulled the pistol from the waistband of his jeans and handed it over to Bill. Bill checked to make sure the weapon was cleared, and it was. Then he inspected it and a deep frown creased his forehead.

"This is a service piece," Bill said, pointing to stamps on the grip, the slide, and the magazine. "See, it's stamped CMPD. Anytime you see a crest and 'PD' stamped on a gun, it's a service piece. You said this guy was a drifter?"

Eric nodded, and Bill shrugged. He handed the gun and magazine back to Eric. "Then how did he end up with a cop's gun?" Bill asked.

Before Eric could think of a plausible answer, Claire and Mike arrived loaded down with bags and guns. Mike had two packs on his back, an AR-15 on each shoulder, and he was carrying a medical bag identical to the one he'd used to treat Christina. Claire had a similar load, but she carried two pump action twelve gauge shotguns instead of rifles.

Bill and Eric went to lend a hand carrying the bags and guns. Claire and Mike were both sweating and very thankful to lighten their load for the last leg of their hike. Once everything was collected under the shelter, the group surveyed their supplies. And set about culling what was unnecessary from what they couldn't afford to leave behind.

The stuff no one was sure about stayed in the middle.

Eric looked at the formidable stack of weapons and turned to Claire and Mike. "What kind of ranger station was that?" he asked.

Claire shrugged. "It's part of DHS regulations now. All park service stations have to be capable of repelling a surprise attack or 'incident' that could be carried out on park grounds. We've got to be able to hold our own until help arrives."

"Of course," Mike said with a sour twist to his mouth. "That's assuming help is coming in the first place."

"Right," Claire said, and she reached into one of the field packs to pull out a large map. She spread the map out flat on the picnic table and put rocks on each of the four corners. "We're here, at the base of these trails," Claire said, pointing to where four lines converged on the edge of the mountain. "And the wind that's carrying the smoke to us is coming from the south west." She pointed on the map, and back over her left shoulder. "That direction. Our best bet is going to be to head east, I think."

Mike was shaking his head before she finished talking. "Look, Claire," he said, pointing with an ink pen to the other side of the park. "I-85 is just a couple of miles down the road if we go this way. We can hit the interstate and be in Charlotte in less than an hour, easy. There's got to be some kind of shelter or something set up in the city. That's our best bet, and it's a straight shot."

"That makes me nervous," Eric said, rubbing his chin absently. "Once you're on I-85, there are concrete dividers and guard rails all over the place. And we'd have to go through some pretty dense places before we get to Charlotte. Given what Claire saw this morning, and what she had to do, I think we'd be better off staying to the back roads. Keep away from people as much as possible until we figure things out."

Claire nodded and traced a line with her finger. "I don't want to go west if we don't absolutely have to. The smoke is getting thicker and it's coming from the west. We don't know how big the fire is, or where it is, or anything else, and I don't want to get caught up in that. We can follow Freedom Mill down to 46-42 and take that all the way to South 49. We'll come into Charlotte from the south end where there are fewer people."

Eric nodded. "Christina and I live in that area, and we know it pretty well. I know a couple of places that we can go if things are rough."

Mike shook his head. "I still say I-85 is the way to go."

"How 'bout it, Bill?" Eric said. "You've been quiet this whole time, and it's your truck. In the end, I guess that makes it your call."

Bill heaved a heavy sigh and ran a hand over the bald top of his head. After a moment, he shrugged a little and looked at Claire as he spoke. "I was a Texas Ranger for a long time. A lot of what I did was chasin bad people up and down interstates, picking up the pieces they left behind, trying to catch up and get ahead of 'em to stop 'em. Weren't none of it pretty, and I don't care to relive it now, to tell you the truth. I gotta go with Eric on this. The longer we can keep to ourselves, the better we'll be."

Each person under the shelter nodded in turn except Mike. For a long, tense moment, he stood glaring first at the map, then at Eric, and finally at Bill. After what seemed like forever, he threw up his hands.

"Ah hell," Mike said, his voice dripping sarcasm. "Fine! Over the river and through the woods. I guess that's our road. Makes me wonder why they built the dang interstates in the first place."

"OH Dear!" Imogene cried, her hand coming up to cover her mouth.

Eric had just enough time to turn and watch as Christina took two shaky steps out of the tent.

Ch. 11

Chain Of Command

Tom rubbed his wrists and shook his head.

"Sorry, man," Joe said with an uncomfortable hitch of his shoulders. "I didn't know what else to do. Someone like you in these tight quarters....well, you could have done a lot of damage to the hardware and everything else. I didn't know how far you'd slipped and I just couldn't take the chance."

Tom nodded. "I know," he said. "You did the right thing. I just didn't know they still taught sailors how to tie knots like that."

All three of the men couldn't help but laugh at that, and it did a lot to ease the unspoken tension in the room. They sat at the long, highly polished conference table in the briefing room. The screens were dark now, and they would likely be that way for a long time to come.

"You were right, Tom," Joe said, and he held up his hand when Tom started to protest. "No, hear me out. Whoever did this, Russia, China, North Korea, Iran... it really doesn't matter more than a hill of beans when you get down to it. The power grid is down, communications are down, and the sat-net is down. They knocked us back to the 19th century with one hit."

Joe paused and took a deep breath. He knew that what he was saying was the truth, but it didn't make it any easier to swallow.

He wanted nothing more than to turn on CNN and watch the talking heads argue. But he knew that wasn't going to happen ever again. Joe knew what he needed to say, but the words stuck in his throat, and the silence stretched.

"I was a para-rescue jumper," Chris said suddenly, breaking the silence. "I jumped into sh*t you wouldn't believe. I graduated PJ School with twenty three guys. Nine of us are still breathing, but we have saved more than four hundred lives among us. That's how we made it all make sense. We knew that each one of us that fell... it was worth it. We put our lives on the line to put our boys back together and make sure they didn't die. 'First there that others may live.' That was our motto, and we lived it."

Chris paused as his voice started to break a bit, and he took a deep breath.

"I spent thirteen years saving other peoples' sons," Chris said after a moment. "Who's going to jump in and save my wife and daughter? Who's going to make sure they make it through the night? The way I see it, if we were going to get orders from higher up we would have by now, especially given Tom's little episode. Hell, the brass nuts in D.C. could have hopped on a high-speed chopper and been here in person to rip him a new one by now. Fact is, they're not coming. And neither are any orders. It's time to face facts.... The U.S. has fallen."

By the end, Chris was whispering. Still, his words seem to hang in the air for a long time. No one spoke. It seemed like no one breathed.

"We only have two options," Joe said at last. "We either sit here and wait for orders that we all agree aren't going to come, or we go. At this point, the lines are down and the screens are dark. All of the things we were put here to watch and to monitor are dead. If we stay here, we'll end up dead eventually too. If this is an all out, full scale attack, then this place will end up being high on the list of targets. We all have families out there, and it's high time we go take care of them."

Tom and Chris nodded, and the three men walked out of the secure briefing room. Joe picked up his Bible and took three wallet-sized family pictures from his computer terminal. They were the only personal effect he had in the office. He looked around the dark watch-room as Tom and Chris gathered their few personal effects.

The three men left the office, and Joe secured the door to the watch-room with the proper code, though in truth there wasn't much at this point to keep safe. With the comm. lines down and no satellite feeds, all anyone would gain access to would be dark computer screens and burned out phone lines. Still, some habits die hard.

"There's an armory down the hall, third door on the right," Joe said. "We'll stop there and gear up. No telling what we'll run into out there on the streets."

Tom and Chris nodded, and the three stepped out into the hallway. Joe led the way as they rounded the wide bend in the plain white hall. The fluorescent lights overhead began to flicker intermittently, and they dimmed almost all the way out at one point. Then, the lights flared back to full strength.

"Backup generator one is dead," Tom said. "No telling how long the coils on number two will hold out."

Joe nodded and kept walking. Finally, he saw the door to the armory ahead, and a lone guard standing watch outside it. Joe took his ID badge from his back pocket and clipped it to the left side of his chest, just under the JSOC logo on his polo shirt so the guard would be forced to look at it. Joe stepped up to the uniformed Marine Corporal without hesitation.

"Step aside, son," Joe said with a wave of his hand. "We gotta get in there."

"Sir, this is my station," Corporal Henderson said in a shaky voice. "I can't let you in without proper clearance."

Joe snorted loudly and took his badge off his shirt. He waived it in front of the Corporal's eyes. "You see what that says, son?" Joe asked, and answered his own question before the Marine could open his mouth. "It says O-6. That's Captain. It also says J-S-O-C. That's Joint Special Operations Command. In other words, I have clearances you never even heard of. Now step aside and let us in that armory before I have to chew you a new ass!"

Corporal Henderson stood for a moment, shaking hard, and finally he stepped aside. Joe put a hand on his shoulder and squeezed.

"Who are you with, Corporal?" Joe asked.

"Base security, sir," Corporal Henderson replied, his voice as shaky as he was. "We got the call to stations, and I came here at a dead run. The other three guys who were supposed to be here with me... they left a few hours ago. I stayed though. This is my station."

Joe nodded, and squeezed the Corporal's shoulder again. "You did well, Corporal. Listen, do you have family around here?"

Henderson shook his head. "I'm from Arkansas, sir. No family here, and not much back home to tell you the truth. Sir, do you know what's happening? I tried to call my sister back home in Bismark, but my phone won't even turn on. The battery was full, but something happened to it."

The Corporal pulled an iPhone from his pocket and handed to Joe. The screen was shattered on the inside, but smooth to the touch. True to his word, Corporal Henderson's phone wouldn't power on at all.

"Bismark's in North Dakota, Corporal," Joe said absently as he inspected the phone.

"Not the one I'm from, sir," Henderson said. "It's a little place near De Gray lake. We grew up there."

Joe handed the phone to Tom, who looked at it and shook his head and handed it back. Tom and Chris stepped into the armory and began loading up field packs with magazines, ammo, and field rations. Joe looked at the Corporal for a long moment, then sighed and pulled him into the armory with them.

"Listen, Corporal," Joe said, "I don't know whose chain of command you were under, and I don't really care. Bottom line is, the chain of command is broken now anyway, so it doesn't mean two shits."

Joe rolled up his left sleeve enough to show his upper bicep and the tattooed Seal globe and trident emblem.

"You know what that means, Corporal?" Joe asked, and Henderson nodded, his eyes wide. "Good, then that will save me some time. We are leaving right now. We're going to find our families and make sure they are safe. You're welcome to come with us, if you want, or you can stay here and man your post. The choice is yours, but you need to understand something. Orders aren't coming down to you. Not any time soon, son. For right now, you're either with us, or you're on your own."

Henderson didn't even hesitate before saying, "I'm going with you, sir."

Joe shook the corporal's hand. "Okay, then here's the deal. You ride with us, you follow our lead. We're going after their families first, then we're moving south after mine. One we get through with that, then we'll head to Arkansas or wherever to find your sister and whoever else. Bottom line, we stick together, we work together, and we watch each others' backs. Got it?"

"Yes sir," Henderson said, nodding his head repeatedly.

"Alright then," Joe replied, stepping into the armory. "Grab guns, ammo, med kits, and food. We'll get water as we go."

"Yes sir," Henderson said eagerly. "Yes sir, I'm right on it, sir."

Joe grabbed a field pack from a shelf and shook his head. "Don't call me sir," he said gruffly. "That's all over with now."

Ch. 12

The Decent Thing

Bill cranked up the old Dodge and the engine roared to life. Imogene helped Christina into the cab and then climbed into the passenger seat. Mike, Claire, and Eric sat in the bed among the various packs, bags, coolers, and water jugs. Once everyone was in the truck, Eric thumped the roof of the cab twice and Bill put the Dodge in drive. He pulled carefully out of the parking spot and down the gravel drive towards the highway.

Freedom Mill Road was nearly empty as Bill made a right turn out onto the pavement. Ahead, a black Taurus was pulled half onto the shoulder the road, the hood up and two doors open. As Bill started to pass the car, Claire began thumping hard on the roof, startling everyone inside. Bill stopped so suddenly that Eric slammed into the half-window in the back wall of cab hard enough to make his ears ring.

"Jesus, Mary, and Joseph, woman!" Bill growled through his window. "What is with all the damned ruckus?"

Claire didn't say anything. Instead she hopped over the side of the pickup and stuck her head in the Taurus. For a brief moment, Eric thought Claire was looting the car, but before he could say anything, she straightened with blanket and a jacket under one arm and tears streaming down her face.

Claire walked around to the front of the car and knelt down out of sight. Eric and Mike exchanged confused frowns, then jumped down and followed her. When they rounded the front bumper of the Taurus, Claire was kneeling next to two bodies. One was obviously a woman in a pale yellow sundress with red flowers. The other was larger and had on jeans and what looked like a red flannel shirt.

Claire had covered their faces.

"I came out to check and see if anyone was driving by," Claire said in barely more than a whisper. "I saw their hood up and started this way to see if I could help. Before I took two steps, that *man* stepped out of the woods a dozen yards down the road from them. The wife saw him first and pointed him out to her husband. The both of them were waiving at him and he just walked up and shot them. She didn't even have time to scream."

Mike stepped forward and squeezed Claire's shoulder, and she reached up to pat his hand. "You were too far away to help them, Claire."

"I know," Claire said softly. "I know. That's why I followed *him*. That's why I didn't wait when he drew his gun on Eric. I couldn't watch him do that again."

Claire reached out and squeezed the wife's hand. Then she stood and wiped her face with the back of her hand and said, "I couldn't just leave these people laying here like this, exposed. I know we can't bury them, but they deserved more than to be just left laying here."

In the distance behind them, a series of four loud pops echoed off the woods. Eric looked at the two rangers and they both nodded at the same moment.

It was time to move.

Eric helped the two rangers back into the bed of the pickup and then climbed up after them. Once they were all settled again and the cargo was rearranged and secure, Eric thumped his fist on the roof of the cab. Bill slapped a huge, meaty hand on the side of his door through the window, and pulled the truck around the Taurus.

Eric glanced through the glass half-window in the back of the cab and smiled. Christina was holding the map, and Imogene was already pointing out the highlighted route they'd agreed on a few hours earlier. After walking around a bit, Christina ate a pack of peanut butter filled crackers. She seemed stronger already and hadn't needed any help walking down the path from the camp site to the parking area. It would take a while for her to get back to a hundred percent, but she was definitely doing better.

With a satisfied smile, Eric leaned back and watched as Crowder's Mountain fell steadily behind them. A cloud of smoke rose into the sky to the south and west beyond the mountain. The cloud was thick, but it was still far enough out that Eric couldn't see the fire or where the smoke was coming from. Ahead of them, the road was empty and so was the sky.

Eric wondered how long it would stay that way.

CH. 13

Checkpoint Tango

Joe walked point as the four men moved through the streets of Norfolk Naval Station. The base was eerily quiet. No engines, motors, or fans were humming in the huge brick and stone buildings. Every vehicle they passed was stopped in the middle of the road, doors open, with the keys still in the ignition.

After the fourth car failed to start, they'd stopped trying. Joe kept his hands on his rifle at all times. He kept his finger near, but intentionally never quite resting on the trigger. Something tickled the pit of Joe's stomach and he recognized the familiar pinch of adrenaline. Somewhere deep down, past his conscious thoughts, past even his training, Joe knew that he was in danger.

Tom and Corporal Alexis Henderson walked about four yards behind him, and Chris brought up the rear. All of the men felt the same thing. Henderson kept glancing back over his right shoulder as if he expected his CO to come around a corner and start yelling. Tom and Chris carried it better. They moved with the same heightened precision and focus that he'd seen before when something major was going on in the watch-room.

Joe rounded a corner and stopped dead still. He dropped his hand by his side quickly, palm out and flat, and the men behind him stopped before the intersection.

"Okay," Joe said, "whatever happens, you follow my lead. If I raise my weapon, we're rolling hot, so be ready for it. Henderson, you keep your mouth shut. No matter what anyone says, you keep it shut, got it?"

All three men nodded, and Joe started walking.

Ahead of him was the guard gate at the entrance to the base. On each side of the gate was a pair of HUM-V's with manned fifty caliber belt-fed machine guns in the back. There were six men standing in front of the vehicles. One of them came striding confidently forward and stopped about twenty feet from the gate.

Joe took a quick survey of the men facing him, marking out details quickly and cataloguing them for mental examination later. The men all had similar tactical gear on in some shade of urban blues and grays or field browns and greens. They all had high end rifles and side arms and they carried them with the practiced ease of men who were accustomed to using them.

None of the men had any patch, badge, or insignia of any kind on their uniforms; not even a company logo.

Joe walked directly up to the man who'd stepped out to meet them.

"You in charge here?" Joe asked before the man could speak.

"I'm the Operations Team Leader," the man said. "Name's Parker. And you are?"

"Tillman," Joe said. "What are you guys doing out here? Where are the regular uniformed guards?"

"They all got called back to the main building for some big thing," Parker replied. "We're a private contractor that augments the regular troops for base security operations and emergency response. Now, who are you with?"

"We're leaving," Joe said simply, and nodded towards the gate. "You mind opening it up for us?"

Parker smiled an easy smile. "Well, I don't know about that now. I was told to hold the gate no matter what. Nobody came and told me to expect visitors. Who are you guys with?"

Joe unclipped his ID badge and handed it to Parker. "That says CC-O6," Joe said. "Civilian Contractor, Officer Level 6. That answer enough for you?"

Parker looked at the badge and shrugged slightly. "Most days, yes sir, it would be. This isn't most days, so I'm going to need more than that."

Joe sighed long and hard but didn't say anything for a moment. Finally, he shook his head slightly, and said, "Have you been to Joint Forces Command, or Joint Special Operations Command recently?"

Parker grunted. "I've heard about both, but I've never been there. We get our orders through...other channels... JSOC's a little bit above my pay grade, I guess," Parker said rather smugly.

Joe reached in his pocket and pulled out a metal coin that was slightly larger than an old Morgan silver dollar. The coin was heavy, and it had enameled crests on both sides. Parker took the coin and looked at it. His eyes widened immediately and he looked back at Joe with raised eyebrows.

"You know what that means, I take it?" Joe asked, and Parker shrugged slightly, but seemed less than convinced.

Joe held out his hand and Parker turned over the ID badge and the coin. Joe nodded towards the gate again, but still Parker hesitated.

"Look," Parker said, "I can send someone to get clearance for you, but as it is I still don't think I should open the gates."

Joe snorted loudly. "Fine, you send a runner. But you know where I work and you see how I'm dressed. Do you really want to try and stand in my way and tell me I can't go? You want to be the one to explain to my *bosses* when they ask me why I didn't carry out my orders? Hell, be my guest."

Parker tightened his grip on his rifle, and for a moment, the two gunners in the HUM-V's seemed much more alert and dangerous. Joe could see Parker wrestling with the decision and had to suppress a smile. If Parker had to wrestle with it this much and this hard, then Joe knew he'd already won.

Finally, Parker turned and whistled a short, loud whistle and the gates began rolling back. Joe turned to the three men at his back and nodded towards the open road. As they passed him, Parker turned and gave a few short hand signals to his men. The contractors on the ground shifted slightly. It was subtle, but they were suddenly poised on the balls of their feet and every pair of eyes was locked on the four men as they approached the gate.

The machine gunners relaxed slightly and allowed the muzzles of their guns to drop to a few feet in front of the vehicles. Still, they kept their hands on their weapons and their eyes on Joe.

"Listen, if you come back this way," Parker said, "I can't guarantee I'll be able to open the gates for you. It'll be dark soon, and I mean darker than it's been in a long time. We've been hearing gunshots every now and then. There was a pretty good exchange an hour ago, but it died out eventually. Who knows what'll happen once the sun goes down."

Joe shrugged slightly and replied, "I know. Orders are orders, though."

Joe stayed on point as the small team made their way down the long road and to the main highway. He didn't start breathing easier until they'd put a few walls between themselves and the contractors. As they walked, Joe expected the tingling feeling of hyperawareness to fade out a bit, but he was wrong.

As the team walked further and further from the naval base, a feeling like charged electricity began prickling across his skin. None of the men spoke, but they felt it just as strong. Their breathing became deep and fast, but not from fear. They were intense and feeding off the tension they could all taste on the back of their tongues every time they breathed in.

The sun was still shining when they found the first body.

D. W. McAliley

Ch. 14

Troubled Waters

The wind whipped through the back of the truck and made it nearly impossible to talk. Eric scanned the countryside as they drove, paying attention to landmarks as they went. He made mental note of where the water towers were as well as tall trees, hills, and other standout features. His father had taught him to note features like that when he was young so if he ever got lost in the woods he would be able to find his way home.

Bill drove out onto a four-lane bridge that had a few cars stalled here and there. He slowed down to navigate among the cars, and Claire tapped Eric's leg and then pointed out over the water. In several places the calm, mirror surface of Lake Wylie was broken by wings or tails of airplanes sticking up in the air at odd angles.

Vultures were already perched on the nearest horizontal stabilizer.

Eric turned his head, not wanting to see what the vultures were feasting on, and he found himself staring at a thick column of black smoke on the western horizon. This fire was different from the one they'd left behind on Crowder's mountain. He wasn't sure, but the location seemed about right for the Coalogix power plant that had burst into flames the night before and then exploded like a bomb.

Eric didn't really want to think about that either, but it seemed wherever he looked there was a reminder of the death and destruction that was all around them. They'd been on the road for less than two hours, sticking to back roads and side streets as much as possible, and still they'd seen stalled cars, burnt out homes and neighborhoods, and several dead bodies lying in the street.

Bill slowed the truck and pulled into a gas station on the North Carolina shore of the lake. There were two cars at pumps and one parked in front of the store, but no people were visible. Eric and Mike climbed down and walked around the store, searching, but they found no one. The two approached the door, and Mike took out a 9mm handgun and held it out to Eric.

"Know how to use this?" Mike asked.

Eric nodded. "Yeah, I've been shooting since I was a kid."

Eric took the handgun, checked the chamber, and clicked the safety off. He motioned to Mike, who pushed open the not-so-automatic doors. Mike stepped inside and swept to the right with his flashlight and pistol. Eric stepped in and did the same to the left, but the store was empty. Mike went to the switch panel for the pumps and started flipping the switches at random, but nothing happened. All of the lights were dark, even the ones in the cooler cabinets.

"Nothing works," Mike said, slamming his heavy Maglite down on the switch panel.

"Alright," Eric said, trying to change the subject. "Let's grab what we can. Get the beef jerky, water, anything we can carry that won't go bad in the next day or two."

"Don't you think they'll have food and water at the shelter?" Mike asked.

Eric grunted. "Never hurts to be prepared," he said noncommittally.

Mike frowned and hesitated, but eventually he took a stack of bags and started collecting water and junk food. Eric took some bags and collected all of the batteries, OTC drugs, and bottles of alcohol and peroxide he could find. He bagged up ten bottles of motor oil and a couple of jugs of antifreeze as well. They carried the supplies outside and started loading them into the bed of the truck.

Bill came around from the cab, a disheartened look on his face. "Fellas," he said, "we're damn near out of gas."

"Better find a fill-up station, then," Mike said with an ironic chuckle.

"Well, yeah," Bill said. "But how are we gonna get the gas out of the ground and into the truck? Pumps are shut down tight."

Eric smiled. "I think I found something that might help," he said, digging around in one of his plastic bags. Finally, he pulled out a small hand-cranked siphon pump with a set of hoses.

"I don't think that little thing will reach down in them big holdin tanks," Bill said, scratching his bald head.

"Probably not," Eric agreed. "But it'll reach into the gas tanks of the cars here in the parking lot. There's a gas can back in the store, if you want to grab it, Bill."

Mike followed Eric to the nearest of the cars. They disconnected the filling hose and Eric set up the pump. They were waiting for Bill to come back with the gas can when Mike nudged Eric's leg with his foot.

"You don't think there's a FEMA shelter in the city, do you?" Mike asked.

Eric shrugged. "I don't know, to tell you the truth," he said honestly. "But I doubt it. I mean, if FEMA was going to be anywhere, don't you think they'd be right here, dealing with all of these downed planes? I mean, think about it, Mike. This happened completely out of the blue. There wasn't any time to set anything up ahead of it, and there's no way to coordinate it now with all of the comm. lines and power lines across the country down."

"Then why'd you agree to come to the city with us in the first place?" Mike asked.

Eric opened his mouth to answer, but was cut off by three loud pops from inside the store. Eric froze and Mike's hand went instantly to his sidearm. They both stood, eyes locked on the door, as Bill came staggering out holding his left shoulder.

Bill took three steps into the parking lot, coughed, and collapsed to the pavement.

Ch. 15

Knock Knock

Joe, Chris, and Henderson formed a three point perimeter, their backs to Tom as he knelt in the massive parking lot of the stitching yard. The lacework of tracks and stalled trains was behind them, and they stood on the broad, flat black-top expanse that separated the railroad yard and the posh Lafayette Shores neighborhood.

Tom breathed heavily through his nose. It was a hot afternoon, and they'd been on the move for the better part of an hour and a half. He had been more used to this kind of pace in his younger years. Still, he didn't run the way his wife, Jen did. She was damned near religious about her 0500 laps around the neighborhood.

The running shoes sticking out from under the blue tarp in front of him weren't Jen's, but he did recognize them. Tom ground his teeth and lifted the tarp. Brown curls framed a middle-aged face that he recognized. He closed his eyes and led the tarp drop.

For a moment, the world reeled, and Tom had to stick out an arm to catch his balance.

Joe glanced at Tom briefly, then turned and scanned his section of perimeter. He caught movement over by one of the parked tractor trailers. Joe whistled and pointed, dropping to one knee. As if on cue, a young man stepped out from in between two trailers, both hands held high.

"You guys Cops?" the young man called, walking cautiously forward.

Joe stood and took two steps forward. "Hands!" he called. "Show me your hands, palms out, arms stretched."

The man did as he was instructed, and he stopped. Joe approached him slowly. Chris and Henderson shifted their position slightly so that their backs were towards each other. Joe knew if he glanced over his shoulder Tom would be covering him from behind. When he got a couple of steps away from the young man, he stopped and lowered his rifle.

"Look," Joe said, "you have two options. I can frisk you, clear you, and we can talk. Or you can turn around and walk back the way you came. Got it?"

"Are you guys the cops?" the young man asked again.

"Do I look like a cop to you, son?" Joe asked, and the young man shook his head. "Okay. So, which is going to be?"

"Go ahead," the young man said. "I got nothing on me."

Joe nodded and stepped forward again, slowly. He kept his right hand close to his sidearm as he carefully swiped his hands down the man's arms, torso, and legs. Satisfied, he took three steps back and held his rifle at the ready, but not quite raised to his shoulder.

"Walk in front of me," Joe said, "and keep your hands where we can all see them. You leave when we say you can go, and you answer questions straight up. We'll do our best to do the same, got it?"

The young man nodded and started walking, arms stretched out. After a few steps, he relaxed a little, and dropped his hands at least. Still, he was careful to keep them well away from his pockets, which was good. When they reached Tom, Chris and Henderson fell in close enough to hear the discussion, but they kept their focus outward.

"Did you know her?" the young man asked.

Tom's head popped up, and he growled, "Yes, did you?"

The young man shook his head slowly. "I never saw her before...before today."

"Were you here?" Tom asked. "Were you a part of this?"

"No, sir," the young man said softly. "I saw it, though. I was up on top of one of the warehouses back there." He jerked a thumb over his shoulder. "And I saw these guys come from the weigh station. They were pushing and draggin her, and they were pretty rough about it. They got her down here, and there was some yelling. I couldn't hear it enough to understand it, but I could hear it. Then this guy, he just shot her."

"What did that guy look like?" Joe asked before Tom could speak.

"I don't know, really," the young man replied. "Short hair, dark sunglasses, and he was with a group of guys dressed pretty much like him; all dark grays and blues. They went and got into two Hum-V's on Hampton Blvd. and drove off in them."

"Wait," Tom said, and suddenly his eyes were intense. "The Hum-V's worked? They drove off?"

The young man nodded slowly. "Yeah. The noise of the engines was what drew me down here to begin with. I stay in a shitty little mill house back up Gleneagles with my grandma. I was on the porch and heard them rumble by when everything else was dead quiet...except for an occasional gun shot."

The young man's eyes dropped for a moment on the tarp, and he suddenly turned his back.

"I put the tarp over her," the young man said after a long moment of silence. "Didn't seem decent to just leave her like that."

"JT," Tom said suddenly, "we've got to roll, and you know it. These guys could decide to roll back through."

Joe nodded and motioned for Chris and Henderson to follow him. Joe squeezed Tom's shoulder once and nodded to the young stranger. He led the men off a little way and they waited for Tom.

Tom knelt and tucked the tarp around the young woman's body so the wind couldn't catch it. When he stood, his eyes were red. He looked at the young man and said, "Mollie. Her name was Mollie. Go home to your Grandma."

Tom turned and walked away from the stranger. He reached the men and broke into a slow trot that would eat distance and preserve as much endurance as possible. Joe brought up the rear guard, and he lingered a moment. He watched as the young man made his way back towards the train tracks and the warehouses. A couple of times he looked back and waved before disappearing between some transfer trucks.

Tom set a hard pace, and it was all the group could manage to stay together. Once they were past the fence that partitioned the port from the residential area, Tom began to gain more confidence with every turn. Finally, he made a left onto Sunrise Cove Court.

There was a Tudor style cottage, an all brick carriage house, and a two story cape cod with a wraparound porch and a bright green tin roof. Tom slowed once they reached the cul-de-sac, and he stopped in front of the Cape Cod style cottage. Joe, Chris, and Henderson watched the houses around them and the street behind them as Joe ease his way up the porch steps. He stepped up to the green door and stood a little to the side of it.

Tom thumped his hand twice on the door and then tapped the glass once with his wedding ring. He repeated the process and whispered, "We will, we will..."

After a long pause, from the other side of the door came a soft, "Rock you."

The double dead-bolt clicked and the door opened. A small blonde woman with large blue-green eyes stood in a nightgown with a twelve gauge shotgun in her hands. One hand went to her mouth, and tears immediately began streaming down her face.

She dropped the shotgun, took two steps, and fell into Tom's arms sobbing. Just then, four young children stuck their heads down from the second floor banister, and shouted "Daddy's home!"

"Baby," Tom said with a small chuckle, "I brought some of the guys from work home for dinner."

Jen's laughter and sobs blended together into one sound as she clung to Tom, and he clung back.

Ch. 16

The Stop-n-Shop

Bill fell forward and hit the sidewalk in front of the convenience store hard. There was a moment of shocked silence, and Imogene let out a bone chilling wail. She ran for Bill, her arms outstretched.

Christina caught Imogene just before she got to Bill. She held the older woman tight, stroking her hair and whispering softly to her. Eric was the first to reach the ex-ranger, and he saw that Bill's chest was rising and falling in shallow gasps. Mike and Claire reached him at nearly the same moment.

Mike carefully pulled Bill's shirt away from his shoulder and tore the fabric where the exit hole was so he could get a better look at the wound. Mike took a deep breath and stuck the end of his finger into the exit wound briefly. Bill groaned and jerked a bit, but Mike took his finger out and wiped it on Bill's shirt.

"No bullet fragments," he said, relieved. "I think it punched straight through. Eric, run grab the medical kit out of the truck; I'm going to need it. Claire, start cutting his shirt off and I'll try and hold him down the best I can."

Eric sprinted to the pickup and dug around a bit in the bed before he found the red and black med kits. He pulled both and found they were surprisingly heavy for their size. Eric ran as fast as he could manage with the awkward load in his hands. By the time he

got back to Bill, Mike and Claire had unhooked his leather
suspenders and cut away his red shirt.

Blood seeped from the small round wound on Bill's shoulder
in a slow, steady stream.

Imogene was still struggling in Christina's arms, trying to
break away and reach her husband, so Eric stood and went to her.
"Imogene, I know you're scared," Eric said, taking the older woman's
face gently in his hands. "But listen. Mike and Claire did a fantastic
job helping Tina, right?" Imogene finally made eye contact with Eric
and nodded slightly, so he moved his hands down to her shoulders.
"They're going to take good care of Bill too. But right now, they
need their space and they need to focus. Can you go with Tina over
to the truck? We're going to need some water and some plain food
like crackers, and she doesn't know where that stuff is. Can you get
that?"

Imogene nodded and finally let Christina lead her slowly back
to the pickup. Eric turned back to Bill, and his stomach lurched.
Mike had a double handful of gauze padding pressed hard against
Bill's back, but it was already soaked through with blood. A dark red
stain was spreading on the concrete sidewalk beneath Bill also. Mike
and Claire exchanged a look that wasn't good.

"If we can't get this bleeding stopped...." Mike said, unwilling
to finish his own thought.
Suddenly, Eric snapped his fingers, and he ran through the still open
doors into the store. Inside, it was still as dark as he remembered.
Along the back wall, two aisles held various fishing, camping, and
cooking necessities for campers who had forgotten to pack this or
that. Eric did his best not to look at the red splatters on the floor or

the small red gas can that lay forgotten against the drink cooler next to Bill's revolver.

A body was laying half in and half out of the storage closet between the restrooms. Eric carefully nudged one of the bright white sneakers, but the body didn't move, so he left it. He ran to the last aisle where the kitchen supplies were stacked, and he grabbed the four bags of sugar on the bottom shelf. He snatched a bottle of rubbing alcohol, six tubes of antibacterial cream, and three bandannas from a rack on the way out.

"I've got an idea," Eric said, dropping to his knees next to Bill. Eric popped open one of the bottles of alcohol and took a deep breath. "You guys will need to hold him."

Mike and Claire put their full weight on Bill's arms and Eric slowly poured alcohol over the wound. Bill groaned some more and tried to move, but couldn't. Eric dried the area with a bandanna and carefully rubbed antibacterial cream all around the wound. He then opened one of the bags of sugar and lifted it over the wound, but Mike grabbed his hand.

"What the heck are you doing?" Mike asked.

"I remember it from history," Eric said. "In the Napoleonic wars battlefield surgeons used sugar to treat bullet and saber wounds."

"How does it work?" Claire asked.

Eric shrugged slightly. "Something about osmotic pressures...I can't remember the details; I just remember that it worked better than any other treatment at the time. If we don't stop this bleeding, Bill's going to die, right? What can it hurt?"

Mike looked at Claire, and they both shrugged. Mike let go of Eric's wrist, and he poured a healthy amount of granulated sugar over the bullet wound. Eric pressed the mound firmly into the wound and then poured more dry sugar on top.

"Okay, let's roll him," Eric said, and he helped Mike and Claire roll Bill onto his side with some difficulty.

Eric dressed the other side of the wound the same way. Once there was a good pack of sugar in both sides of the wound, they pressed gauze pads to both sides and wrapped the wound tightly with rolled gauze. Mike and Claire sat for a moment and watched the wound, expecting it to bleed through immediately.

Much to their surprise, the dressing held and Bill's breathing slowed a bit. After a few minutes, Bill's eyes fluttered and he tried to sit up with a groan. Mike and Eric both jumped forward and held him down. Suddenly, Imogene and Christina were there kneeling next to them.

"What....what am I?" Bill asked, groggily, his eyes half-open.

"You've been shot," Mike said. "Try not to move or you could hurt yourself more."

Bill groaned and tried to say something, but his words were garbled and unintelligible. After a few moments, he fell back, his breathing deeper and slower. Mike checked his pulse and heart beat with a stethoscope and nodded.

"His pulse is stronger," Mike reported, "and his breathing's clear. I think the bullet missed all the main arteries and veins, and Eric's sugar trick stopped the bleeding. He's stable for now."

"Oh, thank you, Jesus!" Imogene whispered, and she collapsed to her knees next to Bill. She began lightly stroking Bill's hair with one hand and squeezing his right hand with her other, whispering to him the whole time. The rest of the group stood and walked a few steps away to give her some privacy.

"Could you tell what happened in there?" Claire asked.

Eric shook his head. "Not really," he replied. "There's a dead guy in a janitor's closet. It looks like he came out and took at least one shot at Bill, maybe two. Bill got him square in the chest with his .357, though, and that put an end to it."

Mike turned his head and cursed hard. "We never cleared the building," he growled after a profanity-laced moment. "I can't believe I did that. I know better than that. I make one lame-brained mistake and Bill gets--"

Claire reached up and squeezed Mike's shoulder. "You didn't know anyone was in there. Don't beat yourself up about it now."

Mike nodded, but his face was still twisted in a grimace.

"Look, there's something we need to consider," Eric said after a moment. "Bill's going to need time to heal before we try to move him, or we risk opening that wound again. Plus, the dressing's going to have to be changed five or six times a day to keep it from getting infected."

"He needs a doctor," Claire said.

"How do you suggest we get him to one?" Mike shot back. "Even if we had a stretcher he could fit on, we couldn't carry him to the truck, much less lift him into it."

"So what are you saying?" Christina asked.

Eric took a heavy breath and let it out slowly. "Looks like our little pit stop just turned into an extended stay."

Ch. 17

Special Delivery

Joe scraped the last bite out of his cold can of Franks-n-Beans. He stuck his spoon in the empty can and leaned back with a wide, satisfied grin. Chris and Henderson both watched him with confusion from opposite ends of the table; neither had taken more than a bite or two of their own dinner.

Tom and Jen were still too busy with each other to pay much attention to anything else.

"What was that about?" Chris asked suddenly breaking the silence.

Tom jumped as if someone had poked him, "What?" he asked, confused.

Joe jerked his head towards the door. "We'll give you two some privacy," he said, ushering the other two men out onto the porch.

Each of them had a side arm tucked behind their waistband and under their shirt, as well as at least one sturdy knife on them. They left their rifles leaning against the inside wall, within arm's reach of the slightly cracked front door.

Chris and Henderson poked at their beans while Joe stared off at the sun as it sank towards the West.

"My best friend for as long as I can remember was Frank," Joe said after a while. "His dad was named Frank too, Frank Sr., but I never called him that. It was Mr. Stewart for forever, and then Mr. Frank after that. I used to work with them in the summers on their farm. We ate Franks-n-Beans for lunch just about every day, and Mr. Frank would always make a joke about it...Two Franks eatin their beans..."

Joe smiled and shook his head. He was quiet for a moment, and when he looked back up at the red sun, his face was more serious.

"I haven't spoken to Frank in years," he said softly. "Last I heard he was doing well in Texas... owned a few physical therapy clinics and a house on some huge lake. I always planned to fly down and see him but never could make the time."

Silence settled over the porch while Chris and Henderson picked at their cans for a while before setting them down. The sun was sinking slowly, but visibly, and a cool breeze was starting to pick up. Joe looked around but couldn't see anyone else out on their porch. A few dogs barked in the distance, but there weren't any other sounds save for the wind and the birds.

It was enough to make his skin itch.

"It's going to be dark soon," Chris said after a while. "We still have a little way to go to get to Allyson and the baby. We need to think about moving."

Joe nodded. "I know, Chris," he said. "We haven't forgotten about you. I just wanted to give them some time. Then maybe it'll go easier when it's time to roll out."

Chris nodded and opened his mouth to say something, but Henderson suddenly held up his hand and hissed an intense, "*Shhhh!*" at them both. He moved to the far end of the porch and cupped his hands around one ear.

"That's an up-armored Hum-V," Chris whispered suddenly. "It's faint, but it's getting close."

"I don't hear anything," Joe said, waving his hand at Henderson. "Just the wind."

Chris was frowning, though, a look of intense concentration on his face. After a few moments, he began nodding his head. "Yeah, I think I'm hearing it too," he said, pointing down the main avenue to the south east. "From back that way, right?"

Henderson nodded. Both men turned and grabbed their empty cans and spoons. Joe did a quick police of the porch to make sure there was no sign anyone had been outside, then the three men quickly stepped into the foyer and carefully closed the door.

"Tom, we have tangos in bound," Joe whispered. "We gotta lock this place down."

Tom immediately stood and blew out the two glass hurricane lamps in the center of the dining room table. He pulled Jen to her feet and led her into the kitchen.

"Jen, we have to get all of the lights out," Tom said as he blew out the other candles. "They can't see anything in here, okay? Then we gotta go up and keep the children absolutely quiet and still."

"What is it?" Jen asked, confused. "What's going on?"

"Someone is coming," Tom said, "and we don't know who it is; that's what has us on edge. They have Hum-V's, though, and they work. I can't explain more right now, there's no time. You have to trust me on this. Go upstairs and get the kids into the back office closet and shut the door. I'll be up in a little bit."

Jen nodded and bolted up the stairs. Tom could hear her moving about on the second floor. He grabbed his rifle from where it sat next to the stairs. Joe nodded to him when he looked, and Tom sprinted up the stairs after his wife. Joe heard him take a position halfway down the upstairs hallway.

Joe, Chris, and Henderson quickly pulled all of the curtains closed on the windows along the back and sides of the house, and then pulled the ones along the front almost closed. They each took their rifles and a position with a clear view of the street.

Joe could hear the faint rumble of the Hum-V's now through the walls, and he looked at Henderson with an appreciative nod. "How in the blue hell did you hear those?" Joe whispered.

Henderson smiled. "When you spend as much time as I did running behind one with a drill instructor screaming at you, the sound kind of gets in your bones."

Joe nodded, and the three men checked through the curtains from in the shadows. They could see out the window in narrow fields, but it would be very hard for someone outside in the fading light to see into the dark house. Joe clicked the safety on his rifle off and heard the other two do the same.

"Tangos in sight," Chris whispered from the southeast end of the living room, and there was the muffled thump of a vehicle door slamming. "Two Hum-V's, gunners on each--holy shit."

Chris looked at Joe, his eyes wide, and whispered, "You're not gonna believe this."

Joe was about to ask what, but just then a man stepped into his field of vision, and he didn't have to. There, in the fading sunset light, a man with a tactical uniform in dark blues and grays walked around to each mailbox in the cul-de-sac. He opened each and stuck a single envelope inside. The man had short dark hair, dark sunglasses, and a very high-end rifle.

Joe took a deep breath, gritted his teeth, and muttered, "Parker..."

Ch. 18

Strangers In A Strange Land

Eric helped Bill sit up and lean his back against the Stop-n-Shop. Bill's face was pale and had a shiny sheen of sweat over it, but his breathing was better and he was able to stay conscious for the most part. Mike had given him two field syrettes of morphine to make the pain more manageable, and for a while Bill had been nearly incoherent from the drugs.

A makeshift sling held Bill's left arm securely across his chest and helped keep the bulky bandage in place over his shoulder. Eric pulled the wrapping aside and checked the wound. The sugar packed in the wound looked moist, but still solid enough to hold for a bit. As it liquefied, the wound would seep and had to be cleaned out. Then fresh dry sugar could be packed in and seal up the wound once more. It had only been six hours, but already the wound was bleeding less with each dressing change and it seemed to be causing Bill less pain as well.

Mike and Claire were setting up tents in a large grassy area between the gas station and a small strip mall with a few empty store fronts and for lease signs. Christina helped as Imogene rummaged through their supplies and began setting aside food and water for dinner. There was more inside the store, but none of them had been able to go back inside since Eric had grabbed the sugar to treat Bill's wound.

"Still attached?" Bill asked through clenched teeth.

Eric nodded. "Yeah, for the time being. How is it feeling?"

Bill snorted. "Like I got shot," he growled.

"Stupid question, I guess," Eric said. "Sorry." There was a brief silence as Eric tried in vain to think up a tactful way to ask his next question. With a small shrug, he whispered, "What happened in there, Bill?"

Bill frowned. "I've been thinking about that a lot," he said after a moment. "And to tell you the truth, it's all kind of a blur. I went in to grab the gas can. I was bent over and I heard something behind me, so I looked over my shoulder to see what it was. There was a guy standing there in a doorway with a gun on me. I remember I tried to tell him not to be afraid, and I started to turn towards him. Then his eyes got real big, and he shot. Th7e first one missed me, but not by much." Bill shuddered. "I turned towards him, and the second one caught me high in the left shoulder. The next thing I remember, I was stumbling out into the sunlight, and then it seemed like a good time to lay down."

Eric nodded and said, "I saw the guy inside. It looks like he was hiding in a janitor's closet. I know it's tough, Bill, but that guy was dangerous. He tried to kill you, and who knows what he'd have done to the rest of us."

Bill just shook his head slowly. "I spent a long time tracking down bad people," he said after a moment, "and I got really good at it. They come in all sizes, shapes, and colors too, you know. Some of the worst of the worst that I ever saw looked like they should be working the counter at the corner drug store or the library at your neighborhood grade school. After a while, you get to where you recognize it when you see it." Bill pointed to the open doors of the convenience store. "*He* wasn't a bad guy. He was scared and backed into a corner, and people do crazy stuff when they don't think there's any way out but swinging."

Bill was quiet for a long moment, and Eric didn't know what to say, so he sat and studied the ground in front of him. After a while, Bill nudged his foot, and said, "You know we're going to have to get him out of there, right? It ain't right to just leave him sittin in there to rot. Besides, there's stuff in there we can use, like the gun he tried to shoot me with."

Eric nodded. "Mike and I will take care of it. I think Mike feels guilty for not clearing the building when we went in the first time, and to tell you the truth, so do I. We should have checked the rooms in the back, Bill."

The ex-Texas Ranger waved his good hand. "Forget that crap," he said dismissively. "Who goes into a gas station and thinks about clearing threats? Hell, I was trained to check doors and I didn't."

Eric thought about that a moment before replying. "I think we need to start thinking about that kind of thing, though," he said. "Between this morning with Claire, and this afternoon with... We're acting like everything is just like it was yesterday, and if we keep it up someone's going to get hurt."

Bill snorted again, and Eric shook his head. "You know what I mean. If that guy had been a better shot....well, I don't want someone else getting hurt or killed because we're too complacent."

Bill touched his left shoulder lightly before replying, "I know what you're saying, and you're right. We've got to be more careful."

Eric nodded. "I'll get Mike, and we'll take care of what's inside," He said. "You rest."

Eric stood and motioned for Mike to follow him. They both carried flashlights and they had their pistols drawn. Mike went first into the store, and Eric followed him, keeping his eyes moving and checking the shadows all around them. The late afternoon sun was slanting through the glass front of the store, and it cast long shadows in the aisles that made Eric jumpy.

The two moved to the back of the store where the body lay. They stood looking down at the deceased man for a long moment, neither really sure what to do next. Eric had to swallow the taste of bile several times.

"Well," Mike said at last, "I don't think we'll be able to dig a grave with the camp shovel I have in my backpack outside. So, what do you suggest?"

Eric shrugged slightly. "I don't know, man. There's a fire exit right there," Eric said, pointing to the back corner of the store a few feet away. "We can drag him outside and at least cover him up."

Mike nodded, then looked back at Eric. "Head or feet?" he asked.

It was the last straw. Eric turned, lurched three steps into the dark bathroom, and emptied his stomach in the dark.

After he collected himself, Eric helped Mike pull the dead body out the fire exit as carefully as they could. If he hadn't already done it, Eric would have lost his lunch several times in the process.

Once outside, they laid the man out as neatly as possible. Mike bent
and began feeling the man's pockets, sticking his hands in them one
by one. Eric was about to object when Mike abruptly stood with a
thin wallet in his hand. He pulled out a driver's license and looked at
it before handing it over to Eric.

"Desandro Rafaella," Eric read softly. "Rest in peace."

"Amen," Mike said softly, and he bent to cover Desandro's
face with a black bandanna from inside the gas station.

Eric turned to go back inside the gas station, but Mike
suddenly caught his arm, "Do you hear that?" Mike said, his voice
intense.

Eric opened his mouth to say no, but stopped. He strained
to listen and caught a very faint, very distant rumble of aircraft
engines. At the same instant he and Mike bolted around the outside
wall of the store to where the others were standing. Eric grabbed
Christina's hand, and they turned towards the southwest where the
noise was coming from.

After a few moments, the sound of the engines grew to a
roar, and a flight of eight C-130 cargo planes broke over the tree tops
on the other side of the lake. They were flying low and fast, all four
props on their wings roaring at max RPM's. Christina and Imogene
both started jumping up and down and waving their arms, screaming
and laughing and crying at the same time. But Eric frowned as he
watched the aircraft fly over. Something didn't seem right, but he
couldn't put his finger on it.

"Where are the markings?" Bill asked suddenly from Eric's
left shoulder, and Eric jumped.

"Jesus, Bill," Eric said. "You'll give me a heart attack!"

"Sorry," Bill said sheepishly. "But look at them. They're all painted jet black with no flags, no numbers, and no markings."

Eric turned back and watched as the last of the C-130's flew overhead, and Bill was right. The planes were painted a uniform, unbroken charcoal black. Another flight of eight followed the first, and they were painted the same way. As the rumble from the C-130's was just beginning to fade, a new noise grew. Eric and the group watched as a flight of six charcoal black A-10's screamed overhead escorting four of the largest aircraft he'd ever seen in his life.

Christina and Imogene had stopped waving their arms.

"What the hell are those?" Eric whispered.

"C-5 Galaxy," Mike said in awe. "Largest military transport the US has in service. I saw one at an air show with two tanks loaded on it."

"What branch were *they* from?" Claire asked.

Mike shook his head. "I don't know. All of the military aircraft I know of have flags and squadron numbers and all kinds of stuff painted all over them. The only exception is the B-2, and none of those looked like a stealth bomber to me."

The group turned and watched as the planes banked and headed slightly to the north east, and Eric felt a lump form in the pit of his stomach. The strange aircraft were headed towards the cargo terminal at Charlotte-Douglas Airport—less than three miles from his house.

Ch. 19

Be Home By

Joe waited until the sound of the Hum-V's had faded completely before he cracked the front door. Even then, he sat with his ear pressed against the thin opening, barely breathing.

All he could hear was the wind.

Joe carefully eased the door open and set his rifle flat on the floor next to the wall, just inside the threshold. He left the door open and darted quickly down the stairs and to the mailbox out front at a low crouch. Joe opened the mailbox, grabbed everything inside, and sprinted back in the house.

He turned and eased the door quickly, but silently closed.

When he stood, Tom was back downstairs with Chris and Henderson. The three men faced him, their faces grim. The envelope from Parker was sitting on top, but it would have been easy to recognize if it had been mixed in with everything else. The envelope was plain white with no address for sender or recipient anywhere on it. Instead, there was a large seal of the Department of Homeland Security on one side, and FEMA on the other.

He handed the rest of Tom's mail to him, but kept Parker's letter. Joe took a deep breath, flipped open a small, very sharp lockback, and slit one end of the envelope open carefully. A letter fell into his hand, and he started reading. It didn't take long for his stomach to start to churn.

The letter read:

Dear Citizen,

I'm sure you are aware that a catastrophic event has occurred. Please, do not be alarmed. The Federal Emergency Management Agency has established protocols to maintain order and stability in just such emergencies. FEMA, in partnership with the Department of Homeland Security, has declared a temporary state of Extreme National Concern, Threat, and Emergency. As such, there are certain mandatory precautions all citizens must adhere to for their own safety.

Some of these concerns are:

1) All persons under the age of 18 must be accompanied by an adult relative if they are to be in public areas.

2) All persons over the age of 18 must restrict themselves to their place of residence from the hours of 6pm to 9am.

3) All gatherings of more than four people who are unrelated by direct blood or marriage are hereby declared disturbances of the peace and a violation of protocol.

4) All persons over the age of 18 must register with the Emergency Response Control Board to obtain information regarding restricted access areas, re-supply rations, and general information.

We understand this is a difficult time, and we thank you for your patience and your participation in the Emergency response. Please, be advised that any violation of the above precautions will result in disciplinary action which may include, but not be limited to:

1) Fines
2) Forfeitures
3) Incarceration
4) Further disciplinary action to be determined

Violators will be apprehended immediately on proof or suspicion of violation by authorized agents, and they will be required to present themselves before the ERCB Disciplinary Review board or the District Coordinator as instructed. All decisions rendered shall be final.

Sincerely,

Reginald Parker
Chief Tactical Security Officer
District 7 ANV 221

Joe resisted the urge to crumple the letter in his fist, but not by much. He felt the pulse begin to race in his temples, and his adrenaline kicked in.

"Welcome to marshal law, gentlemen," Joe said, and he handed to letter over to them. "It's gonna be a long night."

Ch. 20

Midnight Stroll

There wasn't any moon to speak of overhead, and the night was darker than anything Joe had seen in a long time. Only the stars overhead twinkled, and there were so many it was breath taking. Joe wiped his eyes and blinked a few times, then flipped his night vision goggles down and nodded to Chris.

Chris started off again at a brisk jog and Joe took up the rear. They hugged the edge of the gravel bed of the train tracks. The shadows cast by the overgrown fringes that shrouded the intermittent chain link fence were nearly complete. As long as they were relatively quiet, they might as well be invisible.

Twice so far Chris had stopped as a group of six or seven late teen boys had passed within a few dozen yards of them, completely oblivious to their presence. Both times, the young men had been heavily intoxicated and stumbling along in a clumsy attempt at stealth. Chris and Joe had watched through their enhanced vision with safeties off, fingers off the trigger; just in case.

Thankfully, nothing had happened.

Chris set a hard, but steady pace, and Joe ground his teeth and sucked air when he couldn't stand it anymore. He kept a good eye on their back trail, though, and so far they were clear. Joe's right knee was throbbing, and he had a painful stitch in his left side, but he kept putting one foot in front of the other. He pushed the pain down and refused to accept it, cutting it off from his perception. It dulled, but it was still there.

Joe ground his teeth harder.

Suddenly, Chris pulled up to a stop, and dropped his hand flat to the ground. The two men dropped down on their bellies at the same instant, and Joe began moving forward slowly. When he was in reach, he gently squeezed Chris's right foot to let him know he was there.

Once Joe worked his way up to Chris, he followed the other man's gesture and saw a bright glow in his night vision. After a moment, the overload filters on his goggles kicked in and cleared up the image. Joe could see four men crouched together with flashlights attached to their tactical vests. When he looked through his free eye, Joe could just barely pick out the red glow of the flashlights a good hundred yards down the track.

Joe nodded to Chris, and the two crept forward slowly and carefully, bellies flat against the ground. They made quick time at first, sacrificing a bit on silence given the distance between them and their targets. At forty yards out, they started inching forward as quietly as possible.

Chris gave the signal to stop when they were a little more than thirty yards out from the group of men. They could just barely make out what the men were saying.

"It has to look random," the one in charge said, and he knelt next to an indistinct lump. There was a soft click, and the man stood. The other three did similar things, and one gave the lump at his feet a solid kick. The lump rolled, and an arm came out from under the rug it was wrapped in.

The arm twitched a bit, and then started pulling at the rest of the rug.

"Looks like we've got a squirmer," a second man said. The leader walked up, and grabbed one end of the carpet. He stood and yanked; the bundle unrolled and dumped a naked woman on the gravel. Without hesitation, the leader pulled a suppressed side arm and fired two shots into the woman's forehead.

"Not anymore," he said. "Let's wrap this up. We've got four more appointments for tonight."

Chris took a deep breath and brought his gun up, but Joe reached over and squeezed his elbow softly. When Chris shot him a one-eyed glare, Joe shook his head slowly. They couldn't afford to drop these animals, as much as both of them wanted to. If they started leaving a body count all along their trail, they might as well drop some bread crumbs as well.

Chris's whole body went rigid as he fought with the internal struggle for a brief moment, but finally, he nodded, and relaxed. The four murderers finished their gruesome work then walked away and hopped up onto a dilapidated warehouse loading dock. In a few seconds, they disappeared, and the sounds of their boots faded.

Chris waited ten minutes to make sure the men weren't coming back, and then he rose to a crouch and motioned Joe to follow him. The two carefully worked their way up to the warehouse and found three bodies rolled in bloody carpet, and one dumped rudely on the ground.

Joe bent and pulled the carpet up over her face. He knew he shouldn't leave any sign, but he couldn't leave her staring brokenly up at the empty night sky. It twisted his stomach in knots just to think about it. Chris checked the other three for any vital signs, but shook his head sadly.

"What do you think this was? Who would do something like this? Drug gang?" Chris asked, his voice ragged and his face pale.

Joe bent and poked in the leaves and gravel with his knife. After a moment he stood and handed a small piece of black plastic band to Chris.

"How many drug cartels do you know," Joe whispered, "use zip ties to secure a prisoner and a suppressed 9mm to execute a naked housewife? This is something a hell of a lot worse than a drug cartel."

Chris nodded, and both men checked their weapons to make sure they were chambered and ready like they'd done so many times throughout the course of their midnight stroll. Satisfied, Chris turned and took off at the same ground-eating pace he'd kept all night, and Joe tried his best to keep up. They still had more than seven miles to go before they got to Chris's neighborhood.

For Joe, the reassurance that he was locked and loaded wasn't much, but in the field you take what you can get.

Ch. 21

The Sound of Distant Thunder

Eric ran a hand through his hair and heaved a heavy sigh. He was exhausted, but he'd given up trying to sleep in the tent next to Bill. The ex-ranger sounded like a perpetual rock slide when he slept. Eric leaned his head back against the warm cinderblock wall of the Stop-n-Shop. He looked up at more stars than he could remember seeing in decades. Meteorites streaked through the blackness every few minutes, but it was nothing like the show from the night before.

Eric blinked.

Could it really have only been twenty four hours since he'd watched The Blackout roll across the North Carolina country side? So much had happened and so much had changed throughout the day that it was difficult to wrap his mind around it all. So much of his focus and energy over the course of the past twenty four hours had been devoted simply to reacting and staying alive that he hadn't had the chance to really process it all.

Sitting in the near silence of the night, though, none of it seemed real. It was as if he had observed the previous day's events through a lens or a movie. Looking out at the calm, dark surface of the lake a few hundred yards away, though, it was difficult to ignore the stark reality of a half-submerged tail section from a 747.

Eric closed his eyes and tried to clear his head. As he sat there, the night breeze shifted a bit, and Eric caught the faint hint of lavender and honeysuckles, and he smiled. "Couldn't sleep, huh?" Eric asked, and was rewarded by a disgruntled grunt. Christina plopped down on the concrete sidewalk next to him and snuggled her way under his right arm.

Eric opened his eyes and looked up at the incredible array of stars overhead. He squeezed his fiancé close and kissed the top of her head. It all would have been very romantic if it hadn't been for the aircraft wreckage, the utter lack of any sound or sight resembling modern life, and the pervasive smell of old smoke and blood.

Somewhere far off to the north and east, lightning flashed on the horizon and a long time later came the faint rumbling percussion of the thunder that went with it. Christina shivered a bit in the breeze and pushed herself closer to Eric's side and he hugged her tighter.

"You did good today, babe," Christina whispered. "I'm proud of you."

Eric snorted softly. "What, you mean running around scared half out of my mind and worried about you? Yeah, I was the pinnacle of cool thinking under pressure."

Christina pulled back enough to look up at Eric through her eyelashes. "I mean it," she said seriously. "You got help for me when I broke down; you pulled everyone off the mountain when the fire was coming, and you're the one who stopped Bill's bleeding and saved his life so he could keep all of us awake with his snoring."

"Not all of us," Claire said softly, and both Eric and Christina jumped. Claire smiled sheepishly in the pale starlit night and said, "Sorry. I didn't mean to startle you. She's right, though, Eric. I think we'd have been in a lot of trouble today if it hadn't been for you."

Eric shrugged uncomfortably and looked away to the south. Several flashes lit up the sky to the south, and the distant rumble eventually reached them. He didn't like the sudden focus and attention all resting on him; it made his shoulders itch.

"You couldn't sleep either?" Christina asked, motioning for Claire to sit.

"Not with that racket," Claire said, hooking her thumb over her shoulder at the tents. "I don't know how Imogene has put up with that for all of these years. I wouldn't be able to sleep a wink with that kind of noise going on."

"What about Mike?" Eric asked.

Claire shook her head. "He told me a story once about sleeping through a category 4 hurricane in an open garage when he was a kid. I never believed him before, but I do now. He's wrapped up in our tent, sleeping as sound as a baby."

Four quick flashes lit up the night sky to the west, and several seconds later, a deep rumble washed over them. Eric frowned to himself. Something had been nagging him about this "heat" lightening they'd been seeing. He'd never heard of a storm being far enough away that you couldn't see any of the clouds associated with it, yet close enough that you could hear the thunder when it hit.

Eric stood and looked south and west towards the latest of the mysterious flashes. Claire and Christina both stood with him.

"Everything okay, babe?" Christina asked, her hand finding his and squeezing tightly.

"Yeah, it's probably nothing," Eric said, peering into the distance. "Something about that lightening just doesn't seem right."

"What do you mean?" Claire asked, looking off in the direction of the last flashes.

"Well, it's the wrong color," Eric said hesitantly. "Plus it's jumping around a lot. I saw a few flashes to the northeast, then some south west, and now a few just about due west. Storms don't move around like that."

Claire stood. "Come on, let's go down by the lake and see if we can get a better view of what's going on."

Eric nodded and stood. He helped Claire and Christina to their feet and the three walked carefully and quietly past the tents, though any sound they could have made would have been more than drowned out by Bill's unbelievable snores. They walked down the shoulder of the road in the dim starlight. The breeze was cool, but not cold, and with the stars overhead it was really a pleasant night. The only sound was a breeze whispering through the trees and the very far off mumble of what sounded like a jet engine. Eric strained his ears, but the sound of the jet faded before he could pinpoint a direction, and the three walked down to the edge of the bridge in silence.

Eric stood at the edge of the bridge with Christina on his right and Claire on his left. They looked out at the lake and the remnants of aircraft rising like tombstones from a field of grass. Eric could smell the faint, acrid fumes of high-octane jet fuel that was

110

leaking from the damaged fuel tanks on the planes. Every now and then, the breeze would shift slightly, and a more unpleasant smell that he didn't want to think about would waft past.

Suddenly, to the north, there were four flashes of bright orange and yellow light that lit the sky. The rumble that followed was sharper and crisper than anything before had been, and it started in their feet and reverberated up through the air. Eric looked at Claire, a frown on both their faces as they struggled to process what they were hearing. I seemed like it should be thunder and lightning, but there wasn't a cloud in the sky. And the sound didn't quite fit right.

The sound of a jet crept back into Eric's perception, and he turned to the south. "Do you hear that?" he asked, pointing toward the southern horizon. Claire and Christina both nodded and they faced the sound also. The dull moan grew steadily to a roar and somewhere overhead a jet screamed by in full or near full after-burner throttle.

Just as the sound of the jet was passing overhead, a high-pitched whistle and whine to the south grew in a rapid crescendo and there was a flash of bright orange-red fire and smoke. A hard detonation shockwave slammed into the three a heart-beat later as they stood wide-eyed and open mouthed. Two miles to the south, an old rail road bridge collapsed in a deep black cloud of smoke and dust visible even in the darkness.

The jet engine roar was back and growing louder. It took a brief second, but Eric suddenly realized what was happening.

"GET DOWN!" he yelled and threw himself against Christine, knocking them both into the storm ditch next to the road.

Just then there was another ear-piercing whine and whistle. A blinding flash of light and heat accompanied by a near simultaneous crushing shockwave slammed into Eric, and he was stunned for a moment. Sounds seemed muffled as he tried to stand and lost his balance twice.

Eric frantically felt all over Christina, but couldn't find any injuries. He took a small flashlight from his pocket and looked her over, but there were no cuts or bruises. Her eyes were wide, and she tried to tell him something, but he couldn't understand her. The words blended together in a garbled and muffled mumble in his numb ears. Eric put his fingers to his left ear and blinked at the small trickle of blood smeared on them.

His ear drums had likely burst.

Eric turned back towards the bridge, and the ground seemed to spin. He nearly fell again, but managed to catch himself. The bridge that had spanned the entire lake now ended two hundred yards out in a jagged, smoking heap.

Claire knelt in the middle of the road facing the ruined bridge.

When Eric stepped up to face her, he looked down and felt his heart drop into his shoes. Claire sat slumped slightly forward, her hands feebly pulling at a two foot length of twisted steel rebar that had impaled her through the chest at a slightly downward angle. She looked up at Eric, her eyes wide and her mouth hanging open. Claire tried to stand, but the effort seemed to tear something deep inside her. Her body arched with a sudden spasm, and she fell over on her side. Eric knelt and ripped his shirt off to wrap around the rebar and try and slow the blood seeping out around it.

Claire looked up at Eric and moved her mouth as if she was trying to speak, but all that came out was a bubbly froth of blood. She coughed once hard, and then her body went limp. Eric felt for a pulse at her neck, but couldn't find one.

With tears streaming down his face and blood trickling slowly from his ears, Eric reached down and carefully closed Claire's eyes as the sound of distant thunder rolled on past the horizon.

Ch. 22

Better In The Light

Chris leaned over and whispered in Joe's ear, "Are we really going to watch this go down?"

Joe took a deep breath through his nose and let it out slowly. He shook his head. "No," he replied. "We'll take the two on the outside first, the two on the inside next. Get your knife out. I've got my side, you've got yours."

Joe drew his knife with his left hand and his suppressed Beretta with his right. Chris nodded when he was ready. The two crept forward silently and with surprising speed. Years of training took over, and they began rolling their steps and cushioning the impact of their stride with their knees. The result was a low-crouching, shuffling sprint that was quick and quiet.

Just outside the light from the four-man squad's flashlights, Joe and Chris stood in unison. One shot from their twin Berettas dropped the two men on the outside of the semi-circle formation. Their companions turned and stared open-mouthed for a brief heartbeat.

That was all it took.

As the man on the right turned back to the darkness behind him and raised his M-4 carbine, Joe stepped up and smoothly drove home his tactical dagger just under the man's right jaw at an upward angle. The man's body jerked once, hard, as the spinal cord was severed cleanly. Both bodies hit the ground nearly simultaneously as Chris dispatched his guard. Joe nodded to him, and Chris knelt by the four bound captives at his feet. He took off their hoods first and made them focus on him, and not the four bodies. Four young men between seventeen and twenty-two by the looks of them stared wide-eyed at him in shock. Joe kept an eye on the perimeter as Chris took care of the captives.

"Look at me," Chris said softly, but intensely. "I am a United States Air Force officer, got it? This guy, he's Navy Seals, okay? Now, you can tell us who you are when I untie you. If you start making noise or if I think for a second you're lying to us, we will finish what they started."

The oldest of the four blinked a couple of times and then nodded twice. Chris leaned over and loosened his gag. He put the hoods back over the other three, and they squirmed at first, but the young man growled. "Y'all cut that shit out!" After a bit of muffled grumbling the other three settled down, and the bound spokesperson turned back to Chris. "I'm Donovan. Man, I don't give a damn who you are, thank you. Them dudes were gonna kill us, and they weren't shy about saying it."

Chris nodded. "Did any of them say who they were with? Mention a country? Speak in a foreign sounding language?"

Donovan shook his head. "Nah. All I heard was one saying they had to stay on schedule or the TOD would be all over them. Said it like they were sweepin floors or digging ditches. Those dudes are ice cold, man."

"What about you, Donovan?" Chris asked. "You don't seem as shook up as you should be. What do you do?"

"None of your damned business," Donovan spat back. "You don't know me. I don't know you. Let's keep it that way."

Chris shrugged his shoulders just a bit. "Okay. I can appreciate that. Now, can you keep these guys under control? They know who's in charge, right?"

"Man, you cut me loose and leave me a blade or wire snips," Donovan said, shaking his head. "I'll cut them loose after you guys are long gone. You ain't even got to worry about them. They're my problem, not yours."

Chris looked at Joe and shrugged. Joe seemed to think about it for a moment and nodded. He came around and knelt in front of Donovan.

"Look," Joe said, his voice soft and low, "if I even think you guys are behind us, I'll come back for you. I'll put you down and not think twice about it. You're right, I don't know you and you don't know us. Probably best that we keep it that way so everyone can stay healthy. We clear?"

Donovan nodded. "Yeah, we're clear."

Chris busied himself gathering magazines and two rifles from the dead contractors. He left one pistol and two rifles, with one half-full magazine each. He left two strong tactical folding knives clipped to the contractors' belts. It wasn't much, but at least the young men would be able to defend themselves if they ran into trouble....for a while.

Joe took out a three inch lock-blade pocket knife and flipped the blade open. It was small, but razor sharp and well-made. He clipped the ties around Donovan's feet. Donovan held out his hands, but Joe shook his head.

"I don't trust you," Joe said flatly. "Here's the deal. I'm gonna set this knife on the tracks right here. Then I'm gonna put your gag and your hood back on and sit you down five feet in front of the tracks. Then we walk away, and you find the knife and cut yourself out. This way, by the time you and your friends are really free, we *will* be long gone."

Donovan nodded, and Joe was good to his word. Once Donovan was gagged and blind-folded again, Joe left him kneeling just as he'd promised. As Joe and Chris made their way back down the rail road tracks, they checked behind them several times. The last they saw of Donovan, he was carefully pacing forward, placing his feet heel-to-toe slowly and deliberately.

"Four groups of bodies," Chris said softly to Joe as they moved side by side. "Nineteen dead. Those guys would have made twenty three. Whoever these contractors are with, they're trying to make a statement."

Joe nodded, "Most of the time, people say it'll look better in the light of day. When the sun comes up tomorrow there's going to be dozens of victims of 'random violence' all over the city. It'll give them the perfect excuse to come down even harder."

"We've got to get out of here," Chris said. "We can't wait. It's got to be tonight or tomorrow. Any longer than that and they'll have it locked down so tight around here we won't be able to move."

Joe nodded and Chris picked up the pace. They were only a few miles from home now, and it was still hours before dawn. Joe stubbornly refused to acknowledge the burning stitch in his right side as he quickened his steps. As he ran, Joe checked his rifle to make sure it was chambered and ready. So far they'd been able to avoid a hostile exchange of fire, but given years of combat experience, Joe knew that luck couldn't last forever.

Ch. 23

When The Dust Settles

When Eric stood, his legs were steadier and the dizziness was beginning to fade. His ears were still ringing and every sound had an odd echo effect, but even that was settling down as well. Every muscle in his body ached, though, and his head felt like it had been temporarily used as a speed bump for a dump truck or a city bus.

Eric pulled Christina to her feet and helped her up the slope towards the convenience store. Imogene and Bill had come out of their tent, as had Mike. They all stared wide-eyed at the remnants of the bridge they'd crossed just hours earlier. Then Mike noticed Claire's body lying on the pavement at the edge of the bridge.

"Claire!" Mike called, starting down the slope, "*CLAIRE!*"

Eric stepped in front of Mike and grabbed him by the shirt with both hands, forcing him to a stop.

"Mike, she's gone," Eric said. "There's nothing you can do for her, and you don't want to see it."

"NO!" Mike cried. "You're wrong! We've got to *help* her!"

Eric tightened his grip as Mike tried to pull away. "Listen to me, Mike. She's got a two foot long piece of steel rebar through her chest. It pierced at least one lung and part of her heart. She bled out in a matter of seconds. She's gone, man. I'm sorry."

Mike's knees gave way and he collapsed to the ground, tears streaming silently down his cheeks. His face was twisted into a gruesome mask of pain and anger as he stared down at the smoking rubble of the bridge and Claire's body lying on the roadbed. Finally, after a moment, he looked up at Eric with red eyes and fresh tear tracks cut through the dust, sweat, and grime on his cheeks.

"We've got to take care of her," Mike whispered hoarsely. "Bury her, or something. At least get her out of the road like that."

As Eric helped Mike stand, he put a hand reassuringly on his shoulder. "Come on up with the others," Eric said, "and we'll talk about it."

Mike nodded numbly and let himself be turned away from the bridge. The three of them walked slowly up the hill to the parking lot of the Stop-n-Shop. Bill and Imogene were waiting outside their tent. Bill's left arm hung in the makeshift sling across his chest and he had his revolver in his good hand. Imogene's cheeks were wet with fresh tears.

"Claire," Imogene said, her voice cracking, "are you sure she's...?"

Eric nodded. "Yeah, I'm sure. It was over so quick I don't think she really had time to even feel it."

Imogene nodded and buried her face in Bill's massive shoulder as sobs shook her from head to toe.

"What the heck was that?" Bill asked, gesturing towards the ruined bridge.

"I'm not sure," Eric replied, shaking his head. "Some kind of airstrike I think. I heard a jet engine right before it hit."

"Why would someone bring down this bridge? We're not near anything important really," Bill said, confused.

"I can't say," Eric answered, "but I don't think this is an isolated thing. They blew up an old train trellis south of here, and there have been flashes all around the city throughout the night. I was so tired I just wrote it off as lightning from a far off thunderstorm, but it was too scattered for that. I think they're cutting off the city."

"For what?" Mike asked with fear thick in his voice.

"Make it easier to control," Bill said. "They did the same thing in WWII. Go in and bomb all the bridges and roads leading out of a city; save your road in. Then you send in the ground troops and paratroopers to subdue it; no escape for the enemy and no resupply."

Eric felt a sudden knot of fear in the pit of his stomach. "If that's really what they're doing," he said softly, "then the next step is invasion."

He looked around and slowly each member of the group gave some sign of acknowledgement and agreement. "We've got to get out of here," Eric said finally. "If this bridge was important enough to blow up, then they'll definitely be sending a team to make sure the job was done right. I don't want to be up here when they come through."

"What about Claire?" Mike grated through clenched teeth. "We can't just leave her in the road like that."

"We've got to, son," Bill said. He holstered his revolver and put a massive hand on Mike's shoulder. "If we move her or bury her, it'll be a sure sign to the people who come that someone was here. I know it's tough, by try and think it through, Mike. They bombed that bridge in the dead of night when they didn't think anyone would be around to see it. You really think they'll be okay with a group of eye-witnesses walking around breathing?"

"We'll have to leave one of the tents and a sleeping bag," Eric said. "Spread some random supplies around to make it seem like Claire was alone. With any luck, they'll brush her off as random collateral damage."

Mike turned his head, spat, and then stalked off towards the truck. It took the rest of them less than hour to set up the fake campsite. They raided the store for what they could carry and left enough to make a convincing case for Claire being a lone traveler. When everything else was in the truck and ready to go, the eastern horizon was just starting to fade from black to dim purple with the first hints of the sunrise that was still a few hours away.

Mike stood for a long time looking down at the smoking rubble of the bridge and the body of one of the few true friends he'd ever had in his life. Mike said good bye to his partner and his friend while the rest of the group waited in the truck, the engine running. Mike knelt briefly, tears clouding his vision, and whispered, "I don't know if you're there, God. I stopped asking you for things a long time ago, and I don't much give a damn what you think about it. But you took a good woman tonight. I hope you had a good reason for it."

After a moment of silence in response, Mike stood and turned his back on the burning bridge.

Ch. 24

Keys Please

Chris dropped to one knee beneath a stand of oak trees next to the gravel path they'd been following. Joe followed him and dropped to a knee with his back to Chris. He kept an eye on their back trail, watching for any pursuit and finding none. The sky to the east was beginning to turn a light purple with a hint of gray at the very bottom edge. The sun would be up within a couple of hours, and they'd lose the slim advantage night had afforded. Already it was light enough to make out, without the help of the night vision scope, the shapes of a handful of deer moving in the tree line across the park from them.

Chris cursed under his breath and tapped Joe lightly on the shoulder. "There's a Hum-V and four of those contractor assholes in front of my house," he whispered, and handed Joe the small high-magnification spotting scope.

Joe put the scope up to his eye and pressed the activation button. The image in the scope was surprisingly clear, and he could make out the four men standing in a loose perimeter around the Hum-V. The vehicle had a mounted .50 caliber machine gun, but no gunner at the moment. A fifth man came into view from the house with something that looked like a file or a clipboard in his right hand. He reached into the Hum-V and took a radio handset.

"There's a fifth guy," Joe whispered. "Looks like he's getting orders from command somewhere by radio. I don't think they're here by accident, Chris. How do you want to play it?"

"We go around through the trees," Chris whispered. "Come in through the back door. We get Meg and the baby out the back and into the shed first, and then we deal with *them*."

"Look, Chris," Joe said softly, "we can get Meg and the baby and just head out the back. We don't have to go after those guys out front as long as they stay put."

Chris's eyes were hard as stone when he turned to Joe. "They came to my home, Joe. They put my wife and my child in harm's way."

"I know," Joe said, and he put a hand on Chris's shoulder. "I'm just saying if we go in guns blazing, we're going to end up putting them in a lot more danger. We've got to be smart, okay?"

Chris took a deep breath and nodded slowly. He stood and led the way through the trees and around the end of the cul-de-sac. They worked their way slowly and silently around to the back of the house. Chris sat for a minute, surveying the back yard and carefully checking for any contractors, but it was clear. He gave the signal and Joe followed him up the steps to the back door.

Chris carefully unlocked the double dead bolts and the handle lock. He opened the door slowly and sat for a moment by the opening, listening. When he was satisfied that it was clear, he opened the door and stepped inside, sweeping to his right. Joe followed close behind him, and swept to the left. The pair went room to room throughout the first floor, clearing each room as they went.

Chris led the way up the stairs and stopped at the top landing.

"Meg," Chris whispered. "Meg, I'm coming up."

Chris stepped up and into the hallway at the top of the stairs. Joe covered him from the top step and saw a woman with dark, curly hair stick her head out of the bedroom at the far end of the hallway. She recognized Chris immediately and stumbled out of the doorway to him, a bundle of blankets and quilts in her arms.

Chris wrapped his arms around her and half carried the two of them down the hall towards Joe. Just then there was a loud pounding on the front door, and Meg jumped.

"Mrs. Boltzmann," a voice shouted from outside. "I know you are inside, Mrs. Boltzmann, and I know your husband isn't. You have to let us in, ma'am. We have a warrant from the Department of Homeland Security to search the premises. If you don't open the door, ma'am, I have been given permission to break it down. Now I don't want to do that, but you're not giving me much choice. I want you to understand that impeding a federal investigation is a crime, ma'am."

"That guy's been here for a half hour," Meg whispered angrily. "Woke up Sam and she's been fussy ever since. I was going to open the door until I saw the guns they've got. What the hell is going on, Chris?"

Chris just shook his head. "No time to explain it right now. What do you think, Joe?"

"Four man team plus a driver and Mr. Loudmouth," Joe said, shaking his head. "I had hoped we could slip by them, but I don't think that's an option anymore. If they have to breach, they'll come in from the front and back. That will split them up, at least. If we push them to it, though, then there's going to be bullets and blood."

"You got a better idea?" Chris asked, a hard edge to his voice suggesting that he hoped the answer would be no.

Joe smiled a cold smile. "Yeah," he said, and pulled his silenced Beretta. "We let Mr. Loudmouth in and have a conversation."

"How do we do it?" Chris asked.

"Meg, go put the baby in her crib," Joe said. "Then you go down and tell the guy with the clipboard that you're scared, but you're going to let him in, and only him. When he comes in, you tell him to close the door behind him. When he does, Chris and I will step out and deal with him, got it?"

"I'm not scared," Meg said, frowning. "I'm pissed off."

"Fine," Chris said, "be pissed off, but can you do this?"

"Sam's going to fuss," Meg said, patting the baby on the back softly.

"Even better," Joe said. "That'll give Mr. Loudmouth out there something to focus on other than you. Now, if he comes to the door with anyone else, you tell him flat out you're not opening it unless it's just him, got it?"

Meg nodded and walked back down the hall. After a few moments, she emerged from the bedroom without the bundled baby. Sam started wailing as soon as the bedroom door closed, and Meg growled deep in her throat. The look she cast Joe should have been deadly, and she stalked down the stairs. Joe took a position in the office just to the left of the front door, with the door partially closed. Chris slipped into the closet beneath the staircase.

The man outside knocked on the door again, and Meg yelled, "OKAY! Jesus, please, just stop pounding the door! I'll let you in, but only you, okay? I've got a baby in here, and I don't know what to do!"

"Okay, Mrs. Boltzmann," the man outside replied. "But my men will have to come in eventually to conduct the search."

"Okay," Meg said, her voice breaking a little. "But just you first. I need to know I can trust you."

"I'm alone," the man outside called. "My men are standing down. Now, unlock the door, please."

Chris stuck his head out of the closet door and nodded. Meg stepped hesitantly forward, clutching her nightgown close around her. She reached up and unlocked the door, then stepped quickly back away from it. The door opened slowly, and a middle-aged man in tactical gear stepped inside. He held a clipboard in his right hand and had a holstered pistol on that same side. He held his hands clear of his body in a non-threatening gesture.

"Okay, Mrs. Boltzmann," the man said. "I'm alone, just like I said. Now, can my men come do their job?"

"Close the door, please," Meg said, pointing to the front door. "You'll let bugs inside."

With a sigh, the man turned, and pushed the door closed. When he turned back to Meg, he found Chris's pistol in his face. The man's eyes went wide and he opened his mouth, but Chris shook his head slightly.

"You say one word," Chris whispered, "and I'll drop you right here. You make one move I don't like, and I'll drop you right here, got it? The only reason you're breathing right now is cause of him." Chris jerked his head towards Joe, who was just stepping out of the office. "So don't give me a reason to mess up my floors, okay?"

The man with the clipboard nodded.

"Good," Chris said. "Now, three steps forward, then down on your knees. Hands behind you and lock your thumbs."

The man complied, and Joe stepped up behind him. Joe took the man's pistol and handed it to Chris, then patted him down and removed three knives and set them to the side. Joe used nylon zip-ties to secure the man's hands, and he picked up the clipboard. Joe and Chris pulled the man to his feet, walked him slowly to the living room, and dropped him roughly on the couch. Chris pulled a pillowcase from one of the pillows in the closet and dropped it over the man's head, then pulled Meg off to the side.

"Go get the baby quiet," Chris whispered, looking back at the man on the couch. "We're going to have a nice little talk with our new friend over there. Whatever you hear, you keep the baby upstairs until I come get you, okay?"

Meg nodded, tears streaming down her face for the first time.

"It's okay, baby," Chris said soothingly. "I'm here now, and nothing's going to happen. You just go take care of Sam. Joe and I will take care of... *this*."

Meg nodded and wiped away the tears as she climbed the steps. Joe sat on the coffee table across from the man and Chris stood behind him. When Joe nodded, Chris took the man's hood off and held the detached suppressor from his Beretta against the back of the man's head where he couldn't see it, but could definitely feel the pressure. The man's eyes went wide again, and the color drained from his face.

"Good," Joe said. "Now you know we're serious. I've got some questions for you....and for your sake, I sure hope you have the answers..."

Ch. 25

The Beaten Path

Eric turned the pickup onto a gravel road that wound through a thick stand of old growth trees. On the right side of the dirt path, the gray and sagging remnants of a barn were barely visible beneath a shroud of honeysuckle and kudzu vines in the gray pre-dawn light. Briars and weeds grew right up to the edge of the faded road, and decades of hard rain and poor maintenance made for a rough ride. Bill winced and groaned at every bump and jar, but he never said a word. Imogene sat between them, rubbing Bill's shoulder tenderly and looking worried. Christina and Mike in the back didn't fare much better, but they managed to stay in the truck despite the bouncing and shaking.

Eric drove almost to the dead-end of the road and pulled the truck around behind the crumbling ruins of a once massive farmhouse. Three sentry oaks stood in the overgrown wilderness that had once been a yard and they cast deep shadows over the truck and what was left of the house. The second story at some point in the distant past had collapsed, but the first floor had somehow absorbed the impact. The result was a kind of one and a half story tall jumble of old timbers, broken windows, and rusted tin roofing.

"How did you ever find this place?" Bill asked, looking around and shaking his head. "It's like something I'd have see out in Bargersville, Texas growing up. Never woulda guessed you had humps like this in a big city."

Eric smiled. "When I was a kid, I had a cousin that grew up in this area," he replied. "Back then it wasn't all track houses and strip malls. This was country roads, fields, and places like this. I'd spend a few weeks every summer around here with my cousins, and we found this place on one afternoon looking for places to fish. There was a little old lady lived here then, and she let us fish in the pond on the back edge of the woods if we'd keep her yard raked for her."

"What happened to the little old lady?" Imogene asked, looking out the window at the collapsing house."Not sure," Eric replied. "My cousin moved away when I was eleven, and I didn't move to this area for fifteen years. I came here just to see if this place was still here the summer I moved to Charlotte and found it like this."

Mike and Christina had climbed down out of the bed of the truck and were stretching their legs. Eric got out of the cab and joined them as Mike helped Bill and Imogene out of the other side. Eric walked around the yard a bit and peered into the windows of the house with his flashlight, checking for any squatters. There was some new graffiti on the walls and a few empty beer bottles; calling cards for local teenagers, no doubt. Other than that, though, the house was clear.

Satisfied, Eric hopped down from the porch and joined the rest of the group. Imogene was carefully cleaning out Bill's shoulder wound and he was trying not to let the pain show. Mike sat in the leaf litter with his back against the truck and his eyes closed and Christina was idly picking at a broad oak leaf. Every set of eyes turned to Eric, though, and they looked at him expectantly.

Eric cleared his throat, suddenly uncomfortable being the center and focus of so much attention. "Okay," he said at last, "I think we're out of the way enough here that no one will accidently stumble on us. From right here, we're about a mile and a half, maybe two miles from my house as the crow flies. If I stick to the woods, I think I can make it there and back before sundown."

"You're not going alone, are you?" Christina asked.

"Well, I was hoping not to," Eric said, casting a meaningful glance at Mike.

When the silence stretched, Mike looked up from his seat on the ground and shrugged. "I'll go wherever you need me to," he said dejectedly.

Eric nodded. "We can go through the woods and stay off the roads as much as possible. It'll be tough, and it'll slow us down, but I don't want to risk getting spotted or running into people at this point."

"What's so important that you need to get, son?" Bill asked.

"I've got food," Eric said. "Long-term storage food supplies. My dad got it for me for Christmas a few years back. I asked for a flagship laptop for gaming and I got twenty five hundred bucks worth of freeze-dried food instead. I thought it was the lamest present ever, but he told me to stick it in the back of a closet in case something bad happened one day. I never could get him to talk about what he thought might happen where I'd need a six month supply of freeze-dried food. Anyway, I've got a few guns there too, and some ammo. I think we're going to need as much of that as we can get our hands on. There's some other stuff too, odds and ends mostly, but the food alone is enough."

Bill nodded. "Okay, son, I see your point. You're right, we need something more substantial than beef jerky and granola, and I don't think stopping by the local Piggly Wiggly is gonna get it at this point. More likely that would turn into the O.K. Corral or something."

"I want to go with you," Christina interrupted, tears gathering in her eyes.

Eric took both of her hands in his. "Listen, Tina," he said softly, "this isn't going to just be a walk in the woods. We've got to move fast and quiet, and we might run into trouble. I couldn't stand the thought of you getting hurt or something on the way. I'll be back before you know it, okay?"

After a long moment, Christina finally nodded. Mike stood and dusted himself off before digging through the back of the truck. He hesitated then pulled out a bundle and thrust it towards Eric.

"Here," Mike said gruffly. "It used to be Claire's. She wasn't a small woman, and you're not a huge guy, so maybe it'll fit you."

Mike walked off, and Eric unrolled the flannel shirt that wrapped the bundle. Inside was a belt of thick, highly polished leather that held a holstered Beretta 9mm pistol, a leather pouch for two extra magazines, a heavy metal flashlight, and a collapsible tactical baton. There was a detachable leather case with a shiny pair of handcuffs, complete with keys and a small leather pouch for a can of mace as well.

Eric swallowed back a lump in his throat as he buckled the belt around his waist. It was a little tight, but not uncomfortably so. Eric tested the draw on the pistol and found it easy and smooth. Satisfied with the balance and the weight of the rig, Eric gave Christine a long hug and kiss. Before he could stop her, Imogene wrapped him up in a tight, grandmotherly embrace, and she patted his back as if she were trying to burp him. He waved to the two women and turned to go. As he walked down the driveway to where Mike stood, Bill followed with him. The three walked fifty yards or so down the road in silence; then Bill stopped and faced Mike and Eric with a serious frown on his face.

"Listen, fellas," he said softly, "you watch yourselves out there. Don't trust anyone you don't know, and don't let your guard down for a second. People are going to be scared and getting desperate by now." Bill reached up and rubbed his freshly bandaged left shoulder. "And we saw yesterday what can happen when someone gets scared and desperate."

Eric and Mike nodded and the silence stretched for a moment before Eric finally said, "Listen, Bill, if we don't make it back by sundown, you need to take the women and go. Head south from here to Fort Mill, then head east. I saw your roadmap in the truck, and it's pretty detailed. Follow the back roads north from Wadesboro and head for Lillington. I've got family there, and the people are good. They should help you guys."

Bill shook his head. "We'll be here when you get back," he said simply with a firm nod.

Before anyone could say another word, Bill turned and walked back to the truck.

Ch. 26

Cat Got Your Tongue?

Joe leaned forward slowly, carefully, keeping eye contact with the man on the couch the entire time. Neither of them blinked, but the man's eyes widened a little, and the air started coming in and out faster and harder through his nose. His jaw clenched just a little before he caught himself and forced it to relax again. Joe carefully kept even the slightest hint of a smile from his lips; the man was cracking.

"Look," Joe said quietly, almost soothingly, "I don't know what you've heard about us, okay? I don't really care. The truth is I have to hurt people sometimes for my job. I don't like it, but there it is. You do that too, don't you?"

The man just stared hard at Joe for a long moment, the silence between them broken only by the sound of his breathing.

Finally, Joe sat back and crossed his arms in front of his chest. He looked up at Chris and shrugged slightly. "Okay, I guess he doesn't want to play ball. We'll see if the next one will."

Chris came around to the front of the couch, his Beretta in hand. He made a show of attaching the suppressor back to the barrel, and leveled it at the man's forehead.

"You see," Joe said conversationally, "normally we'd use some of those enhanced interrogation tactics you've heard so much about, and we'd draw the truth out of you the same way they draw sap out of a maple tree... one drop at a time." Joe shrugged again. "But we just don't have time for that right now. So, here's the deal. You either start talking now, or my friend Mr. Boltzmann here is going to repaint his living room in a few days. We'll tell your boys you didn't talk, and then shove your body out the door and ask for the next volunteer. Either someone will step up, or we'll take them out while they're trying to figure out what to do next...." Joe paused for a long breath. "Or you can start talking and save us the trouble."

The man was starting to sweat now. A thin, shiny sheen of it coated his forehead and down the side of his nose. He glanced up at Chris and the Beretta in his hand and then looked like he wished he hadn't. Joe sat slowly forward on the coffee table once more until the man's eyes were on a level with his.

With the thumb of his right hand, he hooked a throng of leather out from under his shirt. On the necklace was a row of bottle caps, each pierced through the center with a single bullet hole. The caps at one end were so worn that there was no paint left on them, and the corners were dented and dull. At the opposite end, some of the caps had paint, though scratched and faded.

"Yeah, sometimes I have to really hurt people for my job," Joe said softly. "What do you think each one of these stands for? I don't know their names, but they're here. I've already got to add two to this thing for tonight. Do you really want to make it three?"

The man swallowed hard and dropped his eyes.

"My," the man paused to swallow again. "My name is Charles Ganfield. Tactical Team Leader, Second Team, Confidential Services Division."

"What, is that some kind of rank? What country are you with?" Joe asked, his voice intense.

Charles Ganfield snorted a short chuckle. "You really don't get it, man," he said, shaking his head. "Yours. Your government hired me."

"Bullshit," Joe said flatly, sitting back. "Chris, this guys screwing with us. Time for contestant number two."

Chris placed the barrel of the 9mm against Charles' temple and pushed ever so slightly.

"Wait! WAIT!" Charles called out, flinching hard.

"I'm listening," Joe said patiently, and Chris lifted the gun just a little.

"September 10th," Charles stammered. "September 10th, 2001. Department of Defense announced they couldn't track $2.3 trillion in transactions. No one remembers it because the next day, everything happened, but on September 10th, they laid it all out in the open for people in the right positions, who know what to watch and listen for. I mean, think about it man, 2.3 trillion dollars worth of transactions just up in smoke. What could you build....what could you buy with that kind of money?"

"What are you, X-Defense, Hart, Blackwater?" Joe asked, and Charles started shaking his head.

"You're acting like they're different groups," Charles said. "We're all one big, happy, no compete family. We get our paychecks from the same place, my friend....and they're stamped United States Congress."

Joe cut his eyes at Chris, who gave a very slight shrug. In his experience when a detainee started off on an avalanche, the resulting information was good nine times out of ten. Joe looked carefully at Charles Ganfield's face and watched his eyes as he spoke. There wasn't the slightest bit of hesitation in his voice, no doubt in his eyes either. Whatever else might be said, he believed what he was saying down to his toes.

That didn't make it true, it just meant he didn't know it if it wasn't.

"So what is this, some kind of coup?" Joe asked once Charles had run down a bit.

Charles snorted. "You think they tell me? All I know is my orders came from the Tactical Operations Director himself. They told me to..."

Joe waited, and when Charles didn't continue, Joe leaned forward slightly "Told you to what?" he asked, his tone steely.

Charles shook his head. "Can't disclose tactical directives. That's a violation of the confidentiality statement. I've already said way too much, man. You don't know these people. If they find out I talked, you don't know what they'll do."

Joe pulled one of his short, fixed-blade tactical knives and held it with the point just in front of Charles' eyes. "What do you think I'll do if you don't?" he asked softly.

Charles still shook his head. "Doesn't matter. You kill me, they kill me.... doesn't matter, man. Dead's dead. You're on borrowed time, anyway, you just don't know it."

Charles closed his mouth so hard his teeth clicked. Joe sighed and took the roll of duct tape Chris handed him. Charles had just enough time to register what was about to happen, but Joe moved too quickly for him to do anything about it. Joe wrapped the duct-tape tightly around Charles' mouth several times, and then did the same around his eyes to make an adhesive blindfold. Just to be on the safe side, he even wrapped the zip-ties securing Charles' wrists.

Satisfied, Joe put the hood back on Charles and stood him up. Joe nodded to Chris, who slipped out the back and around the right flank of the house. Joe turned the knob on the door and opened it just a crack. He heard boot steps on the stairs as two of the guards outside came to investigate. When one pushed the door open with his support hand, Joe shoved Charles roughly at the two men. He stumbled and fell into them, carrying one to the ground. The other stood stunned for just a moment, and Joe stepped up to press the barrel of his 9mm against the man's temple.

"Your boss is still breathing," Joe said, pulling the man's weapons from him and using his body as a shield, "and if you want to keep breathing, you're going to tell your buddies to do exactly what I tell them to, got it?"

Just then, Chris stepped up to the driver's door of the Hum-V and jerked the lone occupant out roughly. He used the driver as a shield and held the two guards at gunpoint for a brief, tense moment. The two guards shared a look, and neither decided to be the first to take a bullet at point blank range. Instead, they lowered their weapons slowly to the ground and put their hands behind their backs. Once Joe and Chris had secured the five team members, they left them duct-taped together in pairs, with one man's wrists taped to another man's ankles—back to back.

Eventually, they'd be able to work their way free, but it would take them hours to manage it. Joe and Chris loaded all of the weapons and gear onto the Hum-V along with Meg and Sam. Joe grabbed the discarded clipboard off the couch and hopped in the driver's seat. Chris took over the .50cal machine gun, keeping an eye on the road ahead and the road behind. As Joe pulled out of the neighborhood and onto a main street, the sun was just coming over the eastern horizon behind them. It cast long shadows on the road ahead and bathed them in a deep red light.

"Red skies in the morning," Joe whispered to himself, unwilling to finish the old sailor's rhyme.

Ch. 27

Single File Please

Eric crouched on the high side of the ditch and looked over the crest of the small hill. The park below him was a shallow bowl of grass with dirt embankments on three sides. The fourth side fell in a sharp slop to a rocky dry creek bed. It was scenic and suburban in every sense of the word.

Four black and green camouflage painted trucks were parked in the parking lot and a contingent of guards with big black armbands designating them National Guard soldiers were setting up tents in the green-way in nice, orderly rows. There were little lanes and avenues between them that all led up to the picnic shelter, which was ringed with crates and rolls of what looked like shiny steel wire.

"What is that?" Eric asked.

"FEMA evacuation camp," Mike whispered back. Eric shot him a questioning frown, and Mike shrugged slightly. "I was a rescue swimmer with the Coast Guard for nine years before I became a park ranger. When Katrina hit, I was called up to active duty. I saw camps like that where people were taken before being bused out to the huge trailer parks."

Eric slid down the back side of the slope and motioned for Mike to follow him. The two kept the hill between them and the troops at the park. They followed the dry creek bed to the northwest for a few hundred yards until Eric was sure there was a good buffer of thick woods between them. Then he turned sharply to the right, climbed the bank, and struck off northeast.

Mike was winded, but he was keeping pace with the younger man. He was impressed with Eric's sense of direction in the woods and his confidence in choosing a path. And, after what seemed like an eternity, Eric dropped to one knee and gestured ahead of them.

"On the other side of this field," Eric said between breaths, "just past that thin tree line, is a long wooden fence. That is the boundary for our neighborhood. We should be pretty close to right straight across from my back door, but it's still a little too dark to tell. We might have to follow the fence a bit."

Mike nodded, trying to catch as much of his breath as he could.

"How high is the fence?" Mike asked, trying to buy a few more moments.

"Seven feet," Eric replied. "We should be able to reach the top."

"Not from here," Mike said, as he straitened, wiping some of the sweat from his face.

The sun was still not quite showing, but the morning was already warm and thick with humidity. Steam was rising from the deep, uncut grassy field in front of them, and it formed a misty shroud of the thin tree-line and fence across the way. Eric crept slowly forward, listening for any noise.

Satisfied, he nodded to Mike, and the two of them shuffled forward low and fast across the field. Eric reached the fence first and collapsed against it, panting. A dog on the other side immediately started barking loudly and jumping against the fence. Eric backed carefully, cautiously away from the fence, his hand on his pistol in case the dog made it over the fence.

"Are we close?" Mike panted when he got there.

Eric shook his head. "Not really. That sounds like a dog I'll hear from time to time, but if it is we're about a block and a half too deep in the neighborhood. I usually come at it from the other side, so I guess I got a little mixed up."

"So how far do we have to go?" Mike asked, a little disgruntled.

Eric gave a small shrug. "Quarter of a mile, maybe just a little more," he replied hesitantly, "but, if I remember right, the woods get a little thicker as we go, and this road veers away back towards the lake. So at least we'll be tougher to spot."

Mike opened his mouth, but before he could make a reply, Eric turned and trotted off through the sparse trunks. Mike stood for a brief second, on the verge of yelling after him, but in the end he really didn't have any choice. So, he swallowed his irritation and followed Eric. After a few hundred yards, the trees did indeed begin to close around them, and Mike started to relax a little more with the added cover.

He was just starting to think he shouldn't have overreacted when he almost ran headlong into Eric's back. Mike skidded to a halt and nearly lost his balance. Eric was standing over the bodies of two women and a little girl. Each had been shot twice in the heart.

"I used to see them walking," Eric said softly. "They would always wave back to me."

Mike put a hand on Eric's shoulder and squeezed softly. The other man's eyes popped up, and Mike said softly, "We gotta go, man. We gotta go now."

Eric nodded, wiped hard at his eyes with the backs of his hands, and started trotting away. He moved stiffly at first and almost ran into a tree more than once from looking back over his shoulder. After a while, though, his stride became stronger and he stopped looking back. It wasn't long before Eric dropped to one knee, breathless, and pressed his face against the slats of the fence. After a long moment of silence, he gave Mike a thumbs up sign.

"This is it," he said. "We're here."

Mike nodded. "Okay, how do we tackle this now? I'm exhausted."

Eric took a deep breath. "Me too," he said. "Tell you what...I'll boost you up.... You pull me up and over if....I can't make it..... Okay?"

Mike nodded, and took a few deep, steadying breaths through his nose. He gave Eric an "OK" sign. Eric squatted down and cupped his hands, bracing his elbows against his legs. Mike put his right foot in Eric's hands, and Eric pushed up with his legs as Mike jumped. Mike grabbed the top edge of the fence easily and began pulling himself up. Eric helped as much as he could by pushing on

146

Mike's feet, and eventually the ranger was straddling the top of the fence.

Eric and Mike were both out of breath.

After a moment to collect himself, Eric jumped for the top. Mike grabbed the back of Eric's belt and pulled. When Eric's arms were up and over the edge, and he was able to swing one foot up to catch the top edge as well, Mike slid as carefully as he could down the inside of the fence to the ground. A few moments later, Eric dropped to the grown next to him.

When Eric sat up, he was looking directly into the eyes of his elderly neighbor, Mr. Sheickles. Mr. Sheickles stood in a stark white tank top, faded blue boxers, and a pair of Velcro strapped tennis shoes. His face was pinched in a sour frown.

"Something wrong with your front door, Tillman?" Mr. Sheickles asked in a thin, raspy voice. "You notice the lights are out? I wonder if I should flip my breakers? I'm used to fuses, but breakers don't burn out, so I don't know what to do."

"I don't know what to tell you, Mr. Sheickles," Eric whispered, trying to be as quiet as possible. "If you want to flip your breakers, then you probably should. It can't hurt anything."

Mr. Sheickles made a sound deep in his throat and quirked his mouth into a half-frown. "No sense being quiet now, Tillman. You done woke half the neighborhood kicking around on this fence out here. Your computer top working, Tillman?"

"I doubt my lap top's working, Mr. Sheickles," Eric said with a chuckle, "but I'll check. I just got in, sir."

Mr. Sheickles snorted. "Quit calling me, 'sir' you sister foot," he rasped. "I wore stripes for thirty seven years. I was a workin man, Nancy."

Mr. Sheickles turned and spat to the side. He turned his back on Eric and muttered over his shoulder, "You look like crap, Tillman. Clean yourself up before your woman sees you."

"What the heck was that?" Mike asked from his back, still out of breath and panting.

Eric shook his head and stood. "My neighbor," he replied. "Crazy old Marine Gunnery Sergeant who thinks he's still in the trenches, I guess."

Mike snorted. "The only trenches the Marines liked to fight in were the enemies'. You should have more respect for the guy."

"Oh, I've got plenty of respect for him," Eric said, helping Mike to his feet. "I made the mistake of calling him 'sir' the first time we met and he tore me up one side and down the other for it. His wife had to calm him down."

Eric gave a slight shrug and started for the back door.

"He apologized a couple of days later, though," Eric said, "and we've been pretty much cool since. I learned last year not to ask him if he needs help raking leaves, though."

"What happened then?" Mike asked, but Eric shook his head.

"Oh no," Eric said, "I'm not getting into that." Eric looked around cautiously. "He might be where he can hear us, and I don't feel like listening to a lecture."

Mike started to laugh, but Eric shook his head firmly, a serious look in his eyes.

"I'm not kidding," he said. "I respect the guy, but he scares the crap out of me. He looks all old and frail, but I saw him splitting wood one day. Don't let him fool you, that guy isn't weak. He is old, though."

Eric quickly unlocked the back door to his garage, and Mike followed him through the dark, empty garage and into the house. Eric paused just inside the door, and breathed a deep breath in through his nose, and his face wrinkled a little in a slight frown.

"Even with a kind of refrigerator funk," Eric said with a broad smile, "it's good to be home."

Ch. 28

A Long Row To Hoe

Joe pulled the Hum-V to a rough, sliding stop in front of Tom's house. He reached back and tapped the rough under the gun turret to get Chris's attention. "Chris, keep on that .50 cal. Anything turns down this street that doesn't look friendly, you light 'em up. Don't wait. We'll be out quick."

Chris stomped his foot to let Joe know the message was received. Joe climbed out and held his rifle high over his head. He turned towards the house slowly, keeping his hands in plain view.

"Tom, Henderson," Joe called, "I'm coming in, okay? I can explain about the transport, but you gotta let me inside."

The front door opened just a crack, but no one came out, and no sounds emerged from the house. Joe kept the rifle held high over his head as he walked slowly up the steps to the front porch. He nudged the door open slowly and handed his rifle inside to Henderson. Joe stepped inside the doorway and found both Henderson and Tom waiting and armed.

Their weapons weren't raised, at least.

"Okay, I know it looks bad," Joe said. "We got to Chris' house this morning right before sunrise. There was a team there; looked like a grab-n-go squad looking for Chris. They ended up hassling his wife instead, and we interrupted them. Long story short, the Hum-V was theirs, and we repurposed it."

Tom shook his head. "Wait a minute, you mean they had Chris's address and came after him personally?"

Joe nodded. "Yep. The lead guy had a clipboard with a list of names. I recognized a couple from the Teams. I didn't look through the whole thing, Tom, but if they had Chris in there, then you and I are too. You know that as well as I do."

"What about me?" Henderson asked, his face suddenly pale.

Tom shook his head. "I doubt it," he said. "You're base security, but you're not SOF. What do you think it is, Joe?"

"Do you have a UV penlight?" Joe asked, and Tom nodded. "Then maybe we can find out. Right now, you have to get your kids and your wife, and we have all got to hit the road."

Tom nodded and ran up the stairs. Joe motioned for Henderson to follow him into the pantry.

"Look, we've got to get anything we can get our hands on," Joe said. "Water, canned foods, medicine, alcohol, glass cleaner, sugar and salt. You start at one end of the kitchen; I'll start at the other and we work our way together."

Henderson started to ask a question, but Joe shook his head. "I don't have time to explain it now; just do it, son. We can talk about it later, on the road, okay?"

Henderson nodded and went to the other side of the kitchen with a handful of empty grocery bags from under the kitchen sink. Joe opened the pantry doors and started stacking canned foods in his bags. He bagged all of the rice, sugar, and salt he could find. Two 24-packs of water in the back of the pantry completed his haul.

By the time Joe had everything in the center of the kitchen floor, Henderson finished his round of the kitchen. They had seven grocery bags full of food and supplies along with twenty four liters of water, total. Joe gave a nod of satisfaction and said, "It's a start."

Shortly, Tom came down the stairs with his wife and all four of his children. They all grabbed the supplies and carried them out to the Hum-V together. Chris kept the roof mounted machine gun moving, searching for threats as Tom's family piled into the rear of the vehicle. Tom road shotgun and Henderson sat in the very back of the troop compartment.

Joe pulled out as carefully as he could and turned out of the neighborhood. He kept off of the main roads and the interlacing highways and interstates whenever possible. Burned out cars were scattered alongside some of the streets and thick black columns of smoke rose from more than one neighborhood they passed.

Tom pulled the small UV penlight from his pocket and clicked it on. He took the clipboard of papers and swept the light over the list. Immediately hidden watermarks lit up with phosphorescence and showed the crests of the Department of Homeland Security, FEMA, and from lower left to upper right corners, block letters spelling out, ***COGCON 0.***

He shared a look with Joe and then clicked off the light. Tom started skimming the pages, flipping them quickly. After a moment, he looked up with a sick look on his face.

"Joe, do you know what this is?" Tom asked, his voice shaky. Joe shook his head. "It's an Internment Order. DHS and FEMA have declared a Continuity of Government Condition Zero and they have ordered the internment of all special watch list subjects and their immediate families. Jesus, Joe, I know some of these guys. I've worked with some of them before on ops."

Joe gave him a knowing look. "Yeah, I recognized a few too. Tell me something, Tom... Did you ever get approached for a job as a contractor?"

Tom cast a sidelong glance at Joe and was silent for a long moment. Finally, he said, "I may have had some feelers come my way. I made it clear I wasn't interested though. Why do you ask?"

Joe nodded. "I had the same thing happen when I got out of the Reserves. Three different companies came at me, one right after the other, and they came pretty hard. The only reason that stands out now is because each one of the names that I recognized on that list had the same thing happen to them, and they gave the same response."

"You think that's related?" Tom asked.

"I think they're tying up loose ends," Joe said softly. "Wipe out all the people who said no, or coerce them into saying yes. Either way, it ain't good."

Tom nodded and was silent for a long moment. Finally, he asked, "What are we going to do about the rest of the names on here?"

Joe shook his head as he drove. "There's not a lot we can do right now," he replied, with a meaningful glance back at their passengers. "We've got other responsibilities to take care of at the moment."

"We can't just leave these guys," Tom said softly, but urgently. "They're brothers in arms, Joe."

"I know that," Joe grated, "and we aren't going to leave them. Not for good, anyway. But you weren't out there, Tom. You haven't seen it yet. These guys... it's like back in the Sandbox, but worse. We gotta get these kids out of here first, bottom line."

Tom took a deep breath before answering. "Okay, I trust you, man. It's just going to be a lot tougher to get those guys out once the other side has them; it'll cost more, and I don't mean money."

Joe just nodded. "Yeah, you're right. Sad fact is, Tom, I think we all got a long row to hoe in front of us. No way around it."

Silence fell on them, and Joe drove on through clouds of smoke and empty streets.

Ch. 29

A Leaf On The Wind

Eric handed Mike one trail pack, and he took the other. The backpack was designed for long-trek hiking, and it was built around a light-weight, but rigid and strong aluminum frame. Mike began stuffing reflective Mylar-packaged food in the bottom of the pack. He and Eric split the load from a huge Rubbermaid storage container. The food was bulky and took up a considerable amount of room, but it was much lighter than Mike would have guessed judging from the volume alone.

Two woolen blankets apiece were rolled up and tied to the bottom of the frame for both backpacks. Eric collected all of the extra ammo he could find and began filling the exterior pockets and pouches on both packs with spare ammo and magazines. Mike retrieved two first-aid kits Eric told him about and packed those as well.

Finally, Eric went to his closet and got two rifles, a shotgun, and an old revolver. He handed the semi-auto 12 gauge to Mike. The .22 revolver went into his pack as an emergency backup weapon. Eric tied the .22 rifle onto the top of his pack setup, making sure to carefully pad the scope with a couple of scarves from Christina's side of the closet. He carried the .30-30 lever action Marlin in case he needed it.

The two were headed downstairs to do a final sweep of the house when a deep rumble loud enough to rattle the windows and the dishes in the kitchen cabinets shook the house. Eric sprinted down the last few stairs and out onto the front yard. Every house up and down the street had emptied at the noise, and the spectators were all craning their necks and looking up at the two C-130 cargo planes passing low overhead. Both planes had their cargo ramps down and they were dumping leaflets by the thousands as they flew.

As the small slips of paper floated and fluttered their way down, Eric snatched one out of the air and read it as Mike did the same.

The pamphlet read:

ATTENTION!

A state of National Emergency has been declared. FEMA, under the direction of the Department of Homeland Security, and by authorization of the President of the United States of America, has established an Emergency Response Command Center at the Charlotte Douglas International Airport.

By order of the Secretary of Homeland Security, all local and state public services have been temporarily suspended. Pursuant to Federal law and regulation, all power of police and emergency response has been delegated to FEMA, the Department, and their deputized agents.

Please remain in your homes and await further

information and instructions. FEMA response and
recovery teams will conduct assessment operations
soon. We thank you in advance for your full and
peaceful cooperation.

Eric stuffed the pamphlet into his back pocket and as he
turned back towards the house, he caught sight of Mr. Sheickles
standing in his yard. The old Marine had his standard outfit of
pressed navy blue Dickies and a pressed and creased olive-drab
button down with freshly shined black combat boots. Mr. Sheickles
crumpled the leaflet he held in one hand and turned his head to the
side and spat. He saw Eric watching him, and Mr. Sheickles eyes
narrowed for a moment.

Suddenly, Eric felt very self-conscious standing in his yard,
armed, and with a massive hiking pack on his back. He grabbed
Mike and headed back inside for a few last minute odds and ends.
Eric grabbed a tackle box and fishing pole from his garage while
Mike went through the kitchen and pantry gathering as much salt,
sugar, and dried food like rice and beans that he could find.

In the end, both men were loaded down with about thirty-
five to forty pounds worth of food and supplies, not to mention the
long gun each carried. The packs helped with the weight, though,
and the frames distributed the weight down and around their waists
rather than forcing it to ride high on their back and shoulders.

Eric and Mike were headed for the back door when a loud
pounding on the front door stopped them. Eric drew his 9mm as he
walked to the door, and he heard Mike do the same behind him. Eric

slowly and carefully moved aside the shades that hung over the glass upper half of the door.

"Stop your lollygagging," Mr. Sheickles growled from the other side of the door. "Open up, Tillman. I ain't got all damned day."

Eric heaved a heavy sigh and opened the door. Mr. Sheickles' normally sour face pinched down even farther into a disgruntled frown when he looked down at the gun in Eric's hand. "Bloody well nice to see you too, Tillman," he grumbled, eyeing the packs on Mike and Eric's backs. "You going on a camping trip?"

Eric frowned as he tried to think of a way to answer the question carefully, and Mr. Sheickles grunted a short laugh. "It's never the question that's indiscreet, Tillman; it's always the answer. You remember that," Mr. Sheickles said with a short nod. "Alright, then. You fellas better come with me before I think better of it."

Before Eric or Mike could make a reply, Mr. Sheickles turned and without even a backward glance started walking to his house.

"What can it hurt?" Mike asked.

Eric couldn't find an answer, so the two of them followed the old Gunnery Sergeant across the yard and into his garage. As soon as they stepped inside, Mike whistled softly. The cover had been thrown off of a pristine black and gray 1968 Ford Bronco. The truck had custom rolled steel bumpers on the front and rear, and a trail bar with four round spot lights across the roof.

Mr. Sheickles took a small keychain with a white rabbit's foot from a hook by the door that led into his kitchen. He turned and tossed the keys to Eric, who caught them out of reflex more than anything else.

"You look like you've got a long way to go," Mr. Sheickles said. "A set of wheels might come in handy."

The old Gunnery Sergeant started to turn back towards the house, but Eric called out, "Wait! Mr. Sheickles, I can't take your truck."

"Why not?" Mr. Sheickles growled. "Not *new* enough for you, Tillman?"

Eric was shaking his head already. "It's not that, Mr. Sheickles. I just don't know when I'll be able to bring it back. I don't even know *if* I'll be able to bring it back."

Mr. Sheickles snorted loudly. "You think I don't know that, Tillman? I've marched on three different continents in two different wars. I know when the shit's about to hit the fan hard."

"Well, Mr. Sheickles," Eric said, extending the keys back towards him, "you might need this truck to leave if things get bad."

Mr. Sheickles snorted again, and shook his head. "Look at me, Tillman. I'm ninety two years old. I ain't got any running left in me, and neither does the Missus. I told her twenty years ago when we bought this house that it'd be the one we died in, and I meant every word of it. Don't mean I'll go easy, though. I've got a Garand rifle in there that'll give them boys fits with their little plastic toys if they want to come messin around. But as far as runnin..." Mr. Sheickles turned his head and spat to show what he thought of that.

"I don't know what to say, Mr. Sheickles," Eric said, his voice barely more than a whisper.

Mr. Sheickles turned and looked at the wall to his right, suddenly uncomfortable. "You put up with a cantankerous, crotchety old fart when you had no real call to, Tillman. You're a good man, and I'm glad I knew you. Now you fellas get on out of here and take care of yourselves."

Mr. Sheickles turned and opened the door. Over his shoulder he growled, "You still look like crap, Tillman. And if you scratch my damned truck, I'm taking my M1 and trackin your ass down."

The door slammed shut behind him, and Mr. Sheickles was gone. Eric stared down at the keys in his hands for a long moment, a lump growing in his chest. Finally, he swallowed hard and loaded his pack in the back of the Bronco with Mike's. He climbed into the driver's seat and fired up the Bronco on the first crank.

Eric pulled the Bronco out of the garage and onto the street in the early afternoon sun. There was no air conditioning in the truck, so Eric rolled the windows down and let the wind blow through his hair. A slow smile spread across his face. For the first time since watching the planes fall from the sky, Eric felt like things were finally starting to take a turn for the better.

Ch. 30

Cry Havoc

Joe turned the corner and slowed the Hum-V to a stop. A half mile down the road, the street was lined on both sides with small shops and stores. On the left, two connected brick storefronts were smoking, their roofs caved in and charred timbers showing through the ruins. Broken glass littered the sidewalk along with a handful of shiny chrome rims and two tires. The remnants of one of the signs were barely legible, and it advertised life insurance.

Across the street, a crowd was milling around the front of one of a row of shops. The sign that lay in the middle of the street had once been a RadioShack logo. The closest had once been a liquor store, but the front door had been ripped from the hinges and the windows smashed. Two cars between the Hum-V and the stores had been flipped over and were still smoldering. As Joe watched, a man came sprinting from the store with the crowd in front of it. He had a large bundle under an arm that looked like a boxed television. A couple of the others from the crowd started to chase him but gave up after a few yards and staggered back to the crowd, bottles in their hands.

Joe looked at Tom and shook his head. "We've got to go through it. If we backtrack to another bridge, it'll take hours and we *have* to get out of the city before nightfall."

Tom nodded. "Okay," he said, and he thumped his fist on the wall separating the cab from the passenger compartment.

"Everyone keep your heads down. Henderson, you stay ready. Anyone tries to climb in the back, convince them it's not a good idea," he yelled.

Joe shifted the Hum-V into drive and stepped on the gas. As they drew closer to the crowd, a few people on the back edge heard the engine and turned to see what was coming. They nudged their neighbors and began pointing. The crowd flowed from the storefront to block the road. The faces at the front of the crowd were twisted into soot-stained masks of rage.

When the Hum-V was a couple hundred yards from the front line of the crowd, the looters began hurtling bottles, stones, bricks, and even chunks of black pavement torn from the road bed. The projectiles fell short, but there were an alarming number of them.

Joe thumped his fist on the back wall of the cab and called, "Show 'em we mean business, Chris."

Chris swung the .50cal turret and let out a short burst of fire into the smoking ruins on the left side of the street. The massive rounds tore bricks and mortar apart like sand, sending small explosions of masonry chips flying with every impact. The sound of the weapon was loud enough to be painful, and all of the children in the back began wailing.

Joe gritted his teeth and stepped harder on the accelerator.

Most of the crowd scattered to the right side of the street, taking shelter as they could, but the rocks, bottles, and bricks kept flying. They were bouncing off the hood and the roof of the Hum-V now as the distance closed to less than a hundred yards. A handful of committed looters stood defiant in the street surrounding a large bearded man who looked to be a leader of sorts.

The bearded man raised a bottle of whiskey to his mouth with one hand, and a .45 pistol with the other. He began shooting, the flashes from the muzzle of the pistol clear and unmistakable. There was a loud pop as one of the rounds impacted the windshield of the Hum-V. The bullet left a round scar on the glass, but failed to penetrate. Tom flinched instinctively as another round hit directly in front of his face.

Joe pressed the accelerator to the floor, and the Hum-V surged forward.

The small group of loyal supporters suddenly lost their faith and scurried out of the road like squirrels. The bearded man, however, stood and continued firing shots at the approaching Hum-V. Too late, his eyes went wide with fear. The bottle and the pistol slipped from his hands, and he started to turn to his left. There was a sickening wet thunk as the Hum-V struck the man, and he crumpled under the impact and the right side of the truck bounced roughly once.

Joe never took his foot off the gas.

Ch. 31

The Dogs Of War

The dirt and gravel road was rougher than Eric remembered. The leaf springs in Mr. Sheickles' old Bronco hadn't been upgraded to modern shock absorbers, and he could feel every stone and rut the tires hit. Mike rode next to him, trying not to lose the cold lunch they'd shared at Eric's house. The Bronco hit an especially hard bump that shook Eric so bad he briefly lost sight of the road ahead of him.

When the Bronco settled, Bill was standing in the road about twenty yards away, his revolver in his good hand and leveled at the Bronco.

"Put it in park!" Bill called loudly. "Or I start shootin!"

Eric slammed on the brakes and threw the Bronco out of gear. Just to be on the safe side, he switched the engine off too. There was no way that Bill could see clearly into the cab at that distance, and Eric wasn't interested in testing his marksmanship.

"Hands out the window, both of ya!" Bill called, and when Eric and Mike complied, Bill started forward.

"Bill!" Eric called when the ex-Ranger had cut the distance between them in half. "Bill, it's me, Eric, and Mike! Don't shoot us, all right"

Bill didn't say a word, but he kept the revolver trained on them until he was able to come up even with Eric's window. Bill stayed a good ten feet back, but once he saw who was inside the truck, and that they were alone, he dropped the revolver and relaxed.

"Jesus H," Bill gasped. "I damn near shot you boys. Where'd you get a set like this?"

"His neighbor," Mike said, jerking his head towards Eric, "Mr. Sheickles."

Bill shook his head. "Must have been a heck of a nice guy."

Eric said, "Yes," at the same time Mike said, "Not really."

Bill looked confused but chose not to ask. Instead, he said, "It's good you're back finally. There's something you need to see."

"Yeah, you too," Eric said, and he reached in his back pocket and pulled out the flier he'd kept. "Two C-130's came over dropping these things by the thousands over my neighborhood."

He handed the folded paper over to Bill. Bill read the pamphlet, shook his head, then read it again.

"I don't get it," Bill said. "This thing happened what, a day and a half ago? When have you ever seen the federal government mobilize that quickly on anything?"

"What do you mean?" Mike asked.

Bill handed the pamphlet back to Eric. "Well, do you really think they've just got cargo planes sitting around with these things loaded on them, fueled an ready to go all the time, just in case something like this would happen?"

Eric nodded his head. "I see what you mean," he said slowly. "It'd take the government days just to unpack and ship the flyers, much less load them and coordinate a mass air drop. They had to start that..."

Bill finished the thought for him. "Weeks ago," he whispered.

Eric felt the blood drain from his face. If what Bill was saying was true, it meant that the airplanes they'd watched and likely the ones that had bombed the bridges the night before were all part of the same group that had launched the attack in the first place. The invasion wasn't coming, it was already under way.

Bill swallowed hard. "I know," he said. "And it gets worse. Did y'all see the tanks?"

Ch. 32

A Helping Hand

Joe drove down Highway 17S along the edge of the Great Dismal Swamp. On the right shoulder of the road trees and brush grew thick and heavy, coming almost up to the edge of the pavement. On the other side of the hedgerow were a narrow, but deep canal, and then the swamp itself. To the left, wide open fields planted with soybeans and peanuts stretched to a thin dark line of trees that had to be at least a couple of miles distant.

The shadows cast by the trees on the right side of the road were beginning to stretch in the late afternoon sun, and Joe was looking hard for a place to stop for the night. He had only driven this route to Norfolk a handful of times, and never in the dark. Most of the turns and side roads were familiar to him, but he wasn't sure how he'd manage in the pitch black night. Plus, a moving set of headlights on a dark and deserted highway would stand out to anyone close enough to see them.

Joe snapped quickly out of his brooding thoughts as a small figure stepped out into the road a half mile ahead and started frantically waiving around a white piece of fabric. Joe slowed down, and as they got closer he could see that the figure was a young boy of ten or eleven waiving a white T-shirt much bigger than himself. The boy didn't budge from the middle of the road, forcing Joe to come to a complete stop or hit him.

The boy ran up to Joe's door as he rolled the window down. "Mister!" he called, breathless. "Mister you gotta come help! He's hurt bad, and you gotta come help!"

Joe frowned. "Hold on, son," he said. "Who's hurt bad?"

"My little brother," the boy panted. "He fell this morning and his arm's hurt bad. Momma said come and stop the first people I seen, an you was them."

Before Joe could say anything else, the little boy turned and sprinted down a gravel drive towards an old colonial farm house. The house was set in a semicircle of towering oaks about a quarter mile from the highway. Behind the main house was a large cattle barn and three smaller side barns and out buildings. The boy stopped about halfway to the house and started waving his shirt again.

Joe looked over at Tom who shrugged and said, "Your call, man, but Chris was a PJ and I bet he could help."

Joe nodded and turned the Hum-V off the highway and drove down the dirt driveway after the boy. When he saw the truck was following, the boy turned around and took off running again, glancing back every few yards to make sure Joe was still behind him. The boy bounded up the steps of the wrap-around porch and through the front door when he reached the house. Joe pulled the Hum-V in a wide arc in the flat yard of the house and positioned the vehicle so it was facing out the driveway they'd just come down in case they needed a rapid escape.

As Joe parked the Hum-V, an older man in faded denim coveralls and a flannel button up shirt with the sleeves rolled up to his elbows came out of the farmhouse. He carried a double barrel shotgun in one hand and a massive Browning automatic rifle in the other. The old farmer set the shot gun down against one of the porch columns, but he held the BAR with the ease and comfort that only comes with an intimate knowledge of a weapon system.

"Tom, you stay put," Joe said, "and be ready to jump in the driver's seat and take off if that guy tries to shoot me."

Joe got out of the Hum-V slowly, leaving his M-4 behind. He walked around the back of the vehicle and smiled reassuringly at Henderson and the rest of his passengers. As he came around the rear of the truck, the farmer focused on him and nodded. He didn't raise his gun, which Joe decided to take as a good sign, whether it was one or not.

"Your boy said someone was hurt," Joe called. "I've got a trained Air Force combat medic with me. He might be able to help."

The old farmer leaned casually over the waist high railing that went around the porch and spat thick purple tobacco juice into the azalea bushes.

"I seen you eyeing Betsy here," the farmer said, as he patted the butt of the BAR in his hands. "I carried her from Normandy all the way to Berlin. Marched through six different countries and the damned Ardennes. This ol'BAR put more Krauts in the dirt than the plague. So if things get sideways, I want you to know what's comin."

"I understand," Joe said carefully. "We don't want any trouble, Mister. Just want to help if we can and be on our way."

The old farmer nodded. "Much obliged for the help. The boys are inside. You and the medic can come in; the rest of 'em stays out here."

Joe nodded and Chris hopped out of the back of the Hum-V. They both left their side arms in the truck also, just to be on the safe side. Chris brought the small med kit from the back of the Hum-V, and the farmer led them inside and up a narrow set of stairs to a bedroom on the second floor. The boy from the road was sitting on the floor next to an old wood-frame bed along with a pretty middle-aged woman that looked like the mother. An elderly woman rocked slowly in a weathered wooden rocking chair in one corner of the room. In the bed was a small boy with his right arm propped on a stack of pillows and quilts. The boy's face was pale and sweaty, and his arm was swollen and turned at an impossible angle roughly halfway between his wrist and elbow.

Joe and Chris stepped into the room first, followed by the old farmer and "Betsy." The elderly woman looked up from a bundle of yarn she was crocheting, and her face twisted into a sour frown. "Gilbert, why are you carryin around that damned ol' rifle? You can't see good enough to hit the toilet half the time. God help us you decide to start shootin."

"Maimey, you hush up now," Gilbert growled back. "I can still see good 'nough to knock a walnut out the top of the tree on a windy day. 'Sides, these boys looks like they got trouble followin them 'round like flies on a dog turd. If'n you can't see that, then you's blinder than I am, old woman."

Maimey snorted hard through her nose and shook her head to show what she thought about that. Gilbert sullenly set the BAR in a corner of the room. He leaned against the nearest wall, his arms folded across a barrel chest, frowning and rolling a ball of chewing tobacco around in his mouth and grumbling under his breath.

"Don't mind them," the younger woman said from the bedside. "They bicker like that all the time, but they're harmless. Can you help my boy?"

Chris knelt by the bed. "Ma'am, my name is Chris, and I'm an Air Force medic. I'll do everything I can for him, okay?"

The woman trembled a little and unshed tears filled her eyes. "Thank you," she whispered, patting the young boy's hand. "Thank you so much!"

Chris nodded and began examining the boy's arm carefully. He gently lifted the boy's thin wrist, careful to support the weight of his hand. The boy winced sharply but didn't cry out and didn't shed a tear. After a moment, Chris laid the boy's hand carefully back on the pillows.

"His arm's broken," Chris said, "but it seems to be broken cleanly. I'll need to set the bones and splint the arm. I don't have plaster to make a cast, but a splint should hold it as long as he stays still and doesn't try to use the arm."

The woman tensed, the tears streaming down her face now. The older boy patted his mother's back, trying to hide his own tears.

"What's the boy's name?" Chris asked.

"Steven," the mother said through her tears.

"Okay," Chris said, "I know you're scared, but I need your help, Ma'am. I'm going to need strips of cloth, linen if you can manage it, to wrap the splint. I'll need four pieces of board about two inches by two inches and maybe sixteen inches long or so. And I'll need a wood spoon. As big as you can find, okay?"

The woman nodded and left with the older boy in tow to collect the supplies. Maimey rose slowly and laboriously from her rocking chair, her crocheting project tucked under one arm. She went to the boy and patted his hand.

"Don't worry, baby," Maimey said. "The Doctor here's gonna take good care of my baby boy."

Gilbert leaned down and grabbed his BAR. "I'll get the wood you need," he said gruffly.

The old farmer reached down and pinched the boy's toes through the blankets on the bed, and the little one smiled wanly at him. Maimey sat on the edge of the bed, rubbing Steven's hand and singing softly to him. After a few moments, the boy's eyes drifted closed and his breathing deepened as he drifted into a shallow sleep.

Maimey stood and fixed Chris with a hard glare. "You fix him up, you hear?" she demanded. Chris nodded, and Maimey seemed satisfied. She made her way back to her rocking chair and settled herself back in her seat. She rocked slowly as she crocheted, singing softly to herself.

CH. 33

A Fork In The Road

The shade of the ancient oak trees surrounding the broken farmhouse ruins gave some relief from the late afternoon heat, but not much. The air was thick with gnats, mosquitoes, and the sour smell of people who desperately needed a shower. Without the slight breeze to cool the sweat on Eric's face, it would have been nearly unbearable. Even with the breeze, though, uncomfortable barely described the way he felt and the expression on every face around him. The group was tired, nearly exhausted, but they were still together.

Eric sipped slowly on his bottle of purified water. With the supplies he and Mike had been able to salvage from his house, the group had enough food for several weeks, if they were very careful about rationing. The water was a different story altogether. Even if they were careful and used the water only to drink and not for food preparation, they had at best a three day's supply.

Eric stood and leaned against the Bronco, facing the rest of the group. "We've got to make some decisions," he began, and every pair of eyes turned towards him expectantly. Eric shifted his weight from foot to foot, uncomfortable with the attention and the expectations. He continued, "We have enough food for a while, but our water won't last more than a few days. Besides, with all of the military hardware moving around in this area, I don't think it's going to be a safe place for much longer."

"We could try and find a camp," Imogene said. "There might be one closer to the city, like Mike was saying yesterday."

Mike shook his head. "I don't think so," he replied. "Eric and I saw National Guard troops setting up what looked like a standard FEMA refugee and evacuation center in a city park on the way to his house. I saw what those little relocation camps turned into during Katrina, and that's the last place you want to be, trust me. If they don't have some kind of organized, large scale program going, then we're better off on our own."

"Okay, so what do you suggest, son?" Bill asked, scratching idly at his left shoulder. The wound was clean, and they were still changing the bandage once every few hours, but the sugar wasn't liquefying as much anymore, and the tissue deep in the wound was already starting to mend itself. With the healing, though, came the itching.

Eric nodded to Christina. "Tina and I have talked about this before," he said, "and we're heading to my family's farm. It's about three hours from here, out in the middle of nowhere. We've got plenty of room, good wells, and lots of fields. I don't know what you guys are planning, but that's where we're going."

Bill and Imogene shared a look, and Imogene smiled slowly.

"Eric," she said softly, "the only place we've really called home in a long time is probably in a pile of ashes on the side of King's Mountain. And even if our camper is still there, we can't float the truck across to hook up to it again. A long time ago, Bill and I decided not to take anything on the road with us that we weren't willing to lose except for each other. I think, if you'll have us, we'll go with you a while longer."

Bill nodded his agreement and patted Imogene on the hand. He didn't speak, but everyone was doing their best not to look at Bill's bandaged shoulder. If not for Eric's quick thinking, Bill never would have left the Stop-n-Shop.

Mike shrugged slightly, staring at the ground. After a moment, he said, "I don't have any family that'll speak to me anymore. I tried for a long time, and some bridges are just.... well, burned. Claire had kids around here, though. Two daughters live in this area, and she's got a son in college at the University on the other side of town. They deserve to know what happened to their mom."

Mike didn't look up for a long time, and no one really knew what to say. Finally, after a long moment of uncomfortable silence, Eric leaned into the window of the Bronco and pulled out the keys. He extended them to Mike, but the Ranger shook his head.

"Mr. Sheickles gave that to you," Mike said, with a slight smile. "If he saw me cruising around town in it, he'd probably shoot me...and then you."

Eric couldn't help but laugh at that and found that he suddenly had an uncomfortable lump in his throat. He turned quickly away and started setting aside supplies for Mike to keep. The rest of the group went about saying their good-byes as Eric packed one of his trail bags. He put in three days worth of food rations, but a good third of their water. The rest of the group was facing a three hour car ride, barring any unforeseen complications, but there was no telling when Mike would find another reliable supply of good, clean water.

By the time Eric had the bag packed, the rest of the group was in their vehicles, ready to pull out. Eric handed the bag to Mike, who started to protest when he felt how heavy it was, but Eric stopped him.

"Look, you're going to need it a lot sooner than we are," Eric said firmly. "My family's got two wells and a cow pond on the property. You're lucky I didn't leave all of it for you to carry."

Mike finally nodded and jerked his thumb toward Bill's truck. "I left pretty much everything from the Ranger station," he said. "I kept one of the M-4's, a Beretta, and fifty rounds for each. I've got my own field First Aid kit, and anything else would just be more weight."

Eric nodded, unsure really of what to say. After a moment, Mike took his hand and shook it hard. "I've spent a good part of the last few years trying my best to avoid situations like this," Mike said, "but I guess sometimes you just don't have a choice."

Eric frowned. "You could come with us Mike. You've always got a choice."

Mike just shook his head. "Not when what you do is part of who you are," he said softly.

With one last nod, Mike shouldered his pack and went to sit on the faded, splintered boards of the porch behind him. Eric climbed into the cab of the Bronco and pulled out. His last view of Mike was in the fading red glow of Bill's tail lights as they drove down the rough and weathered gravel road, one hand raised and his rifle in the other.

Ch. 34

Paint Me A Picture

Chris knelt on the bed and looked the little boy squarely in the eyes. He took a deep breath, and nodded. "Yes, Steven," he said, "it is going to hurt. I don't want to lie to you. But your arm will feel better after it hurts, okay?"

The little boy frowned and tears filled his eyes instantly. He bit down hard on his bottom lip, though, and none of the tears reached his cheeks. Steven closed his eyes for a moment and took several slow, deep breaths.

"The bones in your arm," Chris continued, "are in the wrong place, and I have to put them back in the right place. That way they can heal straight and strong. The pain will be quick, but bad. I'll tell you before it happens, so you don't have to worry, okay? I'm a doctor and I can help you, but you have to trust me."

The boy's mother stroked his hair softly, and after a moment he opened his eyes. Maimey stood from the rocking chair in the corner and patted Gilbert on the way out the door. The boy's brother whispered something to him and then quietly slipped out the door. Gilbert extended a hand to Steven's mother, but she shook her head firmly.

"I'm staying with him, Daddy," she said. After a tense moment, Gilbert turned to go.

The old farmer paused to fix Chris with a stare and asked, "Can you really fix his arm?"

Chris nodded slowly, and said, "It won't be pleasant, but I can set it."

Gilbert closed his eyes briefly and placed a rough hand on his shoulder. Then he stepped out into the hall and closed the door behind him. Steven was breathing a little quicker now, so Chris put a hand lightly on his foot.

"Steven," he said calmly, "it's okay. I'm not going to do anything without telling you first. Right now, I'm going to fix some things for the splint that's going to go on your arm to help hold it still when I'm done. It will protect your arm from bumps while it gets better."

Steven took a deep breath, and nodded once. Chris took some linen strips from the boy's mother and lined them next to the boy in the bed. She'd cut up three bed sheets, so the pile was more than enough to serve for wrapping Steven's arm and securing the splint in place. Afterwards, he might even have enough to make a simple sling, assuming she hadn't cut up the pillowcases yet.

"Do you have a special place that you like to play around this farm?" Chris asked as he tied some strips to the wood lengths. Steven nodded once again, and Chris smiled. "I thought you might. I grew up on a farm kind of like this out in Kentucky. My dad was in the Army, and we moved around a lot when I was younger, but there was a farm in Kentucky that always stands out in my mind. I played there a lot when I was about your age, and even a little younger. What is your favorite place, the barn? I bet you can play hide and seek like crazy in a barn like that."

Steven smiled, but suddenly looked shy and didn't give any other response.

Chris shrugged and continued. "We had a silo at our farm. An old round building that was tall and hollow inside. I used to climb in that building, and one day I fell. I got hurt too, but it was my leg. A doctor fixed me up like I'm getting ready to fix you up, and my leg got better. Then, just to prove it was better, I got a job jumping out of air planes and getting paid for it!!"

Steven giggled and the boy's mother smiled.

Chris looked at Joe and motioned for him to come closer. "Okay, you're going to need to hold his legs," Chris said softly. Joe swallowed hard, but gripped the boy's legs just above the knees. "If he moves around, it could do more damage in there," Chris said as he looked at the boy's mother. "Ma'am, are you sure you want to stay in here?"

The woman looked at Chris square in the face, her eyes hard as stone. "My name is Beth Anne," she said calmly and evenly. "And I'm staying with my boy."

Chris decided to let the matter drop. "Okay. You hold his shoulders then."

Beth Anne gripped Steven's shoulders firmly, and Chris put his hand lightly on Steven's head. "Okay, Steven," Chris said, "I have to put the bones in the right place now. Once I do, I'm going to wrap your arm with some of these bandages to help protect it. Then I'll tie the splint on to keep it still. Are you ready?"

Steven closed his eyes for a brief moment and took a deep, shaky breath, but nodded. His eyes were squeezed shut hard. Chris handed Beth Ann the large wooden spoon he'd asked for. The handle was wrapped with a strip from an old leather belt.

"Have him bite down on this," Chris said. "It will help."

Beth Ann took the spoon, her face a little pale. When Steven was ready, Chris took his right arm just below the elbow in one hand. The boy winced but didn't cry out as his arm jostled a bit. He looked Steven squarely in the eye once more. "I want you to do me a favor, Steven. I want you to think about your favorite place to play here on the farm for me. You don't have to tell me about it, but I want you to pretend like you're painting me a picture of it inside your mind, okay? Can you close your eyes and do that for me?"

The boy nodded and closed his eyes even tighter.

"Okay, Steven," Chris said, "on the count of three. One. Two," Chris took the boy's right wrist in his other hand. "Three."

Chris pulled sharply apart and felt the bones in the boy's arm slide against each other. The boy cried out against the leather-wrapped spoon in his mouth; his face twisted in a sharp, but muffled scream of pain. To his credit, though, the boy didn't pull away or jerk. The pain was intense as bone scraped against bone, but Chris had to be sure they aligned.

A simple X-ray would have shown him just how much and to what angle each bone was offset and how he could best align them with the fewest moves. Unfortunately, at the moment, there were probably fewer than two dozen working X-ray machines left in the U.S.

The bones set, Chris quickly grabbed one of the thicker linen strips from the bed next to him. He deftly wrapped the boy's arm twice from elbow to wrist with the bandage. He wrapped it snug but not tight enough to pinch off the circulation. Hopefully the bandages would keep some of the swelling down.

Steven's face and back had relaxed a bit once the bones had stopped moving. He was breathing deep and hard now, tears streaming down his face. Still, he hadn't even tried to jerk his arm back once.

"You've got nerves of steel, kid," Chris said, his voice firm and even. "When the doc set my leg, I kicked him square in the nose with my good foot. Didn't mean to hurt him, but it was just a natural reaction and it happened before I could even think about stopping it."

Beth Ann chuckled a shaky little laugh, and Chris shook his head ruefully. "You laugh now, but he didn't think it was that funny back then. I broke his nose and bloodied up his nice white lab coat. For a while there, when I went to see him for checkups, I had a cast on, and so did he."

Steven giggled between sobs, and Chris winked at him. Chris continued to wrap the boy's arm with two more strips of linen, and then he set the cut and sanded strips of board on either side of his arm. He tied the splint closed just tight enough for Steven to feel the pressure but before it became painful.

"You did good, kid", Chris said.

Beth Ann gave him a full dose of children's Ibuprofen she kept in the bathroom medicine cabinet. Steven swallowed it eagerly, even if he did make a face at the taste. Already his breathing was becoming more rhythmic and even.

"Steven, you're going to feel sleepy now," Chris said. "When your body hurts real badly, your brain releases special chemicals to help you sleep through the pain. You just relax and close your eyes and rest. It will help your arm get better faster, okay?"

Steven nodded and laid his head back, staring up at the ceiling.

Joe and Chris stood and stepped out in the hall while Beth Ann whispered something comforting to Steven. They found Gilbert in the hall, his back against the opposite wall and his face pale.

"Thank you son," Gilbert said. "You boys and your families are welcome to stay here for the night and eat with us. Better than bein on the road out there in the dark, I'd imagine."

Chris looked at Joe who shrugged slightly, then nodded. "Thank you for the hospitality," Chris said. "We've got children with us too, and it might be better to finish our trip in the morning. I promise we won't be any trouble, and we'll be gone early."

Gilbert shook both of their hands. "Least we can do," he said, then turned and walked slowly down the stairs.

Beth Ann stepped into the hallway and closed the door behind her. Tears were streaming down her face as she put her arms around Chris's neck and hugged him tightly.

"Thank you," she said. "It's a miracle you all were coming by when you were! I don't know what we'd have done. None of the cars will start, the phones won't work and I just didn't know what to do."

"You held it together well, Ma'am," Chris said reassuringly. "That story I told about my leg was true...for the most part...and I can promise you that being there for him like that helped a lot."

"Well, thank you again," Beth Ann said, patting Chris on the arm. "And you all are welcome to stay and eat with us."

Chris and Joe smiled.

"Yes Ma'am, your father mentioned that," Joe replied. "We'll be out of your hair first thing tomorrow, though."

Beth Ann made a shooing motion. "Don't worry about that. We don't get many visitors out here, and it'll be good to have the company."

Beth Ann herded the men down the stairs with a wave of her hands. It was a practiced gesture, and one she had obviously perfected through years of dealing with children. Joe and Chris allowed themselves to be ushered outside where the rest of their group was waiting.

"You all talk it over," Beth Ann said, "and we'll be inside when you're ready to come in."

Without waiting for a reply, Beth Ann turned and walked back into the farm house, leaving Joe and Chris on the porch in the growing shadows and the fading afternoon heat.

Ch. 35

Unknown Administrator

Terry Price watched as the process bar slowly ticked up; ninety one percent, ninety two percent, ninety three...

He sat back and ran a hand over his face. The past five days had been a whirlwind, and he'd been running short on sleep for a while now. At 0200, the rest of the staff was sleeping in the dormitory. A skeleton crew in the war room was in charge of monitoring system status and environmental controls until the regular morning shift began at 0700. For the moment, Terry had the entire system practically to himself. Even so, there were some tasks that even the most advanced super-computer couldn't pull off quickly. Searching through millions of individual lines codes and compiling a requested action list was something that just took time. Whoever had entered the commands, though, had hidden their tracks extremely well.

Terry downed half of his mug of cold coffee. He picked idly at the gold foil embossing on the white porcelain with his thumb nail and wondered when he'd find time to go to Annapolis to get another, assuming, of course, that Annapolis and the Academy were still standing.

Finally, there was a series of beeps, and the status bar disappeared from the screen. In its place, the display showed a line item action list. Terry scrolled through the list. Most of the items were regular system maintenance commands carried out either automatically or entered by the technicians on watch at the time, complete with their unique Identity codes and authorization passwords.

On the fourth page, Terry found what he was looking for. A series of commands had been entered and authorized that stood out from the rest. Terry read through the line items and frowned. The commands had been entered by an "Unknown Administrator" with no visible authorization passwords, and yet they had been accepted and acted on by the system. It simply didn't make any sense.

Terry had designed the security protocol himself, and triple authentication was necessary for all system wide actions. Either someone had hacked into the system he had designed with a four thousand and ninety six bit encryption framework, a near physical impossibility, or a back door had been built into the coding without his knowledge. Neither prospect did anything to ease the uncertainty and fear that had been gnawing at him since the system initiated a full data back up and dump of all files from the web and from networked government infrastructure to the secure data vault he was in charge of.

There were four storage facilities like X-Ray Romeo, where Terry served as both Senior Systems Engineer and Operations Director. All four of them would have been activated by the system flash commands Terry had uncovered. None of the other engineers or technicians had his level of write-in clearance, though, and they would have been locked out of all but the most basic levels of access as soon as the dump command was given. Once that switch had been flipped, the system was designed to lock itself down so that only certain people would be able to release it.

Terry stood and drank the rest of his cold coffee in one gulp. He swiped his ID badge to unlock the door to his office and stepped out into the hallway. The concrete block walls were painted a soothing sea-foam green that reminded him of a hospital. To simulate night time conditions two thousand feet beneath the Utah sky, lighting in the hallways was reduced to twenty percent past 2200 hours. Terry walked through the simulated gloom with his empty coffee cup in his hand and brooding thoughts rolling around in his head.

The Snafu-Bar was deserted and the serving counter was dark. Breakfast was still four hours away, and even the cooks hadn't made it to the kitchen yet. Still, along the back wall was a line of vending machines that held everything from individual packs of chewing gum to full microwavable meals. Terry walked to one of the coffee dispensers, swiped his card, and filled his mug with an approximation of Kona Coffee. The best that could be said for it was that it was hot.

Terry swiped his ID card at his office door and stepped inside with his steaming cup of coffee. He sat at his desk still somewhat lost in his own thoughts. When his eyes finally focused on the screen, he almost dropped the coffee mug. Terry's confidential personnel file and his sealed service record were scrolling slowly across the screen like a slide show. The sudden thrill of fear Terry had felt slowly morphed into a burning rage.

Someone had hacked *his* system.

Terry leaned forward and pressed the Esc key on his keyboard, but nothing happened. He tapped several different key commands, but got no response. Finally, on the verge of unplugging the PC, the screen suddenly flashed and a network message window popped up. Terry frowned. All of the systems at the data storage facility were connected to an internal network that was secure and independent from any outside traffic, in theory at least. The one main incoming traffic line that fed the data backup and storage systems was isolated, quarantined, filtered, scanned, and every other trick possible used to keep any unwanted signals from breaking through.

In more than a decade of operation, no facility with Terry's security system in place had *ever* had a breach. Which meant this was either unique, or someone was hacking him from inside his system.

A message appeared in the window.

What are you trying to find, Mr. Price?

The sender listed was "Unknown Administrator." Terry thought again about unplugging his machine, but decided against it. Instead, he began typing, "Who are you?"

Terry hit the enter key and saw the message appear in the window and then fade away. After a moment, he got his reply.

It's never the question that is indiscrete, Mr. Price, only the answer. Knowledge can be a very dangerous thing.

The screen flickered once, and then Terry was again looking at the report he'd requested from the computer's command history log. Terry sat for a moment vacillating between white-hot, foaming rage and cold, clammy fear. Finally, he brought up the system-wide command prompt and keyed in the line, "Cry 'Havoc,' and let slip the dogs of war; A3S1L273." For a long time, Terry sat and stared at the line, but he didn't hit the Enter key.

When he was working on the system years ago, Terry had realized early on what it was intended to be. In the event of a catastrophic crash or an impending disaster, certain commands would execute a complete backup and dump of all information stored, accessed, or transferred over the internet as well as internal security networks. The project coordinators at the time had called it a massive fail-safe, but Terry had always seen it as a weapon.

With a deep breath, Terry pressed the Enter key.

His line of code disappeared. In its place, a message appeared that read, "Command received and authenticated. Full system encryption underway."

Now, whoever was pulling the strings would be locked out. The system encryption would take at least a few days to complete, but once the process was started, it couldn't be halted. Even if all power was disconnected and the system shut down, the first operation in the stack on restart would be the encryption command. Terry had built this in as last ditch fail-safe in the last phase of code compilation after reading a book about Oppenheimer.

Terry unlocked the bottom right drawer of his desk and pulled out a Colt M1911 pistol. His father had carried the same gun through three years of World War II and later in Korea. Terry had carried it since the day he graduated from the Naval Academy in the summer of '72. He laid the pistol on his desk next to his keyboard.

If the "Unknown Administrator" wanted access to the system again, he would have to come to Terry to get it....

And Terry would be ready.

D. W. McAliley

Ch. 36

Lessons Learned

The night air was hot and heavy with rain that hadn't quite started falling yet. Insects and frogs buzzed, chirped, and croaked in the woods around the small gas station, giving the place a surreal atmosphere almost as if someone had dropped a gas station into some primeval jungle. Lightning flashed on the horizon, and Eric flinched. This was natural lightening, though, not the result of an airstrike. Eric counted the seconds from the flash in his head until the rolling boom of the thunder reached him; the storm was still a good four miles from them.

They had time, but they would have to move quickly. Eric stood at the door to the brick convenience store and took a deep breath. Bill stood on the other side, his revolver in his right hand and his left still held up by the makeshift sling. Imogene had made the call to stop treating the wound with the sugar compresses at their last rest stop, and instead had stitched both sides of the wound tightly closed. It was bandaged and had a healthy coating of anti-bacterial cream, but according to Imogene the healing process was already well under way.

Bill shifted his left arm in the sling and frowned.

"Are you sure you're okay with this?" Eric asked.

Bill nodded. "Yeah, I'll be fine, son," he replied "Just a little gun shy is all. Last time I went into one of these places, it didn't work out too well for me."

Eric nodded. "Well, this time you just stay behind me and make sure no one sneaks up on me, okay? I'll clear the rooms one by one, and then we can pump some gas once we're sure there aren't any surprises waiting for us."

Bill nodded, and helped Eric pull open the electrical doors enough for the two of them to slip through. Eric had his small pen light in one hand and his Beretta in the other. They checked each aisle quickly and then went to the store room. Bill stood to one side of the doorway, Eric to the other. On the count of three, Bill turned the handle and threw the door open and then moved aside. Eric stepped quickly into the doorway, shining his flashlight into each corner of the room.

"Clear," Eric whispered, and Bill nodded.

They repeated the process with the bathrooms, checking each individual stall to make certain it was empty. Once they were finished, they went back through and checked each room a second time just to be sure. Satisfied that they were alone, Eric and Bill made their way back outside to the others. Imogene and Christina had kept the engines running just in case they needed a quick get away, but at a hand signal from Eric, they shut off the engines. Without the headlights from the vehicles, the darkness of the night closed in around them, isolating the small pool of light cast by their flashlights.

In the darkness, lightning flashed again, and Eric counted to himself out of reflex. The storm was closing on them and was now a little less than two miles distant.

Bill found a metal cap set in the concrete parking lot off to one side that read '85OCT'. Eric pried the heavy metal cap off with a crowbar and dropped the long hose from their hand-turned pump down into the pitch black opening. With a few turns of the crank, the pump primed and began pouring gasoline into the red plastic gas can they'd taken from the Stop-n-Shop.

They had to fill up the gas can three times to top off both vehicles, and it took nearly a half hour to finish the task. When they were done with the fuel, Eric and Bill went back into the convenience store and took some of the beef jerky, water, and sports drinks. They didn't clean the shelves, though, in case someone came after them in need. When they were done, they loaded the new supplies into the Bronco and paused for a moment to eat a quick snack and drink some water.

Lightning flashed again, and this time the thunder came quicker on its heels. Eric counted out the seconds, and it was less than a mile away, closing in from the West.

"How far out are we?" Bill asked.

"A little less than an hour," Eric replied. "All of the side roads and backtracks we had to make, we've manage to turn a three hour trip into a seven hour journey."

Bill chuckled. "Worth it, if you ask me," he said. "After yesterday, I ain't in a rush to run into too many strangers for a while."

Eric nodded and ran a hand over his face with a deep, heavy sigh. He had been running for days on adrenaline and fear, but the exhaustion was finally beginning to catch up with him. His head was pounding and a muscle just under his left eye had begun to twitch incessantly.

"Do we need to stop?" Bill asked. "We can always go on in the morning, when we've rested a while, and maybe that storm will blow over in the meantime."

Eric shook his head firmly. "We're so close," he replied. "I don't want to stop now... I just want to be home."

Bill nodded. "Alright, Eric. You lead the way and we'll be right behind you."

They all climbed back in the trucks and pulled out of the gas station. As Eric made the left turn onto Highway 24, the skies let loose and rain began to fall in thick, wind-driven sheets. The lightning and thunder that had been sporadic picked up suddenly and began flashing all around them with deafening cracks and booms of thunder. Christina slid closer to him and clutched his arm tightly as the storm raged.

Eric said a quick, silent prayer for his father and for Mike, asking God to keep them safe and dry as he drove on through the wind, the rain, and the darkness.

Ch. 37

Rise And Shine

Gilbert lightly nudged Joe's foot with his boot. Joe's eyes shot open, but other than that he didn't move. Gilbert jerked his head to the side towards the front door, and Joe nodded. He carefully unwrapped himself from the quilt he'd slept under and retrieved his pistol from beneath his pillow. Joe had slept fully clothed with his boots on, so all he had to do was stand, stretch, and holster his side arm. He followed Gilbert out onto the porch.

Outside, the morning air was thick with humidity, and the clouds hung low in the sky. Thunder rolled in the distance, but it was already light enough that he couldn't see the flashes of lightning that caused them. Gilbert had taken a seat in one of the rocking chairs that lined the wraparound porch, and he motioned for Joe to sit in one next to him.

As Joe settled into the faded rocker, Gilbert pulled a small clay pipe from his coverall pocket. He thumbed the bowl full of dark brown tobacco from a leather pouch. With a single cedar match, Gilbert puffed the pipe alight and sat for a moment smoking in silence. The smoke smelled sweet with a hint of cherries and freshly baked cookies.

"Gonna rain today," Gilbert said after a long silence, "and hard, too. You boys headed west, you'll head right into the teeth of it."

Gilbert took his pipe from between his teeth and used it to point at the surrounding fields. "All this used to be family land. My great-granddaddy traded it an acre at the time for a shot o'whiskey in town. Man was dumber than a ten dollar mule, though I guess I shouldn't be bad-mouthin the dead."

"Sorry to hear that," Joe replied, unsure of what to say.

Gilbert shrugged and took another puff on his pipe. "Can't really miss what you never had, I s'pose. 'Cept when people think they need to tell you bout what coulda been."

Joe nodded, and silence fell between them again. A light, drizzling rain began to fall softly in the yard and on the tin roof of the porch. Gilbert woke him up for a purpose and he seemed to be working himself around to it. For the moment, Joe was content to let him build up the courage to say, or ask, whatever was on his mind. Thunder rolled dimly in the distance, and the rain picked up in strength.

Finally, Gilbert turned to Joe. "Look, you boys talked a lot last night without really sayin much," he said around the pipe stem in his mouth. "I get that. With the women folk and kids around, there ain't but so much you can say. Well, now ain't nobody but you an me out here. Whatever you might think bout the rest of em, I know what I've been through. I want the truth, and I'll know if I ain't getting it."

"Okay," Joe said slowly. "What is it you want to know?"

Gilbert hooked one thumb over his shoulder at the Hum-V parked in the yard. "That ain't no family van there, son, and here you are ridin around in it with at least two families packed in there worse than sardines. Now, I don't know where you got it, or how. An to tell you the truth, I don't really wanna know. Just tell me this.... how bad is it?"

Joe took a deep slow breath in and let it out through his nose, trying to decide how much he could say, and how much he should say.

"It's bad," he said at last. "I mean, look...we've both been in combat. I've spent my career in some of the worst places you can imagine. Places they don't even mention on the evening news anymore, they're that rough. And I'm telling you, what I saw back in Norfolk was as bad as I've seen anywhere. And it's gonna get worse."

Gilbert nodded and puffed his pipe for a moment in silence.

"When I was in Europe," he said softly at last, "I seen things...things I spent the rest of my life trying to forget. Some things you just can't un-see, though. People can do some downright evil things, Joe. And I ain't just talkin bout the Nazis, neither. I mean people, real down to earth people. When they get hungry and scared and desperate, people can do some bad things....turrible things..."

Gilbert's voice trailed off as the ghosts of the past revisited him for a moment. Joe had seen many of those same things, he was sure, at different times and different places than Gilbert, but they were all brought on by the same terrible desperation. After a moment Gilbert took his pipe and pressed his thumb into the bowl. He tapped out a few ashes and puffed the pipe back to life again.

"The lights ain't comin back on, are they?" Gilbert asked suddenly.

Joe shook his head slowly. "Not any time soon," he answered, "if ever."

Gilbert nodded. "I figured as much," he said after a moment. "I remember when I was a boy and the electric company was still runnin wires through this part of the country. It took 'em a while to get all the way out here, but they did eventually. I remember the day they flipped the switch and the lights come on. My momma was so happy that she cried so hard you'd a thought somebody had died."

Gilbert leveled his pipe and his eyes at Joe. "You mark my words, people these days ain't ready for it. They ain't got any idea how to live without it. You're right about this, Joe; things are gonna get worse."

"Listen, Gilbert," Joe said, leaning in towards the old farmer, "my family has a farm. It's not huge, but we've got space and fields and fresh water. It's about six...maybe seven hours west of here, and you and your family are welcome to come with us."

Gilbert snorted hard and shook his head. "This house and the thirty acres attached to it's the last piece of my family's land we got left," he said, "and I'll be damned if I'm gonna walk away from it. My girl and her young'uns...well, if things get bad enough I'll see if I can talk them into goin, but she's dang near as stubborn as I am, to tell the truth. I appreciate the offer, Joe, but we'll stay for now."

Joe nodded, but didn't know what to say, and so silence fell between them again. Thunder rolled in the distance, closer than before, and the western sky had gotten dark with the building storm.

After a moment, Gilbert stood and stepped to the porch railing. He tapped the remnants from his pipe out into the wet grass and turned back to Joe.

"I thank ya for talkin to me, Joe," Gilbert said. "Some men woulda tried to make things sound better than they were, but that's no way to get people ready for what's comin. You're a good man, Joe, and you and yours are welcome under my roof any time."

The whole thing had a very formal, almost ceremonial feel to it, so Joe stood and shook Gilbert's outstretched hand solemnly.

"Same goes for you and your family, Gilbert," Joe said, "and I'm serious about that offer. If things get bad...well, I'll leave you directions on how to get to where we'll be. It helps to have people around you that you know and you know you can trust."

Gilbert nodded, and a sudden smile split his face. "Come on, Joe," he said, slapping Joe hard on the back. "Let's go wake these lazy heads up and get some breakfast."

Without waiting for an answer, Gilbert turned and stepped inside the front door, and Joe followed close behind him. He had a lot of road ahead of him, and suddenly Joe very much wanted to be home.

Ch. 38

A Dirt Road Home

Chatham county North Carolina is big; Joe had always known that. He had grown up here, among the trees, fields, rivers, and creeks. He had seen aerial survey and satellite recon photos of the entire area before, so he knew just how large it was in a cognitive sense. However, that knowledge did very little to ease Joe's frustration as he drove across nearly the entire width of the county in the early afternoon heat.

He came into Chatham Country from the East on Hwy 902. It was a small state highway, and seldom used. The black top was pitted with potholes and partially patched cracks. In some places, the lines were only visible as slightly raised matches of pavement down the center line of the road; the reflective paint and tiny plastic reflectors had long since eroded away.

Joe had grown up as a boy out here in the country with hundred acre fields and nothing but forests in between. But he'd grown up on the western edge of the county, in a small community hugging a river that, in places, seemed little more than a deep creek. He knew the ten square miles around his parents' and his grandparents' land like he knew the back of his hand, and he doubted he could ever get lost there.

The eastern half of the county, however, was a different story. He had been to this side of Chatham county so few times that even now, as an adult, he would still find it difficult navigating the small side streets off the highway. Thankfully, he could get most of the way where he was going without turning off of 902W.

Twice Joe slowed down and passed through a dense cloud of smoke that covered the road in areas where the woods on either side looked charred. In one pasture that stretched more than a quarter of a mile of road front, two hillsides were littered with the debris from a downed passenger jet. From the scar across the hills, it looked like the airliner had hit hard and fast.

The fires were all out, though, quenched by the thunderstorm he'd been driving through all morning. Steam rose in thick pillars from the blacktop where the smoke didn't hide the road, and the heat was sweltering. Already, to the west, new cloud towers were rising hot and humid from warm lakes and rivers. It looked like there would be another round of thunderstorms this evening and tomorrow morning.

"You were right," Tom said, softly. They were the first words spoken in the cab since leaving Gilbert's farm.

Joe blinked at him. "I usually like to think so," he admitted, "but what are you talking about in this particular instance?"

"Leaving the guys on that list," Tom said after a long moment of silence. His face was twisted into a sour grimace as he said the words, as if he didn't like the taste of them in his mouth. "You were right, and I shouldn't have questioned you like that," Tom finished.

"Look, Tom," Joe said, "I'm not in command here. You don't have to feel like you're jumping the chain if you disagree with me, okay?"

"Yeah," Tom said with a genuinely warm smile. "You keep telling yourself that, JT."

"Anyway, what changed your mind?" Joe asked, trying to change the subject.

"That guy with the beard," Tom said, pointing to one of the bullet scars in the bullet-resistant wind screen in front of him. "Didn't matter how many kids we had with us; if that mob had gotten hold of us we'd all be dead. So, you were right about getting the kids out of the city being priority number one. Any one of those guys on that list, in our place, would have done the same thing."

"It's not an easy thing to do," Joe said, gripping the steering wheel until his knuckles were white.

"I know it isn't," Tom agreed. "Listen, when you go back to get them, I'm going with you."

"What makes you so sure I'm going back to get them?" Joe asked.

Tom smiled again. "We've known each other too long, Joe. You couldn't leave those guys in enemy hands any more than I could."

Joe didn't speak for a long time. Finally, he said, "And what is your wife going to say about this, Tom?"

"What's yours going to say about it?" Tom shot back.

Joe couldn't help but chuckle. "I guess we'll both find out when we get back, won't we?"

Tom winked back at him and they both laughed long and hard together. It felt good after the past two days just to relax, and drive. Joe rolled down his window to get more air flow as the Hum-V chewed through the miles, and the landmarks slowly began to grow more familiar.

Ch. 39

End Of The Road

Eric stood just inside the doorway to one of the bedrooms in the front half of the small brick house. He flipped the switch on the wall and watched as the LED bulb in the ceiling fan overhead came on and went off. It was such a simple thing to watch as the light turned on and off, but it held such a power now that he couldn't look away from it.

Christina was still asleep in the last bedroom in the front left corner of the farmhouse. The trip had been hard on them all, but it had been harder on Christina than Eric had realized at first. When she finally fell into Eric's mother's arms on the porch, she was trembling and close to collapse.

Eric let her sleep.

He stepped into the living room and looked out the large bay window that took up more than three fourths of the front wall. The glass was slightly thicker at the bottom of the window frame, giving the view through it an odd and distorted look, as if it were seen through the shimmering waves of heat that rise from open fields in the dry summer sun.

Bill and Imogene were on the front porch, laying damp clothes over an impromptu clothes line strung between the brick walls. The two laughed and chatted as they moved around each other. Even in a completely new and strange environment, they seemed at home at each others' side. They had been married so long that one was an extension of the other, and they had truly become one flesh and one person, it seemed. Eric hoped one day he would have that kind of bond with Christina.

The sound and smell of frying chicken drifted through the double glass French doors behind him, and Eric smiled. It smelled like Sunday morning at Nanny's house, a smell that had always meant home to him. Eric leaned his head back in the faded yellow arm chair and closed his eyes. He enjoyed the small glimpse of normalcy in the chaos of the last few days.

The front storm door slammed open hard enough to make Eric jump, and he bolted out of the chair.

"Eric," Bill said, out of breath, "someone's coming!"

Eric didn't pause to ask questions; he simply reacted. In three steps, he had one of the M-4 carbines in his hands. He turned to his mother who'd stuck her head through the kitchen door, a worried frown creasing her face and her forehead.

"Take Nanny, Granddaddy, and Tina into the front utility room," Eric said firmly. "Take the twelve gauge, and if anyone other than me opens that door, you start shooting and don't stop, understand?"

Mom nodded and moved immediately. Eric and Bill stepped out on the porch, and Bill pointed towards the overgrown timber cut that formed the front edge of the broad, flat yard. A small, sandy dirt road ran along the northeast edge of the yard, separating it from the fifteen square acres of field. The dirt road served as his grandparents' half mile long driveway, connecting their small farm with the rest of the world.

Once the driveway cut through the dense underbrush of the cut-over for two hundred yards, it opened up again to fields on both sides that bordered Cutler's Run Lane. The Run, as it was called, had been red clay dirt and gravel when Eric was a boy, but it had always been a 'state' road, unlike the dirt driveway that was maintained by the family. Now, that road was paved with faded and cracked asphalt, making it much more difficult to hear the cars that passed back and forth along its length.

On the porch, Eric could hear the rumble of a large diesel engine roaring on the dirt driveway, and it was getting closer.

He turned to Bill and Imogene. "You two should go around to the back and hide in the top of the old pack house. I'll take this rifle and draw them off through the vineyard and down to the woods at the back edge of the farm. While they're chasing me, you take the rest of them and get out of here, got it?"

"I don't think so, Eric," Bill said, shaking his head. "I'll keep my revolver, and Mother here can pull the trigger on a shotgun as well as anyone else. If they don't take the bait, we'll keep them from getting inside as long as we can."

Eric wanted to argue, but he didn't have time. The sound of the engine was getting closer, and he had to get them away from the house. Eric threw the strap of the M-4 over his right shoulder and vaulted over the waist-high iron railing around the edge of the porch. It was a move he'd perfected as a child, running from his brother while they were playing hide and seek. Eric hit the ground running and sprinted to the edge of the yard.

In front of him was a small cluster of pole-mounted solar panels, forty five of them in total, and the two small power sheds that helped distribute and regulate the power to the house. Eric ran to the broad, flat sandy parking area at the edge of the four acre vineyard. He charged the rifle and knelt, ready to start shooting when the time was right.

Just then, a dark olive green Hum-V broke through the cut-over, nearly going airborne on the low drainage dike that helped form the border between the yard and the woods. There was a large .50cal machine gun mounted on a turret on the top of the Hum-V, and a man stood behind it. Eric put the rifle to his eye, and focused on slowing his breathing. At the rate the Hum-V was moving, it would be on top of him in a few seconds, but he had enough time to squeeze off at least three or four shots to get their attention.

Something didn't seem right, though, as he peered through the red-dot scope. The man behind the machine gun didn't wear a uniform, and he was waving his arms frantically over his head. Eric hesitated and stood. With a gun like that on the truck, Eric's rifle wouldn't even be a nuisance. They could mow him down before he pulled the trigger more than once, and judging by the bullet scars on the windscreen, one shot wouldn't mean much to them.

The Hum-V skidded to a halt thirty feet from Eric, turning slightly sideways as it did. The driver's side door flew open, and a man leapt out of it before the vehicle had even stopped moving. Eric felt the M-4 slip from his hands. He couldn't believe his eyes were seeing what was in front of him, and his breath caught painfully in his throat. Eric took two steps and found himself suddenly running.

The two crashed together, and Eric felt tears streaming hot down his cheeks as he buried his face in his father's shoulder, and wept.

Ch. 40

Breaking Bread

Eric squeezed the handle on the spray nozzle and watched as clear cold water from the deep well next to the farmhouse slowly filled the five gallon bucket. As the water rose past the half-way mark, it lifted the green beans inside with it. When the water and the beans were about two inches from the top, Eric stopped the flow. He washed the beans by pushing them down into the water and swirling handfuls at the time. The leaves and stems from the bean bushes rose to the top, and Eric picked them out. After the beans were washed and clean, he transferred them to an empty bucket. The dirty water was emptied into the massive ancient azalea bushes that bordered the tall pine trees in the back yard. Eventually, it would filter down through the sandy soil to the groundwater table, and would likely wind up back in the well before long, recycled and ready for reuse.

Imogene, Christina, Jen, and Meg were all sitting in a rough semi-circle beneath the shade of a massive oak in the back yard, snapping green beans and talking together as if they'd known each other their entire lives. Tom's children ran and played a game of freeze tag in the vineyard with Nanny's old black lab, Princess, trying desperately to join the game.

Granddaddy sat on the concrete steps of the back porch bouncing baby Samantha on his knee and laughing as she giggled at him. He had been smitten with the small child as soon as he saw her.

He bounced her, tickled her, and even pretended to bite off her little toes one at a time while Sam giggled and laughed the entire time.

It was all so peaceful and perfect that it seemed almost surreal to Eric. Sheltered in the tight ring of trees that bordered the yard and fields, the family homestead could have been on a different planet from the violence and destruction Eric had seen in and around Charlotte, just a few hours' drive south and west. A dense column of black smoke rose to west, however, in the direction of Bennett, the nearest town. That smoke served as a reminder of reality outside of the farm, and every once in a while the ladies underneath the tree would drift to silence and turn to stare at it.

In all, the family farm consisted of the main homestead with the house, four barns, an old chicken coop, a vineyard, and a field that made up about sixty acres total. Another three hundred acres of forests and fields connected to the original homestead provided the income for the farm through corn, soybeans, and tobacco. The land was situated along Cutler's Run, a river that at times seemed little more than a glorified creek. Eventually, Cutler's Run fed into the Neuse River and on into the Pamlico Sound. Eric wondered how difficult it would be to reach the coast following the streams and rivers instead of the paved roads and highways. Rivers had once served as the main transportation network for the whole of humanity, but that had been literally ages ago.

Eric was jolted out of his thoughts as his father set down two more buckets of green beans to be washed. Chris followed behind him with two buckets of plump, red tomatoes. The two had spent the last few hours carrying buckets of produce up from the "small" garden that Nanny and Granddaddy planted every year in the fields just past the old pack house. For most families, the garden would have been massive, covering nearly three square acres in all. They grew sweet corn, tomatoes, beans, peas, turnips, peppers, potatoes, and onions. Frozen and canned vegetables from the garden fed the family year-round, and any extra produce that they didn't need fed the other families up and down The Run. Nanny and Granddaddy were famous for calling people to come pick truckloads of vegetables once their own canning and freezing was done for the year.

"Take care of people when you can," Granddaddy would say, "and they'll take care of you when you can't."

Eric was about to start washing the next bucket of beans, but Joe reached down and stopped him. "Come with us for a minute, Eric," Joe said. "We need to talk."

Eric nodded and stood. He carried the freshly cleaned bucket of beans to the ladies snapping beans under the tree and then followed his father and Chris out to the trucks. Bill and Tom had the hood of the Bronco up, and they were checking seals and fluid levels, making sure the vehicle was ready to drive if they needed it. Corporal Henderson was doing the same for the massive Hum-V. They all stopped what they were doing as Joe and the others approached.

"Okay," Joe said softly, despite them being well out of earshot from anyone else, "here's the plan. There's a list of names that Chris and I took off a guy in Norfolk. It seems that whoever is running that city now had this list of names and was going around rounding up as many of them as possible. These weren't police, either, and I didn't see any warrants when they were trying to scare Chris's wife into letting them inside."

"Snatch and grabs," Bill said, shaking his head. "Cartel guys would do that down in south Texas. They'd find someone they thought had money, tail 'em for a while, then snatch 'em up and demand a ransom from the family."

"Yeah," Joe said. "I don't think these guys were after a pay day. My name is on that list, and so are Tom's and Chris's. We each know guys that are on that list too, and we left them there, knowing someone was coming for them. That doesn't sit too well with me, and I mean to do something about it."

Eric shifted uneasily, but didn't say anything. Joe reached out and put a reassuring hand on his son's shoulder and squeezed. It was a gesture Eric knew well, and it meant his dad was about to deliver some unpleasant news.

"Tom and I are going back," Joe said after a long moment of silence. "We're going to see if we can get to any of those guys and get them out of the city, or at the least find out where they're being held. We've got to do *something*," Joe said, his voice suddenly intense with emotion. "We *can't* just leave them behind like that."

"Okay," Chris said, "when do we leave?"

Joe just shook his head. "You aren't coming, Chris."

"Now wait just a damned minute," Chris began, his face turning red.

Joe raised one hand and cut him off. "We need you here, Chris. Our families, all of them, are going to need someone that can help them if they get sick or hurt. Now, I know you say you're not a doctor, but I saw how you handled that little boy's broken arm yesterday. You're a heck of a lot closer to a doctor than anyone else here, and that means you stay, okay? Please?"

Chris opened his mouth to protest, but after a moment he closed it and left unsaid whatever arguments he had ready. Finally, Chris nodded, though he didn't look happy about it.

"What about me?" Henderson asked, wiping grease from his hands with a faded old denim rag. "I'm sure not a doctor. The only thing I know how to be is a Marine, and there ain't anyone around here to fight."

Joe took a deep breath and replied, "Henderson, this isn't going to be a walk in the park. We're going into a city that's probably in chaos by now with an objective that will probably piss off some well-armed and highly trained operators. I'm not going to lie to you, there's a chance we won't make it back."

Henderson nodded. "No offense, sir," he said hesitantly, "but that's true of pretty much every mission for a Marine."

Joe chuckled. "Fair enough. So it's me, Tom, and Henderson, then. We'll leave late this evening. Even sticking to the back roads and surface streets, we can be in Suffolk in about ten hours. That'll put us getting there right around sunrise."

Just then the back door opened and Nanny stepped out on the porch wiping her hands on a flour stained apron. "You young'uns come on!" she called. "Dinner's ready!"

"What did Mom have to say about this?" Eric asked as the other men started for the small house.

Joe snorted a short chuckled. "I'll let you know when I tell her," he replied.

Eric shook his head. "You know she's gonna flip out, right?"

Joe nodded. "Yeah, I know. But you let me worry about that. Listen, I know you don't really understand this right now, but you will one day."

Eric shook his head and glanced to the west where the column of smoke still rose against the slowly sinking sun. "No," he said softly, "I understand fine. I just don't like it is all."

Inside, the house was warm and smelled like good, home-cooked food. The small kitchen table was packed with serving dishes and pots full to near overflowing. Two bowls were heaped with pieces of crispy fried chicken, and there were three pans of biscuits. A six quart pot of green beans sat next to a huge mixing bowl of mashed potatoes and a Pyrex dish of baked yams. On the four-burner stove was a large cast iron skillet with thick brown gravy and a smaller pot of field peas.

Granddaddy had finally handed baby Sam back to her mother, and he stood next to Nanny in front of the stove.

"It ain't fancy," Granddaddy said, addressing the whole group, "but there's plenty of it, so eat up. If we could all bow our heads, I'll say grace."

Granddaddy reached up and pulled off the faded camouflage hat he'd been wearing and bowed his head. Around the small kitchen table, heads bowed and hats came off. When all was quiet again, Granddaddy cleared his throat and said the prayer.

"Lord, we thank you for the food we are about to receive. We give thanks for this and the many other blessings you have given us, Lord. We are especially thankful for the safe return of family and for the arrival of new friends. Lord, we ask your sheltering protection on all those outside these walls as well as those within, as these are troubled times we face. Lord, we pray for wisdom, understanding, healing, and peace. But, above all, in this as in all things, we pray Thy will be done. In your name we pray, Amen."

In the silence that followed the prayer, Eric's mother opened her eyes and leveled a hard glare and a long-nailed finger at his father.

"And if you think for one second," she said, her voice hard and dangerous, "that I'm going to let you go right after I get you back here safe and sound, you got another thing comin, buddy!"

The only sound was the painful groan that came from deep in Joe's throat.

Ch. 41

Unscheduled Maintenance

Terry Price sat at his desk, keying commands into a code editor. Four thick reference texts were open across his desk, and there was a stack of note cards scattered face down on the printer stand behind him. He had been keeping odd hours lately and found himself working more and sleeping less as he neared the end of his task. It seemed that the closer the objective came, the more difficult it was to stop reaching for it long enough to get a few hours of rest.

There was a sudden knock at his office door, and Terry froze immediately. He went through a quick mental check of the people it possibly could and probably would be, and then he tapped a quick series of commands into his operating window that saved all open data and temporarily locked and encrypted the entire system. The command began running immediately and a status bar leapt onto the display, steadily running through a list of files. His code input system wasn't like most computers. It could execute commands with lightning speed. The small laptop had a staggering 100GB of RAM stacked on four motherboards with BUS networked multi-thread processors and a relatively small 30GB solid-state memory core.

You'd never be able to watch a DVD on the small tablet he was using now, but it was one of his most powerful tools. He tapped another series of commands into the main operating system, and it began the process of factoring an enormously large fractal algorithm, displaying the graphed results as a screen saver of ever evolving geometric patterns. He would lose two hours as the solution process could not be interrupted by any commands, and he would have to wait for it to complete, but in the meantime the system would be utterly secure against any attacks.

"Come in," Terry called.

The door opened and one of his senior team leaders stepped inside the room. Terry recognized the man immediately as Marcus Attledge, an ambitious but principled manager. He was dependable and got jobs done quickly and thoroughly. Right now, though, his eyes were wide and his face a little pale.

"Sir," Marcus said as he came towards the desk, "the Chief Administrator of FEMA is on his way."

Terry nodded his head slowly, his face an unreadable mask. "Well, Mr. Attledge, this facility is a key element in the nation's disaster response. I suppose a visit from the Chief Administrator is to be expected. When will he arrive?"

"Sir, he's landing now," Marcus said. "The senior officer in the Tower radioed me to announce that the Chief Administrator's pilot had just radioed for clearance to land his helicopter. All of the authentication codes checked out, so he had to give clearance."

Terry didn't curse, but he wanted to.

"Very well," he said after a moment, "tell Security that he is to be shown directly to my office. You come inside and wait. Leave the door open, but keep your mouth shut unless I tell you otherwise, got it?"

Marcus blinked and opened his mouth as if to say something, but Terry merely arched an eyebrow, so he closed it. He swallowed hard and stepped over to the side of the office. Terry closed all of the reference books but left them on the table. He set his Colt pistol on top of them, the safety on and the barrel directed at the concrete wall to his left. Marcus took one look at the pistol, swallowed hard, and looked like he wished he were elsewhere. Terry didn't blame him; in fact, he wished the same thing.

Terry sat in his custom-made executive's chair and stared at the ceiling. He idly twisted the thick, heavy Academy ring on his left ring finger. He'd never married, other than the vows he took with the Navy, and so he wore the only wedding ring he had. The style in '72 had been simple and elegant with a sky blue stone set in the antiqued gold. Whenever he was deep in thought, he would twist that ring as his mind worked. At the moment he was running through possible reactions and scenarios for how this meeting would proceed.

He'd had this same reaction as a fighter pilot for the Navy just before a carrier launch. He would sit for a few moments, twisting his ring as he ran through check lists and contingencies in his mind. Then, the steam catapults would kick in, and he was slammed into the back of his seat. The whole thing was over so fast, and he was in the air. Once airborne, the world dropped away, and with it went all distractions. In the sky, Terry was absolutely calm and focused on the mission; it was the waiting to launch that drove him nuts.

Terry caught the sound of footsteps echoing in the hall outside his office door. He straightened his ring one last time and stood. When the head of FEMA stepped through his door, he wanted them to be on equal footing, and standing as the Chief

Administrator entered would have been too much a sign of subordination. As the footsteps grew closer, Terry took a deep breath, and felt the nervousness and uncertainty fall away. He clasped his hands easily in the front within easy reach of the pistol.

Paul Jefferson, the Chief Administrator of FEMA, stepped into the office without being announced. He wore an expertly tailored charcoal black suit with a pin-striped tie of red and blue. He had perfectly combed black hair and a strong jaw line just shy of a dimpled chin. His eyes took in the office as he walked slowly and confidently toward Terry. He noticed the hand-carved cherry wood desk first and then the two espresso-colored leather chairs facing it. There were no framed oil paintings, or delicate carpets, and the next thing he noticed was the pistol on the desk. There was a momentary frown of his eyebrows, but Marcus drew a deeper reaction when he noticed the man standing against the wall.

His smile never wavered.

"Senior Systems Administrator Price," Jefferson said, extending his right hand, "it is good to finally meet you."

Terry nodded and shook the hand. "Thank you, Chief Administrator," he said, adopting the other's formality.

The Chief Administrator sat, and so did Terry. "Please, call me Paul," Jefferson said, and now his eyes went to the gun and stayed. "Do you really think that's necessary?" he asked.

"Mr. Jefferson, if I'm not mistaken," Terry said, "just a few days ago, at least five nuclear weapons were detonated in an attack on the United States. I don't know about you, but that .45 seems hardly enough, in my opinion."

"Fair enough," the other man's eyes narrowed slightly, but he let the matter drop. "How have operations been proceeding here, Mr. Price?"

"Very well, Mr. Jefferson," Terry said, "all things considered, of course. Thanks to the report received by DHS, we were able to execute a full system dump and backup before the devices were detonated. Our hardening and shielding were not penetrated in any way, and our power from the solar farm top-side was never even interrupted."

Jefferson nodded. "It's good to hear some good news, finally," he said, adopting a somber expression. "I understand from some of my own systems engineers, though, that they lost access to the database recently. Is that normal?"

Terry smiled an easy smile. "Yes sir," He replied instantly. "Simply some unscheduled, but routine, maintenance."

Jefferson nodded slowly, a thoughtful frown just barely showing on his mouth and his eyebrows. He steepled his fingers as he thought and was silent for a long moment before speaking. "How can something be both unscheduled, and routine, Mr. Price?"

"Well, this is to address a direct issue with the system itself," Terry said easily, "but it is not a recurring issue, so it won't need to be executed again."

"I see," Jefferson said carefully. "I'm afraid I need you to interrupt this maintenance. My field directors need access to the information in those databases to perform their duties, Mr. Price. I'm sure your security systems are adequate despite this *issue* that you are addressing."

"With all due respect, Mr. Jefferson," Terry said, "I don't take directives from you. This is a Department of Defense facility operated by DOD staff and the military. And while DOD assists and coordinates with your office during emergency response, we don't fall under your chain of command. I am responsible to the DOD and the people, not you. Sir."

There was a brief moment of stunned, icy silence. Mr. Jefferson's smile was gone now and so were his other carefully crafted expressions. His eyes were hard, and his jaw was set. "I see," he said.

"Now that we have an understanding," Terry said calmly, "we can have a conversation, if you wish."

After a brief moment, Jefferson nodded.

"That will be all, Mr. Attledge," Terry said. "This is all classified and sealed, understand?" Marcus indicated that it was, and Terry continued, "Very well. You may go, and close the door on the way out."

Marcus left as quickly as he could without actually seeming to rush. When the door had clicked closed, Terry turned his attention back to Jefferson.

"Mr. Price," the bureaucrat said in a stiff voice, "we really do need that information to do our job. When can we expect to access it again?"

"Once the maintenance is complete," Terry said simply and truthfully. "Until then, even I can't interrupt the process. The system is designed to lock everyone and everything out while it repairs itself."

"I see," Mr. Jefferson said again, his frown deepening.

"Put yourself in my shoes, for a moment," Terry said, leaning forward slightly. "You know the nation is under the most direct and devastating attack in our history, but you don't know who's doing it. However, all of the nation's data...it's deepest and darkest secretes... *everyone's* deepest and darkest secrets... are all conveniently stored in four databases thanks to an early tip that we just happened to get in time to make the backups. And then you discover a vulnerability in that system that threatens the whole thing. What would *you* do?"

Mr. Jefferson's expression was stony and dark. "Protect the system," he replied.

Terry nodded. "Precisely," he said, "and that's what I'm doing. My duty to the people; protecting the system."

Jefferson frowned thoughtfully, but after a moment he gave a slight shrug of his shoulders. He looked as if he believed the two men were speaking about completely different things while using the same words. Terry's replies were all too vague to be certain, though, and that hemmed Jefferson into a corner. He couldn't be the first to tip his hand, of that he was sure.

"Well, in any case," Jefferson said after the silence stretched uncomfortably, "as you said, when the maintenance is...complete...we will have access again."

"As you say," Terry replied, standing. "Thank you for stopping by to check on us, Mr. Jefferson. But please, feel free to call next time so we can offer you a proper reception."

The dismissal was clear, and there was no way that Jefferson could ignore it without it being obvious that he was doing so. After a brief hesitation, he stood and smiled in Terry's direction. Neither man extended his hand, so Jefferson turned to go. When he reached the door and opened it, he paused and turned back, his smile back in place again.

"Thank you, Mr. Price," Jefferson said, "for all of your hard work. Keep up the good results. I'm sure we'll be seeing much more of each other...soon."

"I look forward to it," Terry replied.

Jefferson's smile never wavered, but his eyes bore holes across the space between them. With a deep breath, though, the gaze softened, and the mask was complete again. Jefferson turned, and was gone without another word.

Ch. 42

The Things I Seen

Joe stepped out onto the front porch. The sun was low on the western horizon, and the shadow of the farmhouse stretched long and thin across the entire yard in front of him. In the east, the sky was already turning the deep purple that is really the first sign of night creeping in on the last moments of the day.

Beth stood against the railing, her back to him.

"We're almost loaded," Joe said, "Look, I'm sorry, but—"

Beth shook her head and stuck one hand up without turning towards him. "I don't want to hear it, Joe. Nothing you can say is going to make me understand, and I *don't* want to fight about it again."

Joe took a deep breath but didn't say anything for a long moment. He wanted to go to her, yet experience had taught him better. When her shoulders were set that stiffly, he was safer beyond arm's reach.

"Don't you want to at least say goodbye?" Joe asked finally.

Beth swung around, her eyes narrow, and one finger leveled at him. Joe barely contained a groan.

"*No*," Beth hissed. "I want to yell at you some more. I want to call you names. I want to say a whole lot of nasty things to you, to be honest, but I most certainly do *not* want to say goodbye."

Joe stepped forward to wrap his arms around her. "I love you," he whispered softly, "and I'll see you when I get back."

Beth sobbed into his shoulder, and squeezed hard. "I love you too," she said.

When the two separated, Beth's eyes were heavy with unshed tears. She swallowed hard and stared into Joe's eyes for a moment. Just when Joe was getting ready to say something, Beth squeezed his shoulders once, and before he could get any words out, she was gone.

Joe walked to the edge of the porch and gripped the cast iron railing hard. This was the part he always had a problem with, walking out the door. He knew it was part of the sacrifice that came with making certain commitments and putting on the uniform. But there is a huge difference between knowing something and enduring it.

Joe was about to turn and go back into the house when Levy, Beth's father, stepped up to the railing. Levy didn't say anything; he simply stood and gazed out at the darkening eastern horizon and the first few stars that were just beginning to show. In all the years Joe had known him, he'd never known Levy to just come out and stare at the sky like that.

"I never told you about The War," Levy said suddenly, still looking up at the stars, "but then again, you never asked. Most people do, you know. Ask, I mean. But not you."

Joe blinked but didn't know quite how to respond, so he simply nodded.

"I was nineteen when I signed the papers," Levy said. "Wanted to go out and see the world...and kill some Nazis. I reckon I got what I wanted, funny as that is to say. I killed Nazis. And boy, the things I seen."

Levy turned to face him in silence. His brown Dickies were pressed with a sharp crease, and his blue and red flannel shirt was completely spotless and free of lint. He'd spent all morning working in the garden before the baby arrived with Chris and Meg. He'd spent almost all afternoon playing with Sam in the dirt, but you couldn't have guessed it by his appearance.

"There was this fella," Levy said. "Big corn-fed boy from Nebraska. Nice fella. I met him when we were going through basic and he was in my unit all the way through. Shipped over with us to England and wound up in my landing craft headed for Omaha Beach."

Levy shook his head, a far off look in his eyes. "When we hit the shallows, you could hear the sand on the bottom of the boat. That ramp went down, and all hell broke loose. The boys in the front took it the worst. Bullets flyin every way, and the floors all slick from guys getting sick on the way in, they just couldn't get away from it. Me and one of the Sergeants, we started pushin the other fellas over the side into the surf. Once we spread it out, it wasn't as bad, but it sure didn't get a whole lot better."

Levy turned back toward the yard and gripped the railing. He was quiet for a moment, his face drawn into a dark frown. A whippoorwill called in the woods at the far edge of the field, and its song echoed softly in the darkening evening.

"Water was near chest deep," Levy said softly. "Hard to get through at first. The sand sloped up quick, though, and fore we knew it, we was running up the beach in between obstacles, bullets flying all around us. That guy from Nebraska ended up in front of me. He stumbled in the sand, and fell, so I stopped to help him. They really zeroed in on me quick, then, and bullets were hitting in the sand all around us. So I stuck my arm through the straps on the guy's pack and swung him up on my back."

Levy shook his head. "That boy was heavier than them bales of cotton and tobacco I used to carry out of the fields, but not by much. I ran all the rest of the way up to the sea wall with him like that. I set him down, and we grabbed cover right up against the wall. Poor boy was scared half to death, and he pissed his pants. Ran all the way down my jacket."

Levy looked down at his shoes and actually laughed for a moment.

"And wouldn't you know it," he said after a moment. "Fool boy stuck his head up over the wall for a peak at the German line, and some sniper saw him. Shot the boy clean through the throat. He fell back and we had to sit there and watch him gasp and die, trying to talk. I went through the rest of the damned war with Jonathan Tarrelton's last piss on my back. If he'd a been alive he would've died from laughin."

Levy clasped his hands behind his back and stood for a long time. Finally, he turned to Joe, and said simply, "I know why you have to go, son. I do. I still would have carried that boy up to the sea wall, piss and all, knowin he was gonna get shot. It was just the right thing to do. You going back to try and get people out of there, to save people, that's right too."

Levy shook his head. "You seen some of it coming out of the city, I can tell. Well, I seen the other end of it going into the cities in Europe. When people get desperate, even good people, they can do some terrible things, Joe. Things like you wouldn't believe, just to keep breathing. You find yourself in a spot like that, you turn your tail around and you get out of it, you hear? We need you back here in one piece, buddy."

Levy smiled, and squeezed Joe's hand. Before Joe's stunned mind could think up some reply, Levy had gone back in the house. Tom came around the side porch a few moments later and nodded. The half-rusted 1958 Chevy station wagon was loaded and ready.

Joe took the keys from Tom and climbed into the driver's seat. He took a deep breath, said a quick silent prayer, and cranked up the engine. It didn't exactly roar to life, but the car started. The headlights didn't work, the air conditioner blew hot air, and the thing barely had brakes, but it would get them down the road. And hopefully no one would think it was anything worth stealing if they had to leave it stashed somewhere. Levy had driven the station wagon to town twice a week and to church every Sunday since he'd bought it, but the car had rarely been out of the county, much less out of the state. He swore it was in good running condition, but the farthest Joe had ever personally seen it driven was Surf City for a fishing trip on the North Carolina coast.

The sun was long gone, and the eastern sky was turning a deep, velvety black when Joe pulled the '58 out onto the highway. He turned east, towards the rising quarter moon. Thunder clouds were beginning to rise along the western horizon, but it was so late in the day they would probably fizzle before any serious storms developed. The eastern sky, though, was clear, and the moon and stars lit the road ahead of them. Tom rode next to him, and Henderson was in the back. The men were all silent as they wrestled with things they'd seen, and the things they hadn't.

Ch. 43

The Whippoorwill's Song

Eric stood on the front porch and watched as the quarter moon climbed slowly through the sky. He only realized how high it had reached when he glanced down at the pine trees below. It must be getting late, he knew that, but he had no idea what time it was.

The distant sound of the '58 had faded to silence a long time ago, when the moon was still low on the horizon. Now, the only sounds other than the occasional breeze through the tree tops were the whippoorwills and bob whites calling to each other. The insects and frogs that normally filled the night with a dim, but pervasive hum were strangely silent.

Eric looked down from the moon, and nearly jumped. At the other end of the porch stood his grandfather, silently staring out at the dark woods around the house. Eric hadn't heard the front door close, and he'd thought he was alone. The rest of the house behind Eric was dark and silent, with everyone finally asleep, or so he'd thought.

For a long time, neither of them spoke. The birds sang in the night, and the two men stood quietly as the moon continued its climb. Finally, Levy came down and placed a warm, weathered hand on his shoulder. He squeezed once, and then let his hand fall back to his side.

"Better come in soon, son," Levy said softy. "There's a lot to do tomorrow, and we'll need your help."

Levy stuck a hand in his pocket and handed something metal to him. Eric turned the object over in his hand and frowned. It looked like an abnormally thick piece of copper wire that had been hammered down into a semi-sharp square point on both ends. It shone copper in the moonlight, and it looked either polished or well-worn. It resembled an old iron Ferrier's shoeing nail, but copper and with two sharp ends.

Eric frowned, and looked up at his grandfather, "What's this for?"

Levy simply smiled and patted his shoulder.

"Keep it," he said. "You'll need it tomorrow. I'm going to teach you something, son."

Eric opened his mouth again, but Levy smiled, and winked. He turned and stepped silently back into the house and let the door close slowly and softly behind him.

Eric was alone again.

He turned the small length of copper in his hand a few more times, trying to figure just what kind of tool it was. After a while, though, he gave in and stuck the thing in his pocket. Whatever it was, his grandfather would let him in on the secret when he was ready. Eric turned back and checked the moon's progress. It was now more than halfway to its highest point.

He knew Granddaddy was right; he should get some sleep. He needed the rest, and there would be more work in the garden the next day. Still, he couldn't quite bring himself to turn his back on the night and go inside. So he stood listening to the last whippoorwill that was still calling loudly in the night, and he watched the moon climb slowly higher in the eastern sky.

CH. 44

The Wrong Skies

The half-moon was nearly directly overhead, and Joe could
see the road clearly enough to make out the dotted yellow line in the
middle. Tall pines along the edges of the road cast deep, sharp
shadows that were utterly impenetrable, and Joe watched each one
for the slightest sign of movement that might mean an ambush.
Tom did the same from the front passenger seat, and Henderson
watched behind them.

They had tried talking amongst themselves at the beginning
of the trip, but slowly the atmosphere in the car had changed. As
they drove farther away from the quiet security of the farm, their
awareness had increased. All three men had seen action in combat
zones in the Middle East, though in very different decades and under
very different circumstances. Still, the habits of combat are hard to
break, even twenty years later.

The heightened awareness had quickly given way to vigilance,
and now the men were laser focused on every possible threat source
around them. So far they'd had the road to themselves, but there was
something that just felt off about the night. Joe couldn't put a finger
on exactly what he felt was wrong, but he knew the other men felt it
too. Their shoulders were just a bit too rigid, jaws too tight as they
watched the edges of the highway like hawks.

Suddenly, Joe jammed on the brakes, and the back end of the
station wagon slid slightly sideways. Tom and Henderson both had

D. W. McAliley

their pistols in their hands immediately, scanning the perimeter for the threat, but there was nothing to see. The woods on the left side of the road had fallen away to a large, open field, and on the right was a densely overgrown old timber cut.

"What the hell, Joe?" Tom asked.

Joe was frowning in concentration, and he pointed out his window to the horizon. "Tell me what you see," he said.

Tom and Henderson both stared for a moment, but it was Henderson who saw it first.

"There's a glow on the horizon, really low," He said hesitantly, "It looks almost like street lights, but the wrong color."

Tom nodded. "Yeah, I can see it too now. It's way too early for the sun right?"

"By at least five hours," Joe said, "judging by the moon. Besides, that's the wrong sky. That's north."

The men were silent for a long moment. They were all thinking the same thing, but none of them wanted to say it first. Finally, Joe broke the silence and voiced the fear they all felt.

"Fire," he whispered, "That's Raleigh burning. It's gotta be. I knew there was a reason I got off W64 when I did, I just couldn't put my finger on it. It was something that just felt wrong, and I think it was my brain trying to tell me that I was driving toward that glow on the horizon, and it wasn't right."

"Why would Raleigh be burning?" Henderson asked.

"Three days since it hit," Joe said. "Think about that... three days where you turn on the tap and nothing happens. Whatever food was in peoples' refrigerators and freezers is starting to go bad now, and no way to cook what isn't bad yet except for fire. People are getting desperate."

Tom took a deep breath and let it out slowly. "What's the contingency plan, here, Joe? If it's to that point already that Raleigh's burning, what do you think Norfolk's going to be like in another four or five hours when we get there?"

"If it's too hot, we pull back," Joe said, reluctantly. "Priority one is getting back home in one piece. It sticks in my gut to say that, but we've got families to think about now. The truth of it is, I think before this is all over with, we're gonna need gun hands at the farm; as many as we can get."

As they talked, the glow on the northern horizon grew slowly brighter as the fires feeding it grew unchecked. A sudden flash from below the tree line in the distance illuminated a low, hazy cloud of smoke as it rose over the city. There wasn't one large fire, but a whole host of them with thick pillars of smoke rising to a cloud that was growing dense enough to block out stars in that section of sky. They were a good fifteen miles south of the city, but if the winds shifted, they'd be able to smell the smoke on the wind.

"We'll pick up 64 again on the other side of the Rocky Mount," Joe said. "We might have to detour again, but the highway's the fastest route."

Tom rubbed the heels of his hands hard into his eyes. "If you need me to, I can drive next shift when we hit 64 again. I'm guessing your plan is to use the same route we took in?"

Joe tried unsuccessfully to stifle a yawn. "That way if everything else falls out, at least we might be able to get Gilbert and his family to come with us. We could get them as far away from whatever's about to come out of that city as possible."

Joe shifted the '58 back into drive and sped down the winding country road. The men went back to watching the shadows for movement, but every so often, their eyes were drawn to the northern horizon and the reddish orange glow on the horizon. Slowly, the glow of the fire fell behind them and faded with distance.

Joe rode with his window down, the cool night wind in his hair, and one hand on his pistol. When they crossed an old concrete bridge over a small creek, the clear song of a whippoorwill rang out for a brief moment and then was swept away in their wake.

Joe took a deep breath and tightened his grip on the wheel. He was exhausted, and the constant edginess was beginning to wear on him. With a slight shrug of his shoulders, Joe consciously set that part of himself aside in a small compartment. He couldn't afford to think about it right now, so he wouldn't. Joe stuffed all of his distractions and his second-guesses into that little compartment, and slammed the door hard on them.

There would be plenty of time for doubts and second-guesses when the mission was done. Right now, he had to focus.

CH. 45

Up Before The Sun

Eric woke slowly and reluctantly. He felt the hard floor in his back first and started to shift uncomfortably. The dim sounds of birds outside the bedroom window weren't enough to wake him, but he could hear them clearly. Suddenly, there was a slight tugging on his right big toe, and Eric sat bolt upright in his quilts to find his grandfather sitting at his feet, a broad grin on his face.

"Come on, Doc," Levy said softly. "Time to get a jump on the day."

Levy stood and left the room, trusting to Eric to get himself up and out of his makeshift bed. Christina stirred softly in the bed on the other side of the room, but she was still sound asleep. Eric stood and dressed himself quickly, but quietly, in a pair of faded blue jeans and a loose plaid cotton button down shirt.

When Eric stepped into the kitchen, Levy was pouring two plain white porcelain mugs of coffee from a dented and scratched aluminum percolator. The coffee pot was close to twice as old as Eric himself, but it still made hot, strong coffee. Eric took the mug from his grandfather and then followed him out the back door.

The sky was already pearly shade of gray, but the sun wasn't quite up yet. Along the eastern horizon, a few low clouds were painted bright crimson and orange along their bottom edges, the first hints of the coming dawn. Levy led the way down the concrete stairs and to the old curing barn on the back edge of the farmyard.

"You got that length of copper?" Levy asked as he walked around to the tin lean-to shed on the left side of the tall barn.

Eric frowned for a moment as he dug around and eventually pulled the stiff six inch copper rod from his pocket. He ran his thumb along both points, still puzzling over its purpose even as he showed it to his grandfather. Levy nodded and smiled, then took a seat on an upturned section of oak log that served as his stool. He poked around in the leaves for a moment until he found a large flat section of pottery with a deep brown glaze over it.

Levy handed the piece of ceramic to Eric and asked, "Know what this is?"

Eric examined the piece and turned it over several times in his hands. "It's part of an insulator for a power cable," he answered. "I've found smaller pieces out in the fields around here and the ones out by the road."

Levy nodded. "That's right, Doc," he said. "Way back when the power company was first running lines through this part of the state, they used these thick copper power cables and they used to get hot as all get out. Well, these huge insulators kept the hot cable from burning down the wood power poles."

Eric turned the piece over in his hand and was impressed by its size. If the circle it had broken from had been whole, it would have been twice the size of a dinner plate, and at least four times as thick. And this was part of one section from the original insulator.

"Years ago," Levy said, "before you were born, a bad ice storm came through here. A lot of the lines running through this part of the country got so heavy, they snapped right in half, and brought the power poles down with them. It was so cold that when the insulators hit the ground, they shattered."

Levy took the piece back from Eric and started turning it over and over in his hands, examining every crack and scratch on it. Finally, after several minutes of scrutiny, Levy reached into the leaves on the other side of his stool, and fished around until he picked up a smooth, round stone that had come down from the river bottom. He turned the piece of ceramic over a few more times, then changed his grip on it, and struck it fast and hard with the round river stone in his other hand.

There was a loud snap, and Eric was certain the pottery had shattered. But when Levy opened his fingers, a small sliver of ceramic fell to the ground, and the rest of the piece was intact.

"Your uncle MacBride and I went around while the lines was down," Levy said, half speaking to himself, "and we collected all the copper and insulator pieces we could find. When them power company boys came back through, we played dumb about it, and they just strung up new lines like it weren't nothing. We didn't really know what we was gonna use it all for back then, at least I didn't, but back then you saved stuff just to save it, whether you could use it right then or not. Never know what's gonna happen down the road."

Levy looked up at Eric and winked. He picked another spot and struck the edge of the pottery shard, knocking off thin flake. Levy fell silent for a while, and he worked on the piece of insulator with his stone, moving slowly around the edges. Eric picked up one of the flakes and looked at it in the growing light. It was thin, and razor sharp along the edges. It reminded him of something, but he couldn't quite place it at first.

After about twenty minutes, Levy nodded to himself and handed the piece of pottery back to a dumbfounded Eric. The piece of insulator had been completely transformed. It no longer even resembled ceramics, but had taken on a rough diamond shape a little smaller than Eric's hand. It looked a lot like the stone arrowheads and knife blades he'd found in the fields as a young boy.

"Now, take a look at your piece of copper," Levy said. As Eric did as he was told, Levy reached in his back pocket and pulled out a long, thin stick. At one end of the stick was a hammered point of copper just like the end of Eric's piece. The length of copper line was held to the stick with leather lashings. The entire tool had the weathered and worn look that comes from years of use. Along the copper end of the stick were dark, rusty brown stains that could only be old, dried blood.

Levy took the piece of pottery back from Eric and began working on it again. This time, instead of striking it with the rock, Levy carefully picked at it with the sharpened copper point of his tool. He worked slowly down one side, then the other. Turning it, and examining it between each flake.

The sun was nearly halfway over the horizon when Levy handed the finished blade to Eric. It was smooth, with a regular pattern of zigzagging marks down the full length of it. The edges were razor sharp, and Eric had to make a conscious effort to handle the blade without being cut. Levy smiled and nodded at him.

"You keep that," Levy said. "I'll teach you how to do the same thing, and then you'll have something to measure your work against."

"How did you learn to do that, Granddaddy?" Eric asked, thoroughly impressed.

"Well, it was Bride that did it first, Doc," Levy said shaking his head slightly. "He was a lot better at it than I was. You see, when I was a lot younger than you are now, we'd have to get up 'fore the sun every morning. We had to milk the cow, feed the pigs, check the chickens for eggs, build a fire in the stove... all the kinds of morning chores that you young'uns have growed out of these days. Well, while I was doing all of that, Bride would sneak off somewhere and do this," Levy gestured with his pressure flaker, "and he got real good at it, too. We worked out a deal where I'd do the chores, and he'd make me stone knives, and arrows, and teach me as best he could."

Levy grabbed his cup of coffee that was still steaming slightly and drained it in one gulp without spilling a drop. He chuckled to himself as memories Eric could only guess at danced through his head.

After a few moments, Levy nodded and smiled again. "Well, I ain't had any cows to milk around here for twenty years or more, and we ain't had chickens or pigs in at least ten. I guess I finally had time to start getting good at knapping myself, and I figure it's time to pass it on to you."

Eric shook his head and tried to hand the ceramic knife blade back to his grandfather. "I appreciate it, Granddaddy," he said, "but I don't think I'm going to have a lot of free time to practice this. Like you said, there's a lot to do in the garden, and with everything else going on, I just don't know."

Levy's face suddenly grew serious, and he leaned toward Eric without even moving to take the blade from him.

"Now you mark my words, Doc," Levy said. "You'd better make time. There's gonna come a day in your lifetime when you can't find any more bullets for them guns you carry. And when that happens, you're still gonna need something....something the other fella ain't got. You get my meaning?"

Eric felt the razor sharp edge of the stone knife blade again and imagined a fight where it would make the difference between winning and dying. Finally, he nodded, and said, "Okay, Granddaddy, I understand. Now, can you show me how you hit with the rock, please?"

Levy just smiled and shook his head. "One step at a time, son. We'll practice some more later. Right now, it's time to get to work."

Levy stood and put an arm around Eric's shoulders. The two walked back to the house while Levy laughed and told outlandish stories about the uncle that Eric had never met.

Ch. 46

Familiar Faces

The sun was about halfway up on the eastern horizon, and already the day was hot and humid. No thunderstorms the day before had left the atmosphere with tons of excess energy. When the evening storms finally broke loose, they would be intense.

Tom slowed the station wagon and looked over at Joe, who took a deep breath and thought for a moment before shaking his head. Tom pulled the '58 off to the side of the road and shifted into Park. He switched off the engine a good twenty yards from the foot of the low concrete bridge over the Elizabeth River. They'd crossed that bridge just the day before on their way out of town in the re-purposed HUM-V.

Now it ended a hundred yards out over the river in a jagged heap of charred concrete and twisted rebar. The men got out of the car and walked slowly to the foot of the bridge, their eyes wide in disbelief. Joe nudged a charred chunk of concrete with the toe of his boot and shook his head.

"J-DAM," Henderson said softly. "Two thousand pounder, from the looks of it. They like to roll in and hit center span, weakest point. One hit, and it collapses in under its own weight."

Joe frowned at the young Marine. "Seen this kind of thing before, Corporal?" he asked.

Henderson nodded. "It was classified," he said slowly, "but I guess that's all a bit beside the point now. I was with one of the expeditionary units that went into the Hindu-Kush, sir. Helped call in close support and forward offensive air strikes on strategic targets."

Henderson grinned. "Truth be told, sir, all I really did was track, trap, hunt, and pull the trigger when I needed to. A couple of the other guys...the real scary ones....they did all the radio and satellite communications stuff. I worked with a Seal team and two boys from the Air Force. Anyway, one of the things we had to do sometimes was check and confirm hits on target. So I saw a lot of.... that.... over there."

Joe just shook his head, staring over at the far side of the river. All of the names he'd recognized had lived in and immediately around Norfolk. And if they had gone through the trouble of taking out one bridge with an air strike, the odds are they'd taken out all of them. Joe closed his eyes and said a silent prayer for his brothers in arms.

When he turned back to Tom, his face was grim. "That list," he said. "Were any of the addresses in Chesapeake?"

Tom shook his head. "None of the ones I recognized," he replied. "All of them were Norfolk and Virginia Beach. There was one that was up in Hampton Roads, but I'm pretty sure he moved to Arizona a couple of years ago and never told anybody."

"What about names you didn't recognize?" Joe asked, but Tom only shrugged.

The men turned back to the station wagon to check the papers and froze. Four men stood around the car, examining it from every side. A fifth man leaned on the front driver side fender, his arms crossed, watching them.

"This sure is a *nice* car," the stranger said in a slow, deep southern drawl.

The other four men stopped their scrutiny of the vehicle and turned towards Joe and his companions. Their faces were all grim and dirty. Two of them had the look of bar fighters, with rough chins and crooked noses. One of them looked like a quiet gardener, and the last looked like he desperately wanted people to think he was tough.

Joe shared a glance with Tom and Henderson, and he then started walking calmly and purposefully at the obvious leader. The broad-shouldered man stepped away from the fender and stretched. He made a show of being nonchalant as Joe stalked up on him. When Joe was about five yards away, the man nodded to two of his lackeys, who stepped forward threateningly.

Joe stopped and waited, Tom slightly behind him and to the right, Henderson to his left. He didn't speak, and that began to bother the other man. Whatever was going on here, Joe wasn't going to give the stranger any information he didn't want to part with.

Finally, the large man stepped forward a few paces and pointed to Joe's right hand. "That sure is a fancy ring, Mister. Big, sky-blue stone in it. I know a guy seen a ring like that recently. Said the man wearing it was driving a military transport, and he had a bit of a hit and run. Know anything about that?"

Joe's eyes narrowed and he felt his stomach sink. With a beard added to his face and a bottle of whiskey for his hand, the stranger would have been a dead ringer for the man who had shot at them in the street. Joe swallowed hard and shook his head slowly.

"Now, what's the odds of another fella with the same kind of ring coming through here less than two days later?" The man asked with thick sarcasm. "Not very good, I think," he answered before Joe could speak.

The man reached around behind his back, but he froze when Joe suddenly drew his 9mm FNX and leveled it at him calmly. Tom had his pistol in his hand, scanning two of the men, and Henderson had done the same. No one moved for a moment, as the stranger and his friends stood in stunned silence.

There was soft laughter from behind Joe, and he felt goose bumps run up his neck. "Tom, if this guy's hand moves, drop him," Joe said.

"Roger," Tom replied, and he smoothly swung his gun over to the man, while keeping an eye on his two friends."

Joe turned and found himself looking at another familiar face. The young man from the railroad tracks stood with his three compatriots, their hands all stretched out to their sides. The young man shook his head ruefully.

"I told y'all not to mess with this dude," Donovan said. "I seen him and another cat put down four of the baddest mothas I ever seen. Well, I had a blind fold on, but I heard the guys start falling. Next thing I know, this other cat, that I don't even see is pullin off my hood and givin me the run down. I tried to tell you y'all don't want to mess with these guys. But y'all wouldn't listen to me, damn dumb red-neck."

"He killed my brother," the stranger bellowed.

"Yeah, and if you move they gonna kill you, too," Donovan said, "and what's *that* gonna solve. Your brother was a dead-beat drunk a-hole, and you know it."

Donovan turned back to Joe and shook his head. "Man, I don't want no trouble with y'all," the young man said. "I ain't gonna try and stand in your way, I ain't gonna try to stop ya. Don't mean I gotta help you none, though. Like I said before, you don't know me, and I don't know you. I'd still like to keep it that way, to be honest."

Joe nodded slowly. "That's probably best," he said and fixed the stranger with a hard stare. "You agree, or do you want to die today? Cause I mean to go home to *my* family."

The stranger took a deep, slow breath and seemed to shudder from his head down through to his toes. Finally, he opened his eyes and met Joe's glare. "I'll find you," he grated. "I will find you, you mark my words. You're in North Carolina, a half day's ride from here, maybe a little more. There ain't but so many places it could be, and I *will* find you."

After a moment more, he very slowly took an empty hand out from behind his back and held it out to one side. The men turned together and walked down the road past Donovan and his friends, casting glares of thinly veiled contempt as they moved. For their part, Donovan's friends gave as good as they got, but no one came to blows over it.

With the others moving down the road, Donovan began backing up, still facing the men, "Like I said, you go your way, and I'll go mine."

Joe frowned. "I think we'll be helping each other more than you realize, Donovan," he said.

Donovan opened his mouth to reply but stopped; his eyes widened. He slowly raised his hand to point, and Joe frowned. A dim noise that had been creeping into the edge of his hearing grew, and he turned. A pair of A-10's screamed low overhead, coming out of the south east. Joe turned as he watched them both rock their wings slightly. The aircraft were desert tan with gleaming white teeth painted in a shark-mouth design on the nose cone.

The two jets rapidly climbed over the city, banked into a hard, inverted dive, and fired off four hellfire missiles each. The missiles streaked away on independent flight paths, impacting a few seconds later. Both jets were already on climbing trajectories again. They banked over once more into inverted rolls and ended nose down, streaking towards the ground. The massive nose cannons rattled off a long string of fire like a pair of insanely over-charged buzz saws.

Clouds of smoke rose over the city in the area of the naval base and the freight port. The two A-10's began to climb a third time, but suddenly broke hard for the ground in separate directions. One of them let off a string of burning infrared flares as it climbed and banked at sharp angles. From the North West, a large white streak raced into view, tracing the A-10's path. As it closed, though, the missile changed direction slightly, and targeted one of the flares, detonating in a massive ball of fire two hundred yards behind the A-10.

The two jets, dropped to barely a hundred feet from the ground and raced back the way they'd come. As they passed overhead, they rocked their wings again, and were gone.

"Jesus H.," Donovan whispered softly as the echoes of their engines faded in the distance.

Joe blinked for the first time in what seemed like an hour. The entire thing had happened in maybe three minutes, tops, but it had been like watching a dance in slow motion, each move graceful and coordinated with deadly precision.

"I think we've got a war, fellas," Tom said, his voice thick with emotion.

"Yeah," Henderson said, "but who's shooting at who?"

"The tail on one of the A-10's said 'AZNG'," Joe said, "Arizona National Guard. Whoever we're fighting against, I think those were the good guys."

Tom nodded but didn't say anything in return; there simply wasn't much to say. Tom and Henderson climbed in the car, and Joe sat in the driver's seat. Before he cranked the car, he took the clipboard with the address list and looked over it. Three addresses were from Chesapeake, and two were within fifteen minutes of the bridge.

Joe looked over at Tom, who shrugged with a smile. "We might as well," he said. "I'd hate to get dressed up and drive all the way here without dancing at least one song."

Joe snorted a short chuckle and cranked the engine. He pulled a U-turn in the highway and left the rubble of the shattered bridge behind him. When he looked in the rearview mirror, Donovan was still staring north toward the city and the columns of thick black smoke rising above it.

The angry brother was nowhere to be seen, and that worried him, but Joe decided he'd deal with that problem if it came down the road to him; no need to go chasing after it.

Ch. 47

Halfway Up The Hill

Eric was exhausted.

He carried a half-full five gallon bucket in each hand, careful not to jostle any of the tomatoes on either side of him. The fruit in his buckets was nearly ripe, with just a hint of green-tinted orange along the top third of the grapefruit sized tomatoes. The bottom two thirds of the tomatoes was a deep, ruby red and fully ripe.

Eric set the two buckets in the thin edge of shade at the end of the garden rows. A line of tall, old oak trees bordered the garden field on all sides, and even in the extremes of the seasons, the shadows along that edge would shrink, but they never completely evaporated. Eric picked up two empty buckets and carried them back out into the sun.

Two of Tom's children would take the half-full buckets a little way up the hill towards the farm house and leave them in the shade. The other two youngsters would carry them the rest of the way. Imogene was back at the house with Jen and Meg. The women would wash the tomatoes, dry them, and set them out to finish ripening on two long, low tables that sat in the shade of three old sweet gum trees in the back yard. They laid the tomatoes out with two to three inches between them with the stem scar facing up.

This late in the season, if the tomatoes were left to ripen in the fields, they'd get too hot and begin to cook. The fruit would split from the pressures and then sour and spoil. In the shade of the tall trees, though, they would be protected from the harsh August sun.

In front of him, Eric's grandfather straightened for a moment. He pulled off a faded straw hat and wiped his forehead with a worn, thin handkerchief that stayed perpetually tucked into his back left pocket. He smiled and nodded to Eric, then bent back to the tomato vines. He took each tomato that seemed close enough to ripe and turned it one good time in his hand. If the stem snapped, he would put it in his bucket. Otherwise, he moved on to the next fruit or the next vine.

Eric guessed that they were no more than fifteen yards from the end of the rows, and he desperately hoped that these two buckets would finish them out. His mother worked the right hand row alone, and his grandparents helped each other on the left. Eric's arms and shoulders ached and his lungs burned as he handed the empty buckets over to be filled.

Before the tomatoes, Eric had carried buckets of butterbeans and bell peppers the entire way up to the house. None of the other kids were awake then, so he didn't have anyone to share the load with. Over the day, the buckets had actually gotten lighter, but they felt ten times heavier than the first full ones. It had been years since he'd been available to help with the harvest. Sometimes it was by design, but more often than not it was simply due to happenstance.

Now, he was tired and sweaty. He wished he'd spent more time in the gym and less on the couch the past few years. Finally, they reached the end of the tomatoes, and the three pickers stood. Eric's mother was dirty and sweat-stained, but both of his grandparents looked oddly clean. There was a dark stain around his grandfather's straw hat, and there were a couple of dark sweat spots on Nanny's bandanna, but that was all.

Eric's mother tried to carry the buckets, but Eric shook his head and took them from her. He was tired, but not so tired that he'd let her work while he didn't.

Eric suddenly heard Christina shouting his name from the house, "Eric! Eric!"

He frowned, and started walking back towards the far edge of the garden and the road up to the house a little faster. It was tough to move too quickly with buckets in his hands, but something in Christina's voice didn't sound right. Before he could even reach the edge of the shade, Christina came sprinting out into the sun, breathless.

"Someone's coming up the road, Eric," Christina panted. "They're walking."

Eric turned, and his grandfather nodded once. "Go, Doc," he said. "You can get there quicker than we can. See who it is, and be careful."

Eric was moving before his grandfather had finished speaking. He sprinted for the edge of the field with Christina close behind him. Eric paused just long enough to grab the twelve gauge shotgun that was leaning against one of the thick oak trees on the verge of the garden. The gun was his father's, a Remington semi-auto, and Eric had used it for years to hunt doves and squirrels.

It was only about two hundred yards from the garden to the house so it didn't take long for Eric to reach the front porch. He rounded the edge of the farmhouse, and pointed for Christina to go up and stand by the front door. If something went wrong, he wanted her where she could get inside quickly to warn the others.

Eric trotted out into the white sand of the quarter mile long driveway. He looked down the road and past the first drainage dike; he could see a figure walking towards him. It was still quite a ways off, and the glare from the sun made it difficult to see details, but there was something familiar about the shape and the way it moved.

As the person grew closer, the sense of familiarity grew stronger, until finally a voice he recognized called out, "It's just me, Betsy."

Eric heaved a heavy sigh of relief. 'Aunt' Betsy had lived on the road as long as Eric could remember. She was as much a part of his family as any of his actual aunts and uncles, two of which lived at the far end of Cutler's Run from his grandparents, less than two miles away.

Aunt Betsy moved slowly but confidently down the road. She paused when she got closer to Eric and eyed the shotgun with a twinkle in her eye.

"What you gonna do with that pea-shooter?" Aunt Betsy asked around the Pall Mall hanging from her lip. "I don't see no squirrels around here."

Eric couldn't help but chuckle as he shook his head. "No, but I heard a rumor about some wild Billy goats. Figured you can't be too safe."

Aunt Betsy barked a short laugh at that and shook her head. "Where's yer grandma?"

"Round back of the house," Eric replied. "I'll take you to her."

Aunt Betsy nodded but didn't say anything else. Eric saw a look on her face that he didn't quite understand, but he could tell she was deep in her own mind about something, so he didn't bring it up. He led her around to the back of the farmhouse where Nanny was helping lay out the last of the fresh tomatoes.

When Nanny saw Aunt Bets, she stood and dried her hands. Eric's grandmother came over and the two women greeted each other warmly. After a moment, Aunt Betsy dropped her cigarette and ground it into the dirt.

"Well, there's a reason I come by," Aunt Betsy said. "The other night, when the lights all stopped working, Darril passed away. Only thing we can figure is that his pacemaker just stopped workin right along with everything else. I woke up the next morning, and he looked like he was sleeping. I knew something was wrong. In fifty three years, I never once beat him out of the bed."

Nanny gasped and hugged Aunt Betsy, who assured Nanny that everything was fine and she was okay with everything.

"Actually," Aunt Betsy continued, "I come by to make sure y'all were okay. After everything that happened, and everything with Darril, I just needed to see some faces that were friendly, I guess."

Nanny nodded. "Well, Betsy, you know you can come down here any time," she said, patting the other woman on the back. "Our door's always open for you, you know that. If there's anything you need, you just let us know. Come inside and have a drink of tea, we're just about to fix some dinner."

Aunt Betsy shook her head, though. "Nah, I better get back," she said, lighting another unfiltered Pall Mall. "Like I said, I just wanted to stop by and see ya for a bit."

Nanny shook her head. "Well at least take some tomatoes and butterbeans back with you," she said, already placing some of the vegetables and fruit into a bucket. "Eric, you carry that back for Aunt Betsy."

Eric stepped forward and reached for the bucket, but Aunt Betsy slapped his hand away.

"I don't need no chaperone," Aunt Betsy grumbled, taking the bucket for herself, "and the only reason I'm taking this is 'cause I know if I don't, you'll send Eric after me with it. When you want the bucket back, come get it and I'll fill it up with some corn and chicken eggs for you."

"You sure you don't want me to go with you, Aunt Betsy?" Eric asked.

Aunt Betsy snorted hard. "Boy, I was walking up and down this road before you was even a thought in your momma's head. I think I'll manage."

Aunt Betsy turned and shuffled back down the road, the half-full bucket swinging from one hand, her cigarette clenched in the other.

Ch. 48

0-4

Joe stepped onto the front porch of a single story brick ranch, his Beretta tucked neatly in his hand. Tom and Henderson stood at the foot of the front steps covering both directions down the empty street. Joe cupped his left hand and tried to see through the small window to the right of the door with no luck. There was a thick black film on the inside surface of the glass, and Joe couldn't see a thing.

Joe took the door handle and tried to turn it slowly, but the door was locked. He turned to the two men at the foot of the steps and shook his head.

"Locked down," Joe said. "Just like the other two. Everything's blacked out inside and I can't see a thing through the glass."

Tom shook his head, eyeing the red spray paint on the front door. There was a large red X on the door, marking it out into quadrants. It was the standard Urban Search and Rescue (URS) code that had been used during Hurricane Katrina to clear neighborhoods in house-to-house sweeps. In the left area, in large block letters and numbers, 'TOT KG 117' was painted. The top quadrant was dated the day before, August sixteenth. The right quadrant was the hazards list, with biohazard (Bhz), corrosive chemicals (CC), and explosive flammables (ExF) painted in the same red spray paint. In the bottom quadrant, the body count was listed as zero living and four dead (0-4).

They had seen the same code painted in red paint on each of the three doors from the list of addresses that they'd visited, all with no survivors found. It had also been painted on maybe a half dozen other doors that weren't on the list, all in the same red spray paint. In each of the houses not on the list, there had been at least one living person removed from the home, according to the URS code, but Joe had his doubts.

The three men started walking back towards the station wagon. There was a crash of breaking glass behind them, loud on the otherwise silent street. Joe spun back towards the house, his pistol up and ready. Tom scanned the perimeter, and Henderson checked both ends of the street. There wasn't any movement other than a few shards of broken glass slipping out of the window frame to clink onto the pile on the ground.

Joe gave hand signals to Tom and Henderson to keep a sharp eye out for any movement or threat. He carefully inched his way forward, keeping his gun trained on the shattered bay window. Joe crouched down and crept up to the brick wall directly beneath the window. He heard muffled groans and coughing from inside the home. Joe motioned for Tom and Chris to cover him, and the three made their way back up the steps to the front porch. With Tom and Henderson to either side of the door, Joe stepped in front of it and nodded to Tom. Tom stepped forward and, with a strong backward mule kick, struck the door just to the left of the handle.

The frame splintered, and the door swung in with a snap. Joe stepped smoothly inside and turned immediately to his left. He heard

Henderson come in next and move ahead, with Tom directly behind him and clearing right.

They found themselves in a large, open sitting room with sturdy, though plain, furniture. The hardwood floors were deeply polished walnut and the walls were a desert sand color. A dark rusted brown stain marred the cream colored arm chair and stained the hardwoods in a long smear over to a sofa table along one wall. The sofa table was on its side in front of a broken bay window, and leaning against it was a man clutching his gut. The man's face was pale and slick with shiny sweat. His breath came in shallow, labored gasps, and he groaned incoherently between them.

Joe walked slowly towards the man, his pistol trained on him the entire time. When he was a few feet away, the injured man sat up, and fixed him with a hard stare. There was a solid trickle of blood coming from the corner of his mouth, and he was clutching his gut with both arms.

"You're a little late to the party," the man said. He barked a short chuckled that dissolved into a rough, tearing cough. He turned his head and spat a mouthful of dark, frothy blood to the side.

"Look I'm--" Joe began, but the man cut him off, shaking his head.

"Don't matter who you are," he said, his voice strained. "Won't matter who I am for much longer. Dirty son of a bitch shot me in the gut twice and left me for dead."

The man started coughing harshly again and bloody spittle sprayed from his lips. Joe knelt in front of the man, and lightly touched his shoulder with a hand. When the man looked up, it took a brief moment for his eyes to focus, and when they did he shook Joe's hand off his shoulder roughly.

"Who shot you?" Joe asked quietly.

"Never met him," the man replied. "I guess I should've said yes to the first guy."

"First guy?" Joe asked.

"Yeah, this guy came by with my name on a list," he said, shifting his weight a bit and stifling another cough. "He said I was needed back West for some big operation; a response to this whole thing. I told him I was retired."

"Then he shot you?" Joe asked.

"No, not that one," the man said. "Another guy came with a team a few hours later. I thought they were with the same group, but when I told them I'd already been asked, the head guy got this real serious look on his face. He told me I had one chance to say yes, and I shook my head. That's when he pulled a gun and put two in my gut. Told me he wanted me to die slowly."

"The guy that shot you, did he have a name?" Joe asked.

The man grimaced. "I'm thirsty," he whispered. "So thirsty I can't stand it. Throat feels like it's coated in broken glass."

"Here," Joe said, offering the man his small green canteen. "It's clean and it's fresh."

The man waived his hand and shook his head. "Waste of water," he said. "I'll be dead before I can enjoy it."

Joe took a deep breath. "We've got a field medic that can patch you up," he said.

The man laughed a shallow, rasping laugh again. He lifted his arms, revealing a mass of dark, coagulating blood and thick, yellow bile. The area around the wound was swollen and red, and it smelled like death.

"Can your medic fix that?" the man asked, already shaking his head. "Twelve hours ago, maybe. Nothing's bringing me back now."

"Listen, the man that shot you," Joe said. "What did he look like?"

The man coughed hard, but managed to grate, "He was about your height, short black hair. He had a sharp jaw, and dressed in urban tactical gear with dark sunglasses. His name...."

The man trailed off and slumped slightly forward with blood trickling from his mouth. For a brief moment, his breathing stopped, and Joe felt a chill run through him. After a moment, he reached over and squeezed the man's shoulder, and he jumped as if stuck by a knife. The man blinked, winced with pain, and finally his eye found Joe's again.

"His name," the man whispered, his voice barely audible, "was Parker."

Ch. 49

A Long Shot

Terry sat back in his desk chair, lost in thought. His eyes were on the flat top of the desk in front of him, but they were focused somewhere far away. He had expected a flood of angry calls and demands for access to the system, or at the very least, a few irritated secretaries.

The one thing he hadn't really counted on was silence.

Since the Chief Administrator of FEMA had paid his visit, there had been nothing. Not even one of the other SSA's from the other sites had bothered to call and ask about the situation, which made Terry think they'd already been informed. That left little doubt where their loyalties lay. He still couldn't figure out if FEMA was at the head of this thing, or if they were actually trying to do what they were supposed to and manage the emergency and needed access to the databases to do so.

Terry twisted the class ring on his left hand as the thoughts rattled around like loose boulders in his mind.

When Marcus Attledge knocked softly on Terry's door, he didn't hear it at first, so the engineer stuck his head around the corner and peaked into the open office.

"Mr. Price?" Marcus asked. "You sent for me, sir?"

Pulled from his deep reverie, Terry nodded and stood. "Yes, Mr. Attledge," he said, waiving the young man in. "Please, come and have a seat. Close the door, if you don't mind."

Marcus closed the door as he stepped fully into the office, then walked over to the two chairs across the desk from Terry, and sat in the one on his left. Terry sat once more in his own chair and frowned hard as he tried to find a way to broach the subject he had called Marcus in to discuss.

"Everything okay, sir?" Marcus asked as the silence between them stretched.

Terry shook his head with a small shrug of his shoulders. "If it's obvious enough for you to ask that question, then the answer is quite obviously no," he answered. Terry pulled off this class right from his left hand and held it up to the LED lighting, admiring the detail and the clarity of the sky blue stone. "Do you know what this is, Marcus?" Terry asked, setting the ring down on the desk between them.

Marcus leaned forward and looked at the ring but didn't pick it up. He shook his head, and admitted, "Other than a class ring, not really.,"

"My Naval Academy ring," Terry said slowly. He sat for a long moment, staring at the ring on the table. Finally, he said, "I need you to do something, Marcus. Before I tell you what it is, I want you to know that if there was anyone, and I mean *anyone*, that I could send to get this done, I would. Truth is, I need you here, but there's just no one else I trust to do it."

"What do you need?" Marcus asked without hesitation.

Terry 's more serious tone caught Marcus' attention. "You need to think about this because it's the kind of thing that can get a person killed, Marcus. I don't ask it lightly, and you shouldn't commit to it lightly, either."

Marcus met his eyes with obvious respect. "Sir," he said softly, "you've done more for me in the past nine years than most people I've known my whole life. Whatever it is, I'll do it."

Terry couldn't help but smile at that. He leaned forward, slid the ring towards Marcus, and breathed a deep sigh of relief. "Then you'll need this," Terry said, pointing to the ring.

Marcus picked up the ring, turned it over twice in his fingers, and examined every detail quickly and carefully. Satisfied that he was acquainted with it, he tucked the thick gold band into a buttoned pocket on the left side of his shirt.

"Okay," Terry began, "you know the telemetry file that you said was deleted two days ago? Well, that was me. I deleted the file, and then wiped any trace that I'd done so, though apparently not quite as thoroughly as I'd thought."

"I'm not quite sure I understand," Marcus said. "Why would you delete an aberrant telemetry file and try to hide it?"

"I'm getting to that," Terry said, waiving one hand at Marcus. "Listen, I need you to take a trip..."

CH. 50

The Silence After

Joe stood on the front porch of the house and gave a few hand signals to Tom, "I'll be out in a bit," he said and turned his back before anyone either man outside could speak.

Joe closed the door and walked over to the dying man. His breathing was short and shallow. Judging from the expressions on the man's face, the pain was getting too difficult to bear. The man twitched occasionally and groaned under his breath. Still, when he looked up at Joe, his eyes were clear.

"They take it all?" the man asked, and Joe nodded. "Good. Someone should use it, and Lord knows it ain't gonna be me." The man breathed a little deeper and easier, though it made him wince hard with each exhale.

"Listen, we could help you," Joe offered, one last time, but the man shook his head.

"I told you not to blow your smoke up there," the man grated. "You and I both know these holes in my gut are gonna kill me. It might take another couple of days, but you could drop me on the roof of Walter Reed right now, and it wouldn't matter. Anything strong enough to kill the infection will tank my kidneys and liver, and I'm dead either way."

Joe took a deep breath but didn't speak. After a moment the man continued in a raspy whisper. "You know it, too. You just wanted to be sure. Okay, I don't blame you. Look into my eyes, man. I want you to do it, I know what I'm askin, and I mean it."

Joe swallowed hard, but he met the man's direct gaze without flinching. After a long moment, he said softly, "My name's Joe Tillman."

"Don't matter who you are," the man said. "Don't matter who I am."

Joe shook his head, his eyes grim as he held the man's stare. "I know your name. You should know mine. If I'm going to do this, you should know my name. I don't know *you* but I got that much off a clipboard."

The man nodded. "Yeah, you did. Your name's on it too, right? Don't answer, man, I know it is. Listen....your name was on there, and my name was on there. Look at me now. You've got a family?"

Joe's silence was confirmation enough, and the man closed his eyes briefly. When he opened them, he was calm, but serious. "You gotta get out of here, man. Any one that's on that list would tell you the same thing, if they were sitting where I am now. If you were me, and I was you..... what would you say?"

Joe stared at his hands for a moment. After a long moment he swallowed past the cold knot in his gut and forced himself to look away. His hands had never shaken before.

"I would say the same things you are," Joe replied finally. "Close your eyes, then."

The man shook his head and sat up straighter. "Nah," he said. "I ain't hiding from this. This is my choice. No pain. No suffering. Like flipping a switch. That's my way to go."

Joe stood and drew his Beretta.

The man's eyes focused out the window on the deep blue sky beyond the trees in the yard, and his lips moved silently for a moment. When they stopped, he breathed in deeply through his nose. Just as he began to exhale....

Joe squeezed.....

.....the trigger.....

Ch. 51

After A Good Rain

Levy picked his way carefully along the path through the woods. He paid close attention to where he placed his feet each time he took a step. The path leading down the gentle slope wasn't difficult or steep, and the deep layer of leaf litter and old pine straw made for a soft walking bed. He still had to be vigilant, though, because those leaves could hide copperheads, cottonmouths, and even the occasional canebrake rattler. Levy carried a cricket basket in one hand and two long, thin cane fishing poles in the other.

Eric followed his grandfather, picking his way by carefully following Levy's footfalls. Eric carried a small tackle box and a Cool Whip container of night crawlers in a five gallon bucket with one hand, and a Zebco spinner rod and reel combo in his other hand. The afternoon was hot and humid, but in the shade of the towering oak and pine trees, it felt almost comfortable.

As the pair reached the bottom of the hill, the ground leveled out and became slightly mushy from the rain and thunderstorms of the past few days. A cloud of mosquitoes and gnats followed them every step, buzzing and whining in their ears. Eric breathed a gnat in through his nose, setting off a fit of hard sneezing that left his ribs aching and his eyes watering.

The flood plain stretched a little more than a quarter of a mile from the bottom of the hill on which their family farm sat to the near bank of Cutler's Run. It was an easy walk along the clear, broad path with dense underbrush on either side. Birds scattered in front of them and sang from nearly every tree and bush they passed. The entire forest seemed to be absolutely vibrating with the lush exuberance of late summer.

The path they were following was an old logging road, and it turned to follow the line of the river. For a short time, Eric and his grandfather followed the road as it ran a good thirty yards from the river. After a while, Levy looked up and took his bearings from the towering pines and oaks along the river bank and nodded to himself. Another hundred yards down the road, Levy turned to his left and entered the woods. The road was about fifty yards from the river bank here, and the underbrush was thick. It was difficult to push a path through the river cane and briars, but with a little effort the pair was able to break a path through to the bank.

The river was broad and slow in this stretch, with deep water. On the opposite bank, a massive stone outcrop jutted from the ground, rising sixty feet into the air. It formed a massive rock wall along a two hundred yard stretch of the opposite bank, and the low hill it formed had earned the local moniker 'Little Big Rock'. Levy settled himself onto an old fallen pine tree and began unwinding the fishing line on one of his cane poles.

"After a good rain like we had the past few nights," Levy said as he threaded a worm onto his hook, "the fish will be lookin for food washed into the river. Give it a day or two for the mud to wash out of the water, and the fish start bitin like crazy."

Levy took his cane poll and swung the baited hook in a long arc out into the middle of the river with a plop. The bright orange cork bobbed up and down in the gentle current as the hook settled into the water. The river carried the cork very slowly to the left and

Levy sat back to watch as it floated by. Eric finished tying a larger hook with a synthetic rubber night crawler on his Zebco, and he moved upriver a bit so his casting wouldn't interfere with Levy's bait.

"Gotta be careful with a spinner like that," Levy said, shaking his head. "There's trees and rocks and all kinds of trash piled up deep in this hole. You hit some of it with that hook, and you'll lose your worm."

"I know, Granddaddy," Eric said. "I'll be careful."

Eric cast his lure three fourths of the way across the river and began reeling it slowly towards him. Every few turns, he would jerk the lure a couple of feet through the water to imitate a jittery, injured worm trying to swim. Nothing bit on the first cast, so he tried again in a slightly different spot with the same result.

"I'm gonna move up a little ways," Eric said. "Maybe they'll hit it up where the water's a little less deep."

Levy just grunted. As Eric moved off, Levy's orange cork bobber disappeared beneath the water. Levy stood and pulled up sharply on the cane pole, setting the hook. He pulled a large, flat blue-gilled brim from the water and grinned over at Eric.

"Good luck," Levy said as he pulled the fish from his hook and dropped it into the bucket of river water. The fish flapped and splashed at first but settled down quickly. Eric shook his head and took his tackle box with him as he walked upstream far enough to be out of sight of his grandfather and started fishing.

After more than an hour of trying different spots and different lures, all with the same negative result, Eric was becoming frustrated. He'd lost three complete worm rigs and two shiny spinner baits to hidden obstacles in the murky water. He decided to go back and check on Levy and see if the old timer's luck had held. As he walked up to his grandfather, Eric could hear the fish splashing in the bucket by his side. Eric looked in the bucket and was shocked to see enough fish in the bucket to hide the white plastic bottom from view. Levy never said a word, just looked up and nodded as Eric set his spinner reel down and picked up the spare cane pole.

When Eric had unwound the fishing line and tied on his hook, he added a couple of small split-shot lead weights and a bright orange cork bobber. Levy pulled his line from the water and set his pole next to his log seat as he stood.

"Come with me, Doc," Levy said, and he grabbed the nearly empty cricket cage.

Levy led the way, pushing through the briars and brush until they were back on the old logging road. Levy scanned the trees for a moment, then snapped his fingers and pointed to a young tree that was no more than twenty feet tall at its highest point. The canopy the tree formed was broad and thick with wide flat leaves larger than a dinner plate.

"This here's a Catawba tree," Levy said as they reached the base of the tree. Levy reached up to one of the low-hanging branches and grabbed a broad leaf riddled with holes. He turned the leaf over, and smiled broadly, "And these," he continued, "are Catawba worms."

Levy began plucking the two inch long black caterpillars from the leaf and dropping them into the cricket cage. He left a few of the larger worms and moved on to the next leaf he could reach, repeating the process. Eric followed his grandfather around the tree, pulling worms off where he could reach as well.

"You never want to pick a leaf clean," Levy said, "and it's best to leave the bigger ones, if you can. That way you know there'll be more worms next year."

Eric nodded. "That makes sense," he said, "but what's so special about these worms?"

"It's the smell," Levy said. "You wouldn't believe it, but these things drive fish flat out crazy, Doc. You can have a bad day on every other kind of bait, but drop one of these sticky, stinky little worms in the water, and the fish'll be crawling out onto the bank to get more of it."

When they'd gone around the entire tree, there were about thirty worms crawling around inside the cricket cage. Levy tore off a few pieces of the broad, flat leaves and dropped them into the wire cricket cage with the worms. A few of the remaining crickets were able to use the leaves to mount an escape, but Levy didn't seem to mind.

When they were back at the river, Levy took one of the larger worms from the cricket cage and laid it flat on the log. With his antique Case pocketknife, Levy carved the worm into three roughly equal sections. As soon as he cut into the thick, rubbery hide, a slimy paste squirted out and Eric felt his stomach shift. Levy stuck one of the sections on his own hook and another on Eric's.

They swung the bait out into the water at roughly the same time. Eric turned to ask his grandfather a question and felt a sharp jerk on his line. When he looked back to the water, both his and his grandfather's cork bobbers were nowhere to be seen. For a moment, Eric stood with his mouth open, not quite believing the results he was seeing. Then, his rod jerked again, and Eric's attention snapped back to the water and the present moment. He pulled up sharply on the cane pole to set the hook and pulled a massive brim from the water as Levy did the same.

"You see, Doc," Levy said as they took the fish off and dropped them into the bucket to splash and thrash about, "you're used to fishing for sport and for fun. That's all well and good, but what we're doin now is different. If we don't catch fish, then we don't eat supper. Reelin in that eight or ten pound bass is a challenge, and it's a thrill, but if you don't get that big boy in hand, then all that time spent chasin him is just wasted."

Levy cut another worm, and they baited their hooks with it. Eric dropped his in the water first, and within a few seconds, the bobber bounced once and disappeared again. Eric shook his head but couldn't help chuckling to himself as he pulled another fish from his hook. In less than an hour, the five gallon bucket was so full they couldn't fit any more fish in it. Levy cut a branch and strung a dozen brim on it by running the thin end through one side of their gills and out their mouth.

"Granddaddy, there's just one thing I don't understand," Eric said as they were packing up their poles, the bucket, and tackle boxes to head back up the hill to the house.

"What's that, Doc?"

"Well," Eric said, pointing to the buck and the loaded branch of fish, "you can catch fish like that on your own, so why did you need me down here with you?"

"To carry the bucket back up the hill, of course," Levy replied with a chuckle and a wink.

CH. 52

A Long Way Home

Joe gripped the steering wheel hard, his knuckles white from the strain. The last building of the city fell into the dim shadows deep within his rearview mirror. The old station wagon thundered down the road and the wind tore at Joe's hair. The air was hot and muggy, but at least it was moving, and that helped.

Joe ground his teeth.

Two houses empty, and one he wished had been. They left the Chesapeake and Norfolk behind with many more questions than answers. The man they'd seen, the one they'd found shot, had said there were two groups that came looking for him, and the second one was the violent group. Joe wondered who the first set of visitors had been.

And he wondered who had sent in the A-10's. The National Guard can't respond to a threat with that kind of force unless some very specific conditions had been met. And even with everything he'd seen, Joe wasn't quite ready to go *that* far just yet. He shrugged his shoulders slightly and gripped the steering wheel tighter, trying to silence the doubts rolling through his mind.

Joe wondered which group he'd left hog-tied and without a ride outside Chris's home the day before. Were they the ruthless thugs that had put two bullets in the stranger? Or were they the ones that came first with questions and an open hand? Suddenly, Joe slammed on his brakes. The '58 slid to a halt, the back end starting to slide around to the right. Joe had to cut the wheel hard to keep the car from going into a spin.

He had almost driven past the faded gray mailbox and gravel driveway.

Joe pulled the station wagon into the driveway and started blowing the horn. A grizzled old farmer in dusty tan overalls came around the corner of the porch with a double barrel twelve gauge in his hands. He turned his head and spat a thick jet of dark purple tobacco juice to the side and arched it over the white railing of the porch.

"Whoever you are," Gilbert called, "you'd better stop right there! I'll shoot ya down if I have to, I swear to Christ!"

Joe stomped the brakes again and threw his empty hands out the window.

"Gilbert!" Joe called, "It's me, Joe. We need to talk, old man!"

Gilbert snorted and spat to the side again. "Well, Joe," he said slowly, "there's better ways of sayin that, but okay."

Gilbert flipped the shotgun around so the muzzle was pointing up and to the left, away from anyone in the area. Still, his right hand was close to the trigger, and he could swing the shotgun down quickly from that position. The old farmer fixed Joe with a hard stare.

"Okay, Joe," Gilbert said carefully. "You've got my attention."

"I hate to come at you like this," Joe said shaking his head, "but you need to hear me out, Gilbert. Things are bad in the city now. I watched A-10's dropping missiles and making strafing runs over Norfolk, and I'm pretty sure they were the *good* guys in this. You guys need to get out of here while you still can."

Gilbert knelt by the car and looked Joe in the eye for a long moment. Finally, he shrugged his shoulders a bit. "This is our home, Joe," Gilbert said. "There's a war coming and who would we be if we left our home right at that moment?"

Joe shook his head and thrust his door open. He got out and pulled Gilbert to his feet. He half dragged the farmer to the edge of the yard and pointed to the south. There was a small subdivision of nice, large suburban homes about a mile and a half distant.

"There," Joe said, pointing to the track of homes, "you've got nine neighbors to your south. Do you know any of them?"

Gilbert was silent for a moment.

"I didn't think so," Joe said, releasing the man. "Who do you have out here, Gilbert? Who is there to help you if your grandson breaks his arm or leg? Who's out here to help if you get bit by a moccasin? You got people to look in on or people that look in on you?"

Gilbert didn't reply and he didn't nod or shake his head. He stared sullenly at the farm house and slowly dropped to his knees. He buried his face in his hands for a long time, breathing heavily.

"I know it's hard to leave," Joe said, kneeling next to the old farmer. "You're right, Gilbert. There's a war coming. Who do you have to help keep the war outside and away from your family? Can you do it? All on your own, without any backup, can you keep your family safe?"

A long moment of silence stretched, and it seemed that no one breathed. By now, the rest of the family was on the porch, and Tom was out of the car. The boys' mother glared daggers at Joe, but Gilbert's wife was nodding slowly. She, at least, understood the situation. And it seemed that Gilbert did too.

"We've got nothing to bring," Gilbert said slowly, softly. "We've got nothing to offer."

Joe shook his head and pulled the farmer back to his feet.

"I think we both know that's not true," Joe replied. "You've got decades of knowledge and experience to pass on. You lived and thrived in hardships people my age have only read about in books, if they're lucky. We're going to need your perspective and your experience down the road."

"I never thought I'd be the one to leave this place behind," Gilbert said slowly, looking around the farmyard with a wistful eye.

Joe gripped the old farmer by the shoulder and offered him his right hand.

"Don't worry, Gilbert," Joe said solemnly. "When the time comes, I'll help you take it back."

"I'll hold you to that," Gilbert said, and he took Joe's hand and shook it hard.

There wasn't much left to say after that. In less than two hours, they had secured everything that could be packed and stowed in or on top of the station wagon secured. Joe pulled out onto the road and headed south. The two young boys, one with his arm fresh in a splint and a sling, sobbed in the back seat, as they turned to watch the old farmhouse fade into the background.

Gilbert never turned back once.

Ch. 53

Hand In Hand

The sun was an angry red ball low on the western horizon when Eric took the last slimy fish from the bucket at his feet and laid it on the thin, bowed wooden plank in front of him. He was breathless, and his forearms ached a little. This would be his thirty seventh brim cleaned and scaled, and his grandfather had skinned four long, sleek catfish. Their heads hung from four spikes that had been driven deep into the wood of a massive pecan tree in the back yard. The iron spikes had been imbedded in the trunk so long that it looked as if the tree were weeping rusty tears from four deep black eyes.

When Levy finished filleting the slab of catfish he was working on, he plucked the four heads from the tree and dropped them into a stinking bucket that was encrusted with flies and fish innards. Scales flew from the brim Eric held on the table, and he was almost done with their last fish. Levy dropped the remaining catfish in buttermilk so cold it made the side of the aluminum bowl that held it sweat fat, cold beads of water. The pink chunks of fish floated in the thick liquid like ice cubes.

Levy took a knife with a small, sharp blade and began scraping the scaled and gutted fish. He would hold the cleaned fish in one hand and scrape the last of the thick layer of protective slime from their skin, and then scrape out the cavity that had held the guts. Once they were thoroughly cleaned inside and out he rinsed them a last time and dropped the fish into a large aluminum bowl of ice water. A dash of salt in the water drew out the little bit of blood in the meat, giving it a milder flavor.

Once he was done scaling and gutting the last fish, Eric reached for a knife, but Levy shook his head.

"You go on and take that bucket," Levy said, pointing with the tail of the fish in his left hand at the bucket of guts. "There's a compost pile down at this corner of the garden field. Drop them on top and turn a little of the leaves over to cover it up. Maybe that'll keep the coons and possums out of it for the night."

Eric started to offer a counter proposal, but Levy had already bent back over the fish. With a half-suppressed sigh, Eric hefted the bucket as far away from his body as he could hold it and began the trek down the hill towards the garden.

The small path through the trees to the garden field had nasty roots, several holes, and a good enough covering of overgrowth to hide all of that and more. Eric had to move very carefully to keep from slipping or spilling. Finally, he reached the garden and poured the contents of his bucket into the massive mound of dark brown, steaming refuse. A pitch fork stuck in the ground under a gnarled old oak tree turned the compost easily enough, and Eric soon had the fish guts buried beneath a fresh layer of steaming organic fertilizer.

By the time Eric made it back up the hill to the house, Levy had half of the fish scraped clean and soaking in the chilled salt bath. He motioned for Eric to join him, pointing with another fishtail at the board next to him on the low metal table. Eric took a short paring knife with a thin plastic handle and began to scrape the fish.

After a few minutes, Levy began shaking his head slightly, "Not so deep, Doc," he said. "You don't want to tear the skin. If you do that, you're bein too rough. Just enough to get the thin slime off, that's all."

Eric nodded and adjusted the pressure he was putting on the knife.

"You did well today, Doc," Levy said, after a moment of silence. "You need to learn how to move more quietly, though, if you're gonna spend time walking in these woods."

"I didn't do that bad," Eric grumbled under his breath.

Levy snorted heavily. "Doc, I coulda heard you comin from the next county. You know how to walk quietly in the woods; you used to do it all the time when you was a kid. You just need to remember how is all."

Eric took a deep, steadying breath and pushed down hard on the memories and emotions that suddenly bubbled up. He swallowed and decided to change the subject.

"The fish really tore into those Catawba worms," Eric said, shaking his head. "Never would have guessed looking at them, though."

Levy frowned slightly for a moment, but nodded his head. "Yes sir," he said slowly. "They get 'em every time."

"I'm going to take the catfish inside," Eric said, grabbing for the pan. "Don't want it to get too warm out here."

Levy nodded and went back to scraping the last few fish. Eric carried the wide, shallow pan of catfish nuggets and filets through the screen door on the back porch. Inside, the small farmhouse was bustling with noise and activity. Nanny and Imogene were in the kitchen, each moving with the fluid, smooth motions of muscle memory more than conscious thought. Both women were equally at home in the tiny kitchen, and it was evident they both knew what they were doing.

Nanny was working on green beans and turnip greens while Imogene mixed batter for hushpuppies. The other women were in the kitchen as well, each engaged in their own tasks. Meg was washing and skinning potatoes in a small bucket set in the sink. She handed the slick, freshly peeled tubers to Jen who sliced them into long, finger thick slices to make oven fries. Beth, Eric's mother, was furiously grating cabbage into a massive steel mixing bowl for coleslaw. Her face was red and sweaty, and it seemed as if she were angry at the cabbage, or at least taking out her anger on it.

"Alright, Doc," Nanny said without breaking stride as she worked, "how much longer y'all need out there?"

"I think we're just about ready for the flour to fry the fish," Eric said.

Nanny nodded and handed him a wide, shallow enamel bowl that had a dusty flour and cornmeal mixture in it. Eric took the pan back out on the porch and into the back yard. A long, broad bench held two squat propane burner stoves, each with its own tank of liquid propane attached. Atop the burners were two vats of hot oil. Eric set the bowl of breading next to one of the vats for the fish.

Just then, Levy came walking up to the makeshift outdoor kitchen with the pan of freshly cleaned fish, and at the same moment, Christina came out the back door with a small bowl of milk and egg wash for the fish. Levy looked first at Christina, then at Eric, and cleared his throat roughly.

"I'll go," he began, then coughed. "I forgot something. Be right back."

Levy set the bowl of fish down hard on the bench and turned back toward the metal table a dozen yards away. Christina smiled as the older man walked off and pretended to look for something on the ground around the table, giving her and Eric as much privacy as he could manage. She handed the bowl to Eric and kissed him lightly on the cheek.

"How are things going in there?" Eric asked.

"Not bad," Christina said with a small shrug of her slim shoulders. "I've got Tom's four kids all locked in a cut throat game of Monopoly. The youngest one just bought up three hotels all across one side of the board. I think he's got this one locked."

"Is that the one you've been advising?" Eric asked.

"Maybe," Christina sad with a wink. "I'd better get back and check on them. The others may have him hog tied and held for ransom at this point."

Christina turned and went back up the steps and through the back door to the house. Eric watched her the whole way, unable to take his eyes from her for even a moment. When Levy came back over to the burners, he cleared his throat to catch Eric's attention.

"She's a sweet girl," Levy said, "and pretty too." He fixed Eric with a hard, level stair and said with a serious tone. "Don't do nothing stupid, Doc."

Eric couldn't help but chuckle and nod, "Yes, sir," he said.

"Okay," Levy replied with a nod, "let's cook some fish."

Levy had turned the burners on when he and Eric were halfway through cleaning the fish. By the time he dropped the first egg-washed and breaded fish into the oil, it was perfectly heated. The fish immediately sank but quickly rose back to the top, bubbling and bouncing in the oil. Levy deftly dropped fish after fish into the egg wash while holding their tails. He'd then flop them twice per side in the breading to get a good coating, and into the oil they went.

He turned the fish a few times until the breading turned a crispy golden brown and the meat visible beneath was flaky and white. With a metal basket, he dipped the fish out as they finished cooking. Levy had fried a little more than two thirds of the fish when Imogene came outside with Bill.

"Mind if we use the other stove?" Bill asked.

Levy smiled. "That's what I set it up for. Y'all are more than welcome to it."

Bill nodded and began dropping large spoonfuls of hush puppy batter into the hot grease. The dollops of batter acted similarly to the fish, bobbing and bubbling in the hot grease until golden brown and crispy.

It wasn't long before the pan fish were fried, along with Granddaddy's catfish, and the Texas hushpuppies. When they carried the food inside, the rest of the meal was just being set onto the counters and the sturdy kitchen table. Eric carried the plate of fish and the bowl of fresh, steaming hot hush puppies and set them on the only open spots left on the table. The entire crowd gathered around the table and slowly fell silent, all eyes trained on Levy.

The old farmer stepped forward, his hat in his hand, and looked around the room. He nodded quietly, and said, "If we could all bow our heads."

Every head bowed together. Then, slowly, each person reached out to the one next to them. After the chaos and the fear of the past few days, it felt good just to have simple contact with another living, breathing person. It was as if all of them had taken a deep, heavy sigh of relief at the exact same moment.

"Father," Levy said softly, "bless this food and the hands that prepared it. We thank you for the food we are about to receive, and we pray for those who aren't here to share it with us. Bring them home safely, Lord. In your name we pray, Amen."

The four young children leapt to the front of the line first, of course. Chris followed them with his wife holding their baby daughter. Chris fixed a plate for each of them, balancing his wife's and his on the same arm and using his free hand to serve. The others began chatting together, paying more attention to conversation than to food. They were all tired and hungry, but sometimes there were more important things than food.

For a long time, though, Eric just stood with Christina at the back of the kitchen, his arms wrapped around her waist, watching....and smiling.

Ch. 54

Headlights

Joe pulled the old '58 off to the shoulder of the road and turned off the engine. The gas gauge was reading a little less than a quarter of a tank, but Joe didn't trust the needle to be accurate. Sometimes when the station wagon's lights were turned on, the gas needle would jump a quarter of a tank. The last thing he wanted was to run out of fuel and strand them on the side of the road with no way to reach or even contact help.

As soon as the car was stopped, Tom and Henderson climbed out of the front passenger door. Henderson watched the road ahead of them while Tom kept an eye on their back trail; both men rested a hand uneasily on their sidearm. The road had been empty so far save for a handful of abandoned cars, their doors and trunks standing open, and most of the glass busted out of the windows, but there was no guarantee it would stay that way.

The passengers in the back shifted, and both boys groaned in their sleep. Only Gilbert's eyes were open, though, and he carefully untangled himself from the snarled mass of arms and legs the boys had made in their sleep. He carefully opened his door and slipped out with Joe. The two of them walked around to the trunk and took two of the five gallon gas tanks out to fill the car. Henderson had managed to siphon out a little less than twenty five gallons of gas from some of the abandoned cars in the city to help them on their way south.

"We getting close?" Gilbert asked, stretching his back slowly and carefully. The back seat of the station wagon was wide, but with five people crammed into it, there wasn't really any way to get comfortable.

Joe shook his head slightly. "Probably three more hours," he said, "assuming we don't have to backtrack or detour anywhere between here and home."

Gilbert sighed heavily and nodded. "Where are we headed, anyway?"

Joe's eyes narrowed slightly, but he shrugged and answered. "My in-laws' homestead near Bennett."

"Bennett," Gilbert said softly, one finger tapping his cheek alongside his nose. After a moment, he snapped his fingers. "Chatham County, off of Highway 902, right?"

Joe nodded. "How the heck do you know that?" he asked, setting one empty gas can down, and taking the full one from Gilbert. "Bennett is a hole in the wall town that most people *from* Chatham would be hard-pressed to point out on a map."

"I told you I used to haul equipment," Gilbert said. "I knew every side and back road in North Carolina at one point. Course my memory ain't what it was when I was thirty, but it ain't half bad at that."

Joe nodded, and the two were silent for a while. Gilbert stared through the back glass of the car at his sleeping family, a thoughtful frown creasing his forehead and his face. After a moment, he dug his short, round pipe from his pocket and stuck it unlit between his teeth. The old farmer fixed Joe with a hard, serious stare and seemed to chew over what to say in his mind for a moment before speaking.

"Joe, I don't want you to take this the wrong way," Gilbert said slowly, carefully. "I appreciate all you done so far for me and mine. But I got to ask, are you sure y'all are gonna be able to take care of our family? I don't want us to be a burden too heavy, and I don't want to take my family from the fryin pan to the fire, as it were. I just got to make sure that we're doin the right thing for 'em."

Joe set the can down and turned to Gilbert. "We've got four wells that are deep and have never run dry," Joe said. "There's fields to grow crops, and there's game to hunt. Farms all around us have chickens, cows, and pigs, plus there's wild game in the woods like you wouldn't believe. It won't be easy, Gilbert, but we can help take care of each other."

Gilbert stuck his right hand out. "I'm takin your word on that, Joe. I hope you're right about it."

"Well, think about it this way," Joe said, taking Gilbert's hand, and shaking it firmly, "whatever's coming, the more people you have standing next to you, the easier it'll be to hold the line."

Gilbert nodded and helped Joe finish emptying the second gas can into the car. They put the empty cans back in the trunk, and Gilbert rearranged some of the cargo to better brace the two remaining cans with gas in them. Joe took out two bottles of water for the men to share among the four of them. The night air was definitely cooler without the sun beating down on the car, but it was still warm enough that Joe had broken a sweat putting gas in the car. After drinking half of the bottle that Henderson handed him, Gilbert glared at his pipe as if he wanted to light it, but finally he stuffed it back into the pocket on his overalls.

"Joe!" Tom called suddenly, pointing back the way they'd come, "I saw something way back. It was quick, but I think it was a light."

They hadn't gotten fully into the rolling hills of the piedmont yet, and the road behind them was flat for the most part. A few low hills and shallow valleys were all that broke their line of sight for several miles. As the men all stared behind them, in the distance, a line of small, twinkling lights appeared for an instant over the crest of a low hill, and then sank into one of the shallow low points and out of sight.

For a brief moment, no one moved or spoke, they just stared in shock at the spot where the lights had disappeared. Then they all began moving at once. Gilbert slammed the trunk down, at the same time Henderson and Tom climbed quickly into the front seat. Joe grabbed the two empty water bottles that they'd dropped and did a quick visual sweep of the area as best he could in the dim moonlight. He dropped into the driver's seat, already turning the key to crank the engine. The '58 roared to life, and Joe drove off as quickly as he could.

The sleeping boys never stirred, but both women opened their eyes briefly in confusion. Gilbert soothed them both and reassured them that everything was fine, and they were quickly asleep again, Maimey snoring softly with her head resting on Gilbert's shoulder for a pillow.

"Who do you think it is?" Henderson asked softly, turning as far as he could and straining to see behind them.

"I don't know," Joe said, checking his mirror for the headlights and finding it clear for the moment, "but I'm sure not going to sit around and wait to find out."

The others nodded, and silence returned to the inside of the car. Joe drove with the headlights off to keep them from being seen. The moon was a good ways from full, but it was bright enough to see by with the help of the stars in the crystal clear sky. Joe hoped it would stay that way long enough to keep them ahead of headlights and guide them safely home.

CH. 55

Watching The Road

Eric sat on the wrought iron and wood framed bench that was tucked under the wide eaves on the front porch. The moon was directly overhead, and the shadows under the edge of the roof were deep. Three small metal bucket candles flickered in the corners of the porch, filling the air with thick oily smoke that smelled sharply of citronella. The candles didn't keep all of the annoying mosquitoes at bay, but they helped.

The house behind him was dark, for the most part, and silent. After the fried fish dinner, the conversation had been slow at first and quickly trickled to satisfied silence. Everyone was exhausted from the day's work. While the women were gathering scraps for the dogs and leftovers for the refrigerator, Eric had slipped out the front door. He'd been sitting on the bench ever since, watching the white dirt road as it shone in the moonlight before cutting into the trees where it disappeared.

The front door opened, and Christina stepped out into the night with a steaming cup in one hand. She tiptoed over to Eric and dropped onto the bench beside him.

"Coffee?" she asked, extending the cup. Eric took, and she grimaced slightly. "It's instant, but it's all I could make without waking half the house up."

Eric took a sip and smiled. "Thanks, babe," he said. "It'll do fine. Why aren't you in bed?"

"Cause you aren't," Christina answered, snuggling closer to Eric's arm.

"We're not sharing the same bed here," Eric said, confused.

"I know," Christina said, "but you're still not in bed. I figured you could use some company."

Eric smiled and put his left arm around Christina's shoulders. Part of him wanted to be alone on his vigil. Another part of him desperately needed her warmth and the feel of her breathing against him. And, in the end, Eric already knew which part would win. The coffee was strong, and slightly bitter, but respectable for what it was. Eric took another sip that was still a little too hot for comfort and then set the cup by the bench to cool. The night was warm already, and the coffee gave his forehead a slick sheen of sweat. Birds, frogs, and bugs called to each other in the distance, but other than that the nigh was quiet.

After a while, Christina shifted against him and slid slowly down until her head was resting in Eric's lap. Eric bent and whispered softly in her ear, "You should go to bed, babe. That can't be comfortable."

Christina mumbled something that sounded like, "In a minute," and then rolled onto her side, a half smile on her face.

She was already asleep.

Eric shifted his weight slightly but not enough to disturb her. He ran his fingers lightly through Christina's thick hair as she rested in his lap. The sweet scent of honeysuckle and lavender floated up to him, and he smiled. He had never taken the time to check and see what perfume she used, but Eric could always tell which pillowcase was hers, even when it was fresh from the laundry.

Eric took another sip from his coffee which had cooled some but was still warm enough to be called hot. One of Granddaddy's labs was laying at the front edge of the porch. Eric had thought it was asleep, but suddenly the dog sprang to its feet. It let out a long, low growl and the hair all down its back stood bristling on end. The dog was staring intensely into the night towards the long open field, its entire body rigid.

His hand when instinctively to the M-4 standing by the bench, but Eric didn't stand. He sat absolutely motionless and watched the dog intensely. The dog didn't move, but he had definitely either seen something or caught a scent that he didn't like one bit. After a long, tense moment with the dog trained on the dark night, growling deep in his throat, a coyote called in a raucous, coughing bark that was shrill and echoed off the trees. The Labrador let out a loud, baritone growling bark to let the interloper know who was boss, and Christina jumped in Eric's lap.

"It's okay," Eric whispered softly, kissing her just behind the left ear. "It was just the dog. Go back to sleep."

Christina mumbled something incoherent, already on her way back to slumber. The lab let out a last, muffled grunt of a bark and then lay back down on the porch and rolled lazily on his side. Eric sipped his cooling coffee as his two companions quickly worked their way back to sleep.

Eric sighed softly to himself and settled in for another long night's watch.

Ch. 56

Shaking Out The Bugs

Terry Price sat behind his desk, kneading his forehead with the fingers of his left hand. His head was throbbing and his eyes were grainy from a lack of sleep. Slowly, a noise began to intrude itself into Terry's awareness. It took him a moment to realize that the sound was his watch beeping an alert at him. Terry stared at his wrist for a moment, unable to make sense of the display of zero's across the tiny screen.

The timer had run down.

Terry knew it was significant, but he couldn't quite place why. He closed his eyes tight and forced his mind to work past the exhaustion, and he remembered what he'd been timing. He opened the screen of his laptop and keyed in several pass codes to access the machine. The large fractal factoring program had run its course, finally, and all of the systems' operations and functions had been thoroughly checked and diagnosed in the process. Terry could be one hundred percent certain his machine was clean of all malicious software, tracking programs, and trojans. Any programming not personally signed and authenticated with Terry's own pass code would have been immediately flagged and isolated by his systems check.

Terry logged into the main system and keyed in a pre-set one hundred and twenty eight character pass code. Four layers of encoding took Terry's pass code and expanded it into a mind-numbingly large string of apparently random characters that would take even the most advanced super computers in the world decades to crack. The encryption and decryption process took a few moments, and Terry waited as patiently as he could manage.

Finally, the system opened, and Terry gained access to the massive information databases and processing banks secured within the bowels of his facility. Immediately, Terry ran a search deep within his own personal database files and brought up a hidden and secure file named simply "Transit."

Terry opened the file, keyed in the necessary password, and the command and control interface for the antiquated NAVSAT network loaded a line at the time onto his screen. A brief status check established a working connection, and Terry sat for a moment staring at his command cursor. He hesitated for a moment, weighing his options. It didn't take him long to realize that there just weren't any.

Terry keyed in the transponder number written on a small slip of paper in front of him. The NAVSAT program spun for a few minutes as it did computations and brought up records of received signals. After a minute or two, the screen shifted to a split view. On the left hand side was a table of Latitude and Longitude coordinates. The right side of the screen displayed a featureless map of the United States, with a dotted track line that ran from Utah east, all the way to the extreme western border of Tennessee.

The blinking dot on the screen marked the farthest recorded point the transponder had reached, and Terry sat staring at it. For a long moment, the dot didn't move at all. Then, finally, it shifted ever so slightly to the right, and a new set of numbers appeared in the column to the left.

Terry sat back slightly with a deep, relieved sigh. Mr. Attledge and his companions wouldn't reach their destination for at least another eight to ten hours with re-fueling time factored in, and at most it would be another day and a half if there were no unforeseen problems or delays. Terry quickly signed out of his programs and closed the connection to the mainframe databases.

Once disconnected, Terry reclined fully in his comfortably padded executive's chair. He smiled to himself and let his eyes slip closed, pleased with the fact that no matter what else might have gone wrong, Mr. Attledge was still on the move. With any luck, a key part of Terry's plans that had nearly slipped through his fingers would once again be within his grasp.

In no time at all Terry was snoring softly as the exhaustion he'd been fighting finally overcame him.

Ch. 57

If The Worst Should Happen

Joe climbed the brick steps to the front porch slowly and quietly. The old lab sleeping in one corner of the porch raised his head briefly, his tail thumping the concrete floor twice before he flopped back over on his side and drifted off to sleep again. Joe walked over to the bench and gently squeezed Eric's knee. Eric immediately jerked awake, his right hand reaching instinctively for the rifle leaning against the brick wall next to him, but Joe caught his arm.

"It's okay, son," Joe said softly. "It's just me."

Eric blinked a few times, and his eyes finally focused on Joe's face. Joe smiled back at him and then gently gripped Christina's shoulder. The young woman's eyes fluttered open sleepily, and she smiled up at him.

"Mr. Tillman," she said groggily. "you're back!"

"Come on, hun," Joe said softly. "Why don't you go inside and lay down. You'll be a lot more comfortable in your bed. Eric and I are going to take a walk."

Christina mumbled something that might have been agreement, and she climbed slowly and somewhat shakily to her feet. Eric helped her to the door, and she kissed him on the cheek as she stepped into the still dark house. He caught the heavy screen door as it swung closed to keep it from banging loudly in the metal frame.

Joe jerked his head towards the field when Eric turned back to him.

"Come on son," Joe said. "There's something you need to see. Bring your rifle."

Eric frowned slightly and rubbed his eyes as he picked up the M-4 and slipped his head and arm through the single point sling. Joe turned and led the way down the steps and across the broad front yard. Even though the eastern sky was just beginning to show hints of sunrise, it was still dark enough to make walking somewhat of a challenge, but both men knew the ground and the land well enough to make do without a light.

When they reached the edge of the field, Joe turned to the left and Eric followed him around to the old tobacco curing barns that sat at the edge of the woods. The barns were made of thick steel and aluminum sheeting with massive double doors that swung outward on simple post and barrel hinges. They were constructed so each barn was divided down the middle, with independent doors for each side to create four separate curing chambers. When the farm was running at its peak, both of the barns would have been packed from back to front, floor to ceiling with several thousand pounds of bright-leaf tobacco slowly drying for sale.

Now, though, most of the fields were rented to other farmers who grew soybeans, corn, and cotton. The barns hadn't been used to cure tobacco in more than a decade. Still, when Joe unlocked the massive padlocks on one of the doors and swung it open, the inside smelled faintly of the thick, sweet-sharp tang of good tobacco. Joe stepped up, and clicked on a small LED flashlight. Eric followed him, and they made their way to the back of the barn where plastic crates were stacked in neat rows, most of them halfway up to the ten foot ceiling. Joe pulled one of the gray crates down and popped the lid off. Inside were neatly packed Mylar packages with nutrition labels pasted on the outside.

"Each of these crates," Joe said, pulling one of the packages out, "has enough freeze-dried food for one adult for one month, eating three meals a day. You could stretch one of these packs another week or two if you limited yourself to two meals a day, but that's about the limit if you want to keep yourself healthy. There's enough stocked up to last the whole family for a little more than a year."

Eric looked around at the stacks of crates, his eyes wide. Joe tossed him the shiny package he was holding, and Eric caught it. It was surprisingly light considering the label said it contained seven full dinners complete with a main entrée, three sides, and a desert. Eric handed the pouch carefully back to his father, who dropped it into the plastic crate and snapped the lid closed.

Joe led the way back outside, where he closed and locked the one door and opened the left door of the same barn. Joe shone his light inside, revealing stacks of solar panels still in their protective packaging. There were piles of cables to one side, and smaller boxes stacked in racks against the left wall of the barn.

"There's enough in here to repair our solar grid," Joe said. "As long as we don't lose more than half of the panels at once, we should be good. There are backup batteries, power inverters, and cables too. If we needed to, we could add another thirty percent or so to our power production and still have spares for repairs."

The next barn held stacks of ammo cans grouped by caliber from front to back on the right side, and basic supplies like woolen blankets, first aid necessities, sleeping bags, and the like on the left. Once he was done, Joe carefully locked each door with two heavy padlocks, each with separately ground keys. When he was finished, Joe pulled a key ring from his pocket with eight small brass keys attached and handed to Eric.

"These are the only spares I have," Joe said, fixing Eric with a serious stare. "Put them some place safe. Don't tell anyone, and I mean *anyone* what I just showed you."

"I don't understand," Eric said, looking at the keys in his hand like they were a poisonous snake. "Why did you show all this to me? What's it for?"

Joe took a deep breath and gripped Eric's shoulder with one hand, his face troubled. "It took me thirty years to put that together, son," Joe said seriously. "But it'd take someone thirty minutes to take it all. I didn't know what was coming back then, but something told me to get ready. I've spent most of my adult life neck deep in the worst, most dangerous and unstable environments on the planet. I've been scared before, but never here at home. Not until..."

Joe's voice trailed off, and for a long moment he stood staring at something Eric couldn't see. Finally, Joe shook his head and snapped back to the present.

"This," he said, gesturing to the barns behind them, "well, you need to know what's out here, son. In case the worst should happen."

Ch. 58

Word From Outside

"Tower, this is inbound," Marcus Attledge said into his headset again. "Request authentication code: Utah Kilo 166 Yankee. This is a FEMA priority one task flight, you are required to respond. Please copy, over."

Marcus sat and waited for a moment, listening to the static on the other end of the line. He had repeated the message four times now and had so far gotten the same static in return. He was beginning to lose his patience.

"Look," Marcus said into the headset, "I can see the lights in the windows, and your radar is scanning right now. You've got power, and I know you can hear me. Open up, guys."

"Roger, Ghostrider, we copy," a voice finally replied into the headset. "Your code is authentic. Response: Romeo Charlie 449. Welcome to Tennessee. I've got to admit, we weren't exactly expecting visitors."

"I can imagine," Marcus replied. "Request permission to land?"

"Come on down, Ghostrider, the skies are clear," the controller responded.

Marcus tapped the pilot lightly on the shoulder, and he began maneuvering the chopper to the flat paved helipad outside the National Guard control tower. As soon as the wheels touched down, Marcus hopped out and sprinted across the landing pad towards the door leading to the control tower. When he was out from under the rotors, Marcus stood, but he pulled up short. A squad of soldiers had deployed from the base of the stairwell and had their rifles trained on him.

"That's far enough, sir," the man from the radio called. "You have an authentic code, but we don't know you. I need to hear a little more before we give you access to the base."

Marcus nodded, careful to keep his hands well away from his body. He was wearing a tactical vest and body armor with impact plates, but that wouldn't mean a thing to a well place shot in the head from one of the rifles trained on him. The forty five caliber pistol at Marcus' hip might as well have been back in the helicopter for as much good as it would do him to reach for it.

"Okay," Marcus shouted over the sound of the helicopter. "What do you want to hear?"

"What are you doing out here in a working Blackhawk, for starters?" the commander asked.

"Classified, Captain," Marcus replied, noticing the two silver bars on the man's fatigues. "We're just here for refueling, and we'll be on our way."

"Who are you with?" the Captain asked, his eyes narrowing. "You don't seem like the FEMA type."

"Private contractor," Marcus replied, noticing a sour twist to the Captain's face. "Can't be more specific than that. We are on contract with FEMA and DHS, though, and operate under their authority."

The Captain frowned and thought for a moment, his eyes troubled. He had to know that there was only one way Marcus could possibly have the valid authentication code he'd used. Those codes had been changed immediately after the blackout, and new sets of go codes and confirmation codes had been disseminated from the very system Marcus helped design and maintain under Terry Price. Marcus knew without a doubt the codes were authentic, and so was the Captain. With that knowledge, there wasn't really a whole lot the Captain could officially do to stand in his way.

"Do you have any word from outside?" the Captain asked finally. "Anything at all about what's happening?"

Marcus nodded slowly. "That I can tell you," he replied, and the Captain visibly relaxed a bit. "I'm Marcus Attledge."

"Withers," the officer replied, stepping forward and extending his hand. "Captain James Withers. Like I said before, welcome to Tennessee."

Marcus nodded and shook the Captain's hand.

Ch. 59

A Quiet Sunrise

Joe sat in the family room listening to the soft tick-tock of the antique Regulator hanging above the fireplace. The brass pendulum rhythmically marked out the seconds just as it had for more than fifty years. The rest of the house was silent save for the sounds of sleep and snoring. Joe could hear the big fellow, Bill, who was sleeping outside on the side porch in a sleeping bag. He had helped settle Gilbert and his family on the front porch with some sleeping bags from the stockpile. It wasn't the most comfortable place to make a bed, but that was temporary, and they had been more than grateful just for a place to stretch out and rest their heads.

The white porcelain cup of instant coffee in Joe's hands had cooled enough that he was able to drain it in two large gulps. He sat for a while staring into the empty mug, his thoughts rolling around in his head like loose bowling balls. Outside, the sky had turned a pearly gray that hinted at the coming dawn.

Later, Joe couldn't be sure how long, the door across the family room opened, and his father-in-law stepped into the room. Levy was neatly dressed in a pair of dark khaki work pants and a buttoned plaid cotton shirt. Levy's Velcro tennis shoes had been brushed clean of dust and dirt from the previous day's work in the fields, and his hair was neatly parted to the right. If he was surprised to find Joe awake ahead of him, it didn't show.

"Good morning, Joe," Levy said, taking his glasses off to wipe the lenses clean. "Good to see you back safe and sound. Did you find what you were looking for up north?"

Joe shook his head, still staring into the coffee cup.

"What happened, son?" Levy asked softly. "Do you want to talk about it?"

Joe shook his head again, looking up and meeting Levy's eyes. "Not yet. I will, but not yet."

Joe stood and set the coffee cup on the mantle and scooped four fresh bottle caps into his hand. He picked up his scoped bolt action rifle, slung it over his shoulder, and grabbed a roll of duct tape and a paper match target from the hearth. Levy watched him quietly from across the room, his eyes and face full of concern and unasked questions.

"Can you do me a favor?" Joe asked, and Levy nodded slowly. "Don't let anyone go past the garden field until I come back. We'll talk then, okay?"

Joe started for the door, but Levy placed a hand gently on his shoulder and stopped him.

"Whatever you done," Levy said slowly, looking Joe square in the eyes as he spoke, "it got you home safe, son. You're a good man. Don't you doubt it for one minute," Levy said as he squeezed Joe's shoulder and then patted it softly.

Joe wasn't quite sure what to say, so he swallowed past the hard lump that had formed in his throat and nodded. Levy turned and went into the kitchen to fix some coffee, and Joe stepped out on the back porch. He took a deep breath of the cool morning air and started walking. The rough road that led down the hill to the garden field was still in deep shade beneath the towering oaks and pine trees on either side. Spider webs outlined in thick drops of dew stretched across the road in several places, but Joe avoided them easily.

At the back edge of the garden field, Joe stepped into the woods. The shadows were dark beneath the canopy even though the sky had begun to lighten considerably. There was a road that ran down to the river fields that Joe could have used, but he felt like stretching his woodsman's legs this morning. He picked his way carefully and silently through the thick leaf litter that covered the forest floor as birds and squirrels scattered into the trees ahead of him.

At the bottom of the long slope of the hill, the ground flattened out into a broad flood plain. The trees thinned out a little, and Joe stepped out onto the same road that Levy and Eric had walked the day before on their fishing trip. Joe followed the road around past the big rock fishing hole until he came to the last of the river fields. The field was two hundred and thirty yards long and around eighty yards wide. The far end of the field was raised slightly, and years ago he'd built up a shooting platform there.

Joe took the target to a mound of earth that had been piled with a backhoe just at the edge of the thin line of trees that separated his end of the field from the river. A broad, flat piece of plywood riddled with holes lay flat against the steep side of the earthen bulwark facing the opposite end of the field. Joe taped the paper target to the center of the board, and then taped one of the bottle caps to each of the four corners of the paper.

The soybeans planted in the field were waist high and a deep emerald green. The stalks swayed in the light morning breeze, and they would serve as a wind indicator for Joe once he was in place. He walked slowly through the field, making note of the deer, rabbit, and raccoon tracks that littered the soft soil. Some of the tracks were faded and washed out from weeks of rain, but others were deep, crisp, and no more than a day old. A few tracks from coyotes ran through the field also, tight on the tracks of a rabbit or squirrel. Joe knew that at least three bobcats lived on the family's property, but they were much harder to track than the coyotes. The soft fur and padding on the cats' paws made their tracks shallow and soft, and they washed out completely with even a light rain.

When Joe reached the flat-topped dirt mound that served as his shooting platform, he climbed to the top and began setting up his shooting area. He placed a small plastic ammunition box where he'd be able to reach it easily with his right hand. A pair of spotting binoculars went to his left to check his shots. Joe flipped down the bipod attached to the fore end of the rifle and set it on the mound. Then he carefully settled himself into a prone position with his legs extended behind him and spread slightly more than shoulder width apart.

Joe sighted down the scope first, and then reached up to turn the dial while counting the faint clicks in his head. The scope had been zeroed in at one hundred and fifty yards, so he had to raise the point of impact slightly for the extended range. He guessed the wind speed at no more than five miles per hour to the right, and adjusted his reticule accordingly. Finally set, Joe loaded one of the .25-06 cartridges that he'd hand-loaded months earlier. The powder was carefully measured and packed to provide the best speed, longest range, and flattest trajectory possible for his bullet weight.

Joe shifted his weight slightly and sighted through the scope again. He slowed his breathing, taking deep and even breaths in and out, counting in his head to set a steady rhythm. He breathed in deep one last time, and let a little more than half of the air out of his lungs and held the rest. As he began squeezing the trigger slowly, meticulously, Joe became acutely aware of his heartbeat. In the space between one beat and the next, Joe squeezed the last little bit, and the round fired.

The rifle was loud, but the recoil was easily absorbed by Joe's body and the ground he was resting on. The targeting reticule barely moved, and Joe could clearly see the point of impact on the neon "splatter" target; three inches low and two to the right. The first shot was always off, though, thanks to the cold barrel. Joe sighted on the center of the bull's-eye again and controlled his breathing. At just the right moment, he squeezed off another round. This time, his shot hit just slightly below center. Joe clicked the elevation dial on his scope one time to the right to raise the point of impact slightly. This time, though, instead of aiming for the center of the target, he aimed just a hair below center. He sent three rounds down range, and then checked his accuracy with the binoculars; all three of his last shots were nearly on top of each other and tightly clustered in the very center of the red bull's-eye.

Satisfied that he was dialed in on the target, Joe moved his aim over to the bottle cap in the top left corner of the target. He slowed his breathing and carefully squeezed the trigger smoothly, evenly. The shot rang out, and Joe knew it was a hit before the bullet even reached the target. He repeated the process on each corner of the target. When he reached the last cap, though, he hesitated. For a brief moment, as Joe sighted down the scope at the last bottle cap, he thought he saw a face staring back at him, pale and drawn in a twisted expression of pain and suffering.

Joe squeezed his eyes shut and took three deep, long breaths. Suddenly sweat stood out on his forehead and the back of his neck, making the slight breeze feel clammy against his skin. After a moment, his breathing and his hands steady, he forced his eyes open, and looked through the scope. He refused to allow his emotions to overwhelm him again. There would be time to deal with those feelings one day, but this was not that day.

Joe took a deep breath and slowly exhaled half of it. He timed his heartbeats and squeezed the trigger slowly and evenly until the hammer fell once more, and his round was sent down range. Before the round left the gun, Joe knew it would be a hit. He stood and collected his things, carefully brushing the dirt from his binoculars before replacing them in the field case that hung from his left shoulder.

When he reached the target board, there were five holes in the paper target, three of them nearly stacked on top of each other in the dead center. And all four bottle caps were neatly pierced through the center with a perfectly round hole. Joe took the bottle caps down, and with shaking fingers he tied them with the others on the leather thong around his neck as the first rays of the sun fell on the river bottom.

Ch. 60

Deep Shadows

Marcus stood in the break room on the bottom floor of the control tower, a fresh cup of coffee in his hands. The room was large enough to double as the mess hall for the small Tennessee Air National Guard base with extra folding tables stacked against one wall. Right now, the four small square tables set up in the room were only half full, with the Captain standing off to one side from his men.

All eyes were on Marcus.

"There's only so much we know for sure," Marcus said carefully, "and even less that I'm allowed to actually talk about for security concerns. What I can tell you is that this was a deliberate attack, not an accidental failure or natural catastrophe."

The men in the room all nodded slowly, some whispering softly to each other until the Captain cleared his throat loudly. He nodded to Marcus to continue once order was restored.

"We don't know who attacked us," Marcus said, "but there is an active and ongoing response and investigation. More than that, I can't say."

"Is help coming?" the Captain asked. "The people around here are getting anxious. Some of them are still on well water, and a lot of them use wood stoves for heat, but enough are hooked into the utilities that are now down that we're running out of the supplies to

help them. We need things like water, food, blankets, generators....
when can we expect help and relief?"

Marcus took a deep breath and looked into his coffee cup for
a moment, trying to compose an effective answer. His stomach was
twisted in knots, and he felt ill.

"We are actively working on that," Marcus said finally, and
grimaced even as the words were coming out of his mouth.

The Captain's faced hardened, and his eye narrowed. "In
other words," he said quietly, "you don't know. We're on our own."

"Captain Withers," Marcus said with a meaningful glance at
the dozen or so other uniformed men in the room, "maybe we
should talk amongst ourselves? Some of this information is
sensitive."

The Captain shook his head flatly. "I told these men when
they agreed to stay that I wouldn't hide anything from them. Half of
the guys on the books at this base never even showed up when the
lights went down, and *more* than half of the ones who did took off
back to their homes after the first day. We stayed, all of us. They
deserve to hear it just as much as I do, and this way I don't have to
retell it."

Marcus took a deep breath and let it out slowly. He could tell
in the Captain's voice and his eyes that he meant every word he'd
said. Finally, Marcus gave a slight shrug of his shoulders and met the
Captain's gaze.

"I guess 'need to know' has changed in the past few days,"
Marcus agreed. "You're right; we don't know when help is going to

come. But I wasn't lying when I said we're working on it--we really are-- it's just not number one on the priority list. For the moment, you need to do your best to maintain order locally and keep people safe. Try and get the residents who have wells to provide supplementary supplies to the ones that don't."

The Captain's jaws clenched and he looked as if he could have chewed a ten penny nail in half if he'd had one. Just at that moment, there was a knock at the closed door, and the pilot stuck in his head and gave Marcus a thumbs up signal.

"Well," Captain Withers growled, "I'm sure glad we could fill up the tanks for you, *Mister* Attledge. Of course, if we get a call and have to use *our* choppers for a search and recovery op, then we might be 'up the creek,' so to speak. And so will the person on the other end of the line."

"Look, I get it," Marcus said. "You're pissed. But all I did was tell you the truth. Would you rather have that or an answer that you wanted to hear?"

Captain Withers was silent for a long moment, but he finally shrugged his shoulders slightly. "The truth," he said, "but you're right, I *am* pissed. We need real help out here, and you're basically telling me to take a number. Is this what it's like everywhere?"

"No," Marcus said simply, "most places; it's worse; a lot worse. All I can do, Captain Withers, is give you my word that I will do whatever I can to get you and your men help and relief. Beyond that, I can't make any promises."

Captain Withers looked Marcus deep in the eyes for a long
time and finally nodded his head once. "Okay, Mr. Attledge," the
Captain said, extending his hand again, "I'll take you at your word."

Marcus breathed a deep sigh of relief and shook the Captain's
hand.

For a brief moment, the Captain's grip tightened. "And I'll
hold you to it, too," the Captain said.

Marcus swallowed hard and drained his cup of cool coffee in
one long gulp to cover his discomfort. He thanked the Captain for
his hospitality, and the two men walked back outside, leaving the rest
of the soldiers to talk in tight, hushed conversations among
themselves. Outside, the sky was light enough for it to be morning
already, but the sun was nowhere to be seen.

"The sun is up already," Captain Withers said, following
Marcus's eyes upward, "but we're in deep shadows here in the valley.
Sunrise for us comes a few hours later than the rest of the world."

"Stay in the shadows," Marcus said as the pilot fired up the
Blackhawk's engines behind him. "I wasn't lying when I said it's
worse out there. I didn't want your men to hear this, but we had to
bypass Knoxville and Memphis. They're both burning bad, and we
couldn't get anyone to return our calls. You guys were our last stop
before we had to set the chopper down to avoid a crash."

"I understand," the Captain said, leaning close so Marcus
could hear him. "I didn't mean to take it out on you. I know you
didn't do this. You're just the one who showed up; that's all."

Marcus nodded. "One last thing, Captain," he said, shouting now over the roar of the engines, "I gave you the truth, even though you didn't want to hear it. Be very wary of people who come and give you promises."

Before Captain Withers could ask what he meant, Marcus ducked and ran over to the open door on the Blackhawk's cockpit. He climbed in next to the pilot and slid the door closed. The engines throttled up, and the chopper slowly climbed into the air. The pilot stayed low, barely over the trees, and as they banked away, Marcus looked back. Framed in the lit doorway of the control tower, Captain James Withers snapped to attention and gave a salute. Then, the trees passed between them and Marcus lost sight of the 5th Mountain Rescue Wing of the Tennessee Air National Guard, and their commander.

As the pilot navigated the valley, Marcus closed his eyes and said a short silent prayer asking God to protect all those waking up in deep shadows.

Ch. 61

A Working Relationship

Terry Price sat at his desk, his fingers arched in a steeple on his chest. The silence in the office stretched, and Terry could hear the second hand on his watch ticking away. His guest took a deep, deliberately loud breath slowly in through his nose and out through his mouth.

Terry waited.

"*Mister* Price," Jefferson grated, "are you going to answer my question?"

Terry gave the Chief Administrator of FEMA a wry half smile and said, "You know, I don't think I will. I once heard someone say that it's never the question that's indiscreet, it's only the answer. It kind of stuck with me."

Jefferson's jaw clenched slightly and one of his eyebrows crept up just a hint. For any other man, Terry would have said that was nothing, but Jefferson was a practiced and schooled press conference politician straight through his core. He could fake a smile with the best of them, and to see that façade slip even a hair was worth noting.

"You said the system would be up and running shortly," Jefferson said, his voice tight. "That was more than a day and a half ago, and we still don't have access. What is wrong with the system, Price?"

"Oh, nothing's wrong with it," Terry said with a slight shrug. "The unscheduled maintenance was completed without any problems."

"Then why can't I access my system?" Jefferson grated through clenched teeth.

Terry sat for a moment, meeting Jefferson's gaze calmly and evenly. The silence between them stretched again, and Jefferson's irritation began to show at the corners of his eyes and his mouth. He was losing his patience, albeit slowly.

"What you need to know," Terry said after another few moments, "is that I *do* have access to the system. And right now, *only* I have access to the system."

Jefferson's eyes narrowed. For a moment, he didn't speak or show any other reaction. Finally, he smirked slightly and shook his head. "I don't believe you."

Terry shrugged. "That's fine by me, you don't have to."

Jefferson's eyes narrowed again, and the carefully crafted smirk evaporated.

"I can't effectively do my job without full and unfettered access to the information and control systems," Jefferson said carefully. "I'd hate to have to arrest you to force your cooperation, but I do have the authority to do so."

Terry smiled slowly, and said, "What kind of person wants to be Chief Administrator of FEMA?"

Jefferson blinked and sat back in his chair for a moment, taken aback. He frowned and opened his mouth, then frowned again before answering.

"I was approached and asked to serve," Jefferson said, "and I accepted the request by the President."

"Really?" Terry asked, "because that's not what I saw on C-Span. You were asked in your confirmation how you first got offered the job. You admitted that you asked the President for consideration for the appointment in return for what you called 'advice and assistance' in his campaign. You were one of the President's best fund raisers, and by most accounts, one of his most trusted advisers. He didn't make a move without first running it by you. In return for that kind of guidance, you could have had any spot in the administration you wanted, and you *chose* FEMA. I just can't figure it out."

Jefferson's face darkened. Terry had come far too close to truths that Jefferson had thought were well hidden. The only way he could have found some of that information out would have been to read some very private communications, which of course meant that he did have complete access to the system as he claimed. Jefferson opened his mouth with an angry retort, but Terry spoke right over top of him.

"In any case," Terry said, "you're wrong about your authority at this facility. The funding for this whole system was somewhat controversial, so the Department of Defense agreed to pay for half out of its own bloated and conveniently classified budget. In return the DOD retained control over the first site to come online. This site, in fact. That means that this site and the people who run it. I and my fellow contractors alike, all fall under DOD chain of command, not yours. So your legal authority stops when you enter our air space."

Jefferson regained control of himself, and the only visible sign of his irritation now was the fact that his lips were pressed into a thin, white line. After a long moment of silence, his eyes rose and took in the two security officers, one at each of Terry's shoulders. It was the first time Jefferson had acknowledged their existence, but he still didn't comment on them.

"When I tell the President about this," Jefferson said, "and explain why I'm not able to do the job he hired me to do, I'll be sure to tell him it was all because you didn't feel like acknowledging a little interagency courtesy. I can only imagine what his reaction will be."

Terry snorted. "You get the President in this room with the two of us, and I'll answer any question he has for me with the truth, as long as you swear to do the same. You and I both know you won't do that though."

"And why is that?" Jefferson asked.

"Because you have a lot to hide," Terry said carefully. "I don't. I told you the first time you came here, I detected a threat to the system and I took action to defend it. That's my job; it's why I'm here. When I took that action, the other sites linked into this system initiated their own action simultaneously. It's a security measure to make sure all of the backup systems are locked out and protected any time there is a threat on one of them. Beyond that, I can't say."

Suddenly, Jefferson stood, and the two security officers shifted their position slightly in response. Jefferson eyed them again, but this time with clear annoyance. Terry remained in his seat, reclining slightly, with his fingers steepled on his chest. He hadn't moved the entire time.

"I had hoped we would be able to develop a working relationship," Jefferson said stiffly. "I'm sorry that won't be the case, Mr. Price."

Terry nodded. "I'm sure you are," he said. "I will be in contact when we have finished our investigation into the breach of system security. I'm sure you'll want to know what we find out."

Jefferson turned on his heel and strode to the door but he stopped when Terry said, "Oh, and if you *do* talk to the President, let him know that I have been trying to get in touch with him for some time now. For some reason, none of the official comm. channels seem to be functioning at the moment."

Jefferson looked for a brief moment as if he would say something, but then his jaw clenched, and he was gone through the door. After a few minutes of silence, Terry dismissed the two security officers but asked them to stay posted outside the outer doors of his office for the next hour and to make sure he wasn't disturbed under any circumstances. Surrounded by the silence, Terry sat deep in thought. With the fingers of his right hand he rubbed his left ring finger, itching to spin the academy ring that wasn't there.

Ch. 62

Lines In The Sand

In the back yard of Levy and Blossom's farmhouse was a towering live oak with massive branches that spread over an area the size of a baseball's dirt infield. The trunk of the oak was nearly four feet in diameter, and its wrist-thick gnarled roots jutted through the bare earth in the shade beneath it. In the summer seasons, thousands of slender, dark green leaves wove a tight canopy that blocked out most of the sunlight. Joe stood in the Live Oak's circle of shade at the head of a long metal banquet table the family used when they had barbecues and other large gatherings. This morning, though, there were no heaping bowls of mashed potatoes or steaming pans of baked beans, only somber faces. Joe had just finished describing the moment the four missiles had detonated on the radar screen in the watch room.

"There's more," Joe said, somewhat hesitantly. "We ran the footage back and checked it closely. Shortly after the launch in New York Harbor, it seems a secondary device was detonated. The satellite image cut out before we could see just how bad it was, but the explosion was definitely nuclear and pretty high yield."

Around the table, eyes widened and there was a near collective gasp. Tom and Chris both stared hard at their hands. Joe's wife, Beth, had tears streaming down her face, and Levy's face was grim. They all wore mingled expressions of shock, horror, and anger alternating with fear. Joe took a deep breath and steeled himself for what was to come. He'd already delivered a hard blow, but the worst was still unsaid.

"With this kind of attack," Joe said softly, and the table grew quiet again except for the echoes of the children's laughter as they played in the front yard, "there's no telling *if* the government is going to be able to start putting things back together, much less *when*. For the foreseeable future, though, we are on our own."

"What do you mean on our own?" Gilbert's daughter, Beth Anne asked. "You said there's a town right a half an hour from here, so why not just go get help?"

Gilbert patted her hand softly and shook his head. "Listen to what the man's saying, hun," he said softly, pointing to the horizon behind Joe. "You see them big clouds of smoke there, and there, and there? That ain't forest fires, hun. Those are cities burning. I seen it before in Belgium and Germany in the War."

An uncomfortable silence fell as the people slowly began the long and painful process of letting go of the life they'd all known. Some of them whispered prayers, some cried silent tears, and some just stared off into space, their mind working too hard and too fast for the process to show. Joe knew what they were going through because he'd felt it himself in that moment that the satellite images slowly winked out as the sat-net was destroyed. It was a sense of numb uncertainty and distant fear too overwhelming to be confronted directly.

Joe wished there was something he could say to make it easier, something to take the sting out of his words and the knowledge they brought. But this was a pain that was necessary.

They needed to feel it, needed to know it in order to accept it as real. Hiding from the truth now could only lead to disaster down the road.

"So what do we do now?" Maimey, Gilbert's wife, asked in her high-pitched, reedy voice.

"Survive," Joe replied simply. "We've all had a long four days, I know. I wish I could tell you things are going to get better now, but we've all got a long row to hoe. We're blessed with being somewhere that can support us, if we're smart. But there are some things we need that we don't have. Sugar and salt for preserving food, dry goods like beans and rice, flour, batteries. We need to make a run into town and get what we can now before it gets too bad to risk it."

"You're talking about stealing!" Jen, said, and Tom rolled his eyes slightly. "I don't think I'm comfortable with that," she continued, slapping Tom in the stomach. "I mean are we really ready to just throw society away and grab stuff because we need some stuff and we can get away with it? If that's all it takes for us to turn into thieves, then doesn't that say something about us?"

"A lady came down the road yesterday," Chris said. "Her husband had died in his sleep the moment those nukes detonated in the atmosphere. His pacemaker was fried by the pulse. A hundred and ninety thousand other people died right along with him. Around five hundred thousand people get daily dialysis treatments because their kidneys are failing for one reason or another. I'd be surprised if ten percent of them were still alive after four days without it."

Jen's face was pale as she sat back in her seat, but Chris wasn't done.

"My father had a pacemaker," Chris said. "My Uncle, his brother, was on daily dialysis, and both of Meg's parents are diabetic. Insulin goes bad without refrigeration, and there are twenty nine million diabetics in the U.S. That means by the end of the week you're looking at thirty million Americans dead or dying, and that's just three things taken down by this attack. Three small, tightly contained things, and ten percent of the population is gone inside a week."

Joe swallowed hard and said, "I know it isn't pretty, but it's the truth. Now think about what it's going to be like when the other ninety percent of the population realizes that they're on their own, and their water is running out....their food is gone..."

"Desperate people," Levy said softly, his first words so far, "will do the worst things to try and stay alive, and there's people out there getting desperate right about now. We ain't desperate yet, and I can tell you this much....I'll do any damn thing in the world to make sure we don't ever get that way."

"This feels like the kind of thing we should decide together," Joe said, looking around the table. "So how about it? I think we should go into town for supplies today, before it gets dark. All those in favor, raise your hands."

One by one, their hands went into the air. Jen was the last one to relent, but she finally gave a small shrug and raised her hand with the rest. There was a soft sigh of collective relief that the matter was settled. It was comforting to make a decision that would actively direct at least a small portion of their fate that was still within their control.

"Okay," Joe said, "I'll need three volunteers to go with me. If we can get what we need without taking it, then that's what we'll do. But whoever volunteers needs to be ready to do what is necessary, whatever that means. We'll meet by the..."

Joe trailed off, a frown on his face. A noise had been growing at the edge of his awareness for a while now, and he still couldn't quite place it. It came at first as faint bursts of sound half imagined on the wind like a barely heard echo. Now, though, it was steady and growing, and it felt to Joe as if he should know it. Just at that moment, Henderson came sprinting down the road, Eric close on his heels. The two young men had been keeping watch at the far end of the quarter mile long driveway. Both of them were winded when they skidded to a halt beneath the oak tree and couldn't speak for a moment.

"There's a helicopter," Eric panted finally, Henderson nodding in agreement, "flying low, headed this way. Henderson caught a glimpse through the trees."

"That's right." Henderson said, "Blackhawk with a side gunner at least."

Joe nodded and the soft, rhythmic sound he'd been hearing suddenly crystallized in his mind as the chatter of the rotors on a Blackhawk in fast flight. Without conscious thought, Joe ran down the list of options he had available, and chose a plan of action.

"Henderson, you take Bill and go up the left edge of the bean field," Joe said pointing as he spoke. "Tom, you and Eric get in the edge of the vineyard, down the right side of the bean field. All of you direct your field of fire to the far end, down by the tree line in the far left corner of the field. If they're going to set it down, that's where they'll do it cause it's the most open and the farthest from the trees. No one shoots unless I do, got it?" They nodded and went to get their rifles. Joe turned to the women and children. "Chris, you come with me. The rest of you, get in the house for now."

Joe was already walking by the time his words sank in, and people started moving. The stunned silence suddenly shattered into a thousand murmured voices at once. As he passed his wife, Beth reached out and caught Joe's arm, stopping him.

"Do you really think they're coming here?" Beth asked, a worried frown creasing her forehead.

Joe nodded, and looked for a moment at the Hum-V. "Chris," he said as Beth released him and began herding the rest of the crowd into the farmhouse, "you'd better get on Ma Deuce."

Chris turned without hesitation and sprinted over to the transport. He climbed into the back and quickly loaded the massive mounted machine gun. He jerked the charging handle back and released it. The heavy spring loaded a round, and Chris swung the barrel around, pointing it towards the approaching sound of the helicopter.

Joe grabbed his bolt-action rifle and trotted over to the old, battered '58 station wagon. He popped the trunk, raising the large metal lid to use as cover if the need should arise. Then he knelt by the driver's side rear fender and used the car as a bench rest for his rifle. The sound of the helicopter grew steadily, and in a few short moments, the aircraft broke over the tops of the trees, flying low. It pulled a long, slow loop around the farmhouse and field, and Joe tracked it through his scope, watching for a clear shot at the pilot or co-pilot.

Joe frowned.

Something wasn't right.

The helicopter was low enough that he could see clearly into the back passenger bay and the cockpit as it circled the farm. There was a pilot in the cockpit and a passenger with his open palms pressed against the clear glass of the window, but other than that the helicopter was empty. The bay doors were all open on the chopper, allowing him to see straight through to the other side. There was definitely a mounted machine gun, but no one was sitting in the bay to man it. The gun could be remote fired, of course, but if they meant to do that he felt the bullets would be flying already. Instead, the helicopter just circled slowly with Chris targeting his own machine gun on them.

Joe stood slowly and propped his rifle against the station wagon as the helicopter began to descend in the far corner of the field.

"Keep your gun on them, Chris," Joe called. "If they make a move, try and take out that helicopter without taking me with it, okay?"

Chris winked at him and grinned.

As the helicopter dropped, it kicked up a thick cloud of dust and torn soybeans. Joe stepped out into the edge of the field as the passenger door on the cockpit opened. A man stepped out, keeping his hands well clear of his body, fingers splayed open. The engines slowed as the pilot throttled everything down, but the rotors still spun rapidly. The man ducked and trotted forward enough to be clear of the long, whirring blades, and then stood with his hands

334

raised and outstretched. The stranger walked slowly forward to meet Joe, and they stopped with twenty feet between them.

The stranger was dressed in tactical clothes that didn't quite come to a uniform. Comfortable, but durable pants, close fitting button down shirt with what looked like a discretely Kevlar vest over it. There was a .45 caliber pistol in a drop-leg holster on his right side. It wasn't an over the top gear kit like he'd seen on some of the more tactically aspiring contractors, but it was functional. And the man looked like he knew how to wear it and move in it.

"Are you Captain Joseph Tillman?" the man called.

Joe's hand automatically dropped to his own holstered 9mm Beretta. He frowned and asked, "Who wants to know?"

The stranger's face drained of color as his eyes followed Joe's hand. He swallowed hard twice, then shouted over the rotors, "Terry Price says hello!"

Ch. 63

First Impressions

Marcus stood frozen for a brief moment and wondered for the first time if he'd made a terrible mistake. The man certainly fit the description Mr. Price had given him, and he was in the right place. But as soon as he said the man's name, his hand dropped to his gun, and he suddenly became intense and focused. Those hard eyes were boring into Marcus's skull right now.

"Terry Price says hello," Marcus said.

For a brief moment, the man didn't move. Marcus wasn't even sure he'd been heard, and he was about to repeat himself, when suddenly there was a slight ease in the set of his shoulders. His right hand still rested on the pistol at his hip, but he wasn't gripping it with white knuckles anymore. He straightened slightly and regarded Marcus with a curious and thoughtful frown creasing his forehead and his face.

"I guess you'd better come with me," the man said, and he turned back toward the house.

Marcus had taken three steps before he realized he hadn't actually received an answer. By then he had the choice of stopping like a petulant child in the middle of the field or continuing to follow the man towards the house and farther from his route of escape. Marcus eyed the younger man behind the .50 caliber machine gun mounted to the roof of the HUM-V and swallowed hard. There were two men on the left edge of the field, and one of them followed him with the scope of an M-4.

Finally, near the white sand road that separated the field and the yard, the man stopped and turned to Marcus, his hand still resting lightly on his side arm.

"Okay, son," he said, "you'd better explain yourself."

"Are you Captain Joe Tillman?" Marcus asked again, wishing he had a canteen of water.

The man's frown deepened, and he didn't speak. Finally, after a long moment, he nodded twice. Marcus figured he had gotten all of the confirmation the man was going to offer for the moment, so he took a deep breath, said a quick prayer, and let the breath out slowly.

"Okay," Marcus said slowly, "I have to reach into the outside right pocket on my vest. I'm going to do it slowly, so please don't shoot me, okay?"

Captain Tillman leaned forward and said softly, "If I even think you're making a move, son, I'll drop you where you stand. Got it?"

Marcus tried to swallow, but couldn't. Instead, he nodded. Very slowly, and very deliberately he reached into his outside right pocket and held out his open hand. In the palm was a heavy gold ring with a sky blue stone the size of a man's pinky nail on the faceted oval face of it. Captain Tillman picked up the ring with his free hand and turned it over in his fingers, examining the inside and the outside carefully in the sunlight. Satisfied, he nodded to himself.

"Okay," Captain Tillman said, "I believe that Terry Price sent you. Nothing else would have worked, but I imagine he told you that. I guess you want to go inside and talk alone, right?"

Marcus shook his head, and the Captain's eyes widened slightly. "No sir," Marcus replied. "I can't stay. Mr. Price sent me to tell you he needs your help. The nation is under attack, and he needs your help to stop it."

Captain Tillman snorted a chuckled. "Terry always did have delusions of grandeur."

This time, Marcus raised an eyebrow, and Captain Tillman caught the expression. His frown immediately shifted into a scowl.

"Look, son," he said, "I don't even know you, and I don't know what Terry Price told you, but I haven't seen or heard from the man in twelve years. I'm not about to leave my family and get on a helicopter with you just because you bring me a ring. Jesus, I'm not an idiot."

Marcus blinked, and paused unable to think of what to say next. Mr. Price had told him that this man was one of his best friends. He'd assured Marcus that there would be no issues and no problems. The ring was supposed to be significant and elicit Captain Tillman's immediate cooperation. Instead, he seemed to be digging in his heels.

"Captain Tillman, my name is—"Marcus began, but the Captain held his hand up, shaking his head.

338

"Son, I don't want to know," Captain Tillman growled. "If I don't know who you are, then it's safer...for the both of us. I told you, I'm not going with you. There are people here that need me now, and I'm not going to leave them. I suggest you don't push the matter."

Captain Tillman paused for a moment, and Marcus could only nod in shock.

"Good," the Captain said, slipping Mr. Price's ring into his pants pocket. "Now, you can come inside and have a bite to eat, and we can talk. Your pilot's welcome to come too, if he wants. You'll have to hand over your side arms, though."

Marcus shook his head slowly. "We have to get airborne, sir, I'm sorry. I have to get back over the Appalachians before nightfall. Mr. Price swore to me that you'd come without hesitation."

Captain Tillman just shook his head. "Then he lied, son," he said. "Don't feel bad. He's good at it. You tell Terry Price that if he wants to talk, he obviously knows where to find me. I'll keep his ring safe for him until he comes to collect it."

"Will you try to stop me from leaving?" Marcus asked, casting a meaningful glance at the HUM-V.

Captain Tillman shook his head. "No, you're free to go, son. Just remember what I said before. If I even think you're making a move on me or mine, I will drop you. If I have to track you over half of God's green Earth, I'll find you, and I'll put you down."

He said it with the calm assurance of a man who knew he was making a promise he could and would keep if it ever came down to that. Most men couldn't have uttered words like that without at least the impression of false bravado. With Captain Tillman, it was a simple statement of fact. Marcus nodded, and the two men began walking back towards the still running helicopter.

Marcus pointed over to the HUM-V, and said, "Mr. Price also said to ditch the Hummer. It has a GPS tracking chip imbedded in the engine works that can be switched on remotely. He's deactivated it and removed its reference from the database, but it is still there. If someone manages to dig up the reference ID, they'll be able to track you. The .50cal is clean, though."

Captain Tillman nodded, but didn't speak. Marcus felt like he should say something or try to convince the man once more to join him. Something about the set of the Captain's jaw stopped him, though. He could read it in the Captain's firm body language that he meant to stay put. Marcus had seen how quickly his hand had gone to the pistol at his side, and he knew he didn't want to push until he wore out his welcome.

So, in stunned silence, Marcus climbed back into the cockpit and strapped himself in. He put the headset on and gave the signal for the pilot to take off. The pilot shrugged slightly, throttled up the engines, and coaxed the chopper slowly into the air. As the Blackhawk banked in a low circuit of the farm one last time, Marcus looked down at the Captain standing alone in the field, and the man raised his hand to waive once, and then they were gone.

Ch. 64

Best Laid Plans

Terry woke with a start. He blinked eyes that felt like they were filled with grit and slowly straightened. A small drop of drool on the mirror-polished desk marked where he'd fallen asleep. Terry shook his head hard and rubbed his eyes with the heels of his hands. After a moment, when he could see straight again, Terry checked his watch, and had to blink some more.

He did some mental math slowly in his head and worked out the time differences involved. It would be mid-afternoon in North Carolina, and Mr. Attledge would have long since completed his mission, one way or another. Terry swallowed hard and tried not to let his fingers shake as he keyed the necessary commands into his personal terminal to access the data base. He executed a pre-set series of commands and the old NAVSAT system was called up once again. When the tracking screen resolved, Terry sat back and smiled a satisfied smile. There, on the screen, was a steadily blinking dot set firmly in the middle of the state of North Carolina.

The blip wasn't moving.

Epilogue

Mind Your Business

Mike stood in the narrow strip of deep, dark shadows between two houses. The lamp-style street lights that lined the winding road into the cul-de-sac were dark, of course. None of the windows up and down that dark street were lit. The only lights visible were the stars overhead and an angry orange glow on the horizon to the north over downtown Charlotte. The wind had changed so the acrid smell of smoke wasn't as thick in the air, but it still coated the inside of his nose and mouth.

Across the street, a shadowy figure moved, and Mike's nerves instantly stood on end. But whoever it was passed by quickly, and disappeared before he could make out much other than their silhouette. Another shape followed a few minutes later, but this one stopped in the middle of the rounded end of the street. The shadowy figure turned one way, then another. Finally, it seemed to notice the one solid door, and it charged. There was the solid thud of heavy impacts as the shadowy figure began trying to kick in the door.

Mike gritted his teeth and checked to his left and right. Nothing stirred, and no other sounds reached him other than the solid thunk of blows against a heavy wooden door frame. Mike had only seconds to make a decision before one of those kicks succeeded in caving in the door.

He broke cover and sprinted across the street. Without pausing to think, Mike ran up to the person kicking the door. He grabbed a handful of hair and shirt, pulled back, and rammed the person's face into the door jamb hard. There was a sickening crunching noise as the person's nose and probably their jaw were crushed under the blow. The stranger crumpled in a limp, gurgling heap at Mike's feet. He turned, scanning the street with his M-4 at the ready in case the would-be looter had any friends following behind.

Either the assailant was alone, or his ragtag followers had seen the carnage and run for the hills. The street was dark and silent again, with just the hint of a breeze blowing through the pitch black night.

Mike reached behind his back and tapped softly on the door twice. He waited, and then tapped again.

"Alyssa," Mike whispered, "my name is Mike. I knew your mother, Claire. Are you in there?"

Silence answered him, so Mike tapped softly again. He stood and tried to see into two dark windows next to the door, but there were towels up to block the glass from the inside.

"Alyssa," Mike whispered again, "Clair told me about you and your sister. She used to talk about you two all the time at work. Are you there? I have fresh water and food...kind of..."

Still, silence was his only answer. Mike heaved a heavy sigh and took a step towards the street. There was a soft rustling sound behind him, and Mike froze in his tracks. He turned as the deadbolt softly clicked, and the door opened a crack. A woman's dirty, sweating face peaked through the slim opening, her brown eyes wide, and rimmed with tears.

"You said you knew my mother?" the woman asked, her voice cracking. "Knew…as in, past tense?"

Mike took a breath to answer, but he couldn't. He dropped his eyes heavily and nodded, unable to face Alyssa's eyes, so much like Claire's own.

A chain on the door rattled, and it opened fully. Alyssa stood in cut off jean shorts and a white tank top stained dark with sweat. She stepped to one side, and took Mike's hand tentatively. She glanced down at the unconscious attacker and said, "Maybe you'd better come inside?"

Mike was still staring at his feet. He let Alyssa lead him inside and the door clicked closed behind him.

EMP Commission Executive Report:

http://www.empcommission.org/reports.php